THE DAMNED YARD

Ivo Andrić was born in Travnik, Bosnia on 9th October 1892, attended schools in Višegrad and Sarajevo, and studied at the Universities of Zagreb, Vienna, Krakow and Graz. He was imprisoned for 3 years during World War I for his involvement in the Young Bosnia Movement which was implicated in the assassination of Archduke Franz-Ferdinand in Sarajevo. A diplomat from 1919–41, he served in Rome, Geneva, Madrid, Bucharest, Trieste, Graz and Belgrade, ending his career as Minister in Berlin on the eve of World War II. Although richly influenced by his foreign travels, most of Andrić's fiction is set in his native Bosnia. He wrote 6 volumes of short stories and 5 novels, including *Na Drini ćuprija* (The Bridge on the Drina), *Travnička hronika* (The Days of the Consuls) and *Gospodjica* (The Woman from Sarajevo), as well as poetry and reflective prose. His great contribution to twentieth-century European writing was recognised in 1961 when he was awarded the Nobel Prize for Literature. He died in March 1975, and his Belgrade funeral was attended by 10,000 people.

Celia Hawkesworth is Senior Lecturer in Serbo-Croat, School of Slavonic and East European Studies, University of London. She graduated from the University of Cambridge in 1964 with a degree in French and Russian, then took an M.Phil in Serbo-Croat Studies at the University of London in 1969. Amongst her recent translations are *The Damned Yard* (Forest Books) and *Conversation with Goya* (Menard), both by Ivo Andrić, and *In the Jaws of Life* by Dubravka Ugrešić (Virago).

fiction
(short stories)

This selection first published in Great Britain in 1992
by Forest Books
20 Forest View, London E4 7AY, UK
PO Box 312, Lincoln Center, MA 01773, USA
and simultaneously in Belgrade by Dereta
Vladimira Rolovica 30, 11030 Beograd, Serbia

Original stories © Zadužbina Ive Andrića

The acknowledgements on page xi constitute an extension of
this copyright page

Typeset at London University
Printed by Dereta, Belgrade

A CIP record for this book is available from the British Library

ISBN: 1–85610–022–7

Published with the generous financial support of
Zadužbina Dure Daničića

096791

The Damned Yard

AND OTHER STORIES

Ivo Andrić

Edited by Celia Hawkesworth

FOREST
BOOKS
London & Boston

DERETA
BELGRADE

CONTENTS

Introduction   v

Note on the pronunciation of Serbo-Croat Names   x

Acknowledgements   xi

The Story of the Vizier's Elephant   1
translated by Celia Hawkesworth

The Bridge on the Žepa   41
translated by Svetozar Koljević

In the Guest-House   49
translated by Joseph Schallert and Ronelle Alexander

Death in Sinan's Tekke   61
translated by Felicity Rosslyn

The Climbers   71
translated by Svetozar Koljević

A Letter from 1920   107
translated by Lenore Grenoble

Introduction to *The House on Its Own*   121
translated by Celia Hawkesworth

Alipasha   125
translated by Felicity Rosslyn

A Story   137
translated by Felicity Rosslyn

The Damned Yard   143
translated by Celia Hawkesworth

For Dušan Puvačić, and all our friends in Bosnia

INTRODUCTION

This selection of Andrić's short stories and the novella 'The Damned Yard' highlights a number of recurrent themes from his work. Their primary setting is Bosnia, where Andrić spent the formative years of his life: he was born in Travnik on 9th October 1892, he spent his childhood in Višegrad, near the border with Serbia, and his secondary school years in Sarajevo. Travnik, which was the seat of Ottoman power in Bosnia, is the setting of Andrić's novel, *The Days of the Consuls* (previously published as *Bosnian Story*), while Višegrad provides the context for numerous short stories and the novel *The Bridge on the Drina*. While Andrić's work includes some timeless stories and some set in a neutral post-Second World War urban context, much of it is set in Bosnia and is closely dependent on this setting.

A leitmotiv of Andrić's work is the material nature of human experience: wary of abstraction, he roots his stories in a specific geographical and historical context which has the effect both of qualifying the statement and, more importantly, of stressing the fact that all universal truths that may be abstracted from human experience are lived through in a specific context. Andrić suggests that there are recurrent patterns of behaviour and a number of essential truths, which form the core of legend and myth, to be rediscovered in new forms by succeeding generations.

This approach may be seen illustrated in 'The Bridge on the Žepa', where the Grand Vizier who has the bridge built leaves it to stand on its own, without further comment, as a complete statement: 'Seen from the side, the bold span of its white arch ... took the traveller by surprise like a strange thought, gone astray and caught among the crags, in the wilderness.' The 'thought' is not articulated, but what is communicated by the stone bridge are such abstract concepts as: harmony, beauty, reconciliation, the surmounting of obstacles. In 'The Damned Yard', the rivalry between the two contenders for the Ottoman throne at the heart of the work is described as 'the age-old story of two brothers' and the way in which the younger brother, Cem, is thwarted and manipulated by forces beyond his control is echoed in a different form in the story of Kamil.

'The Damned Yard' represents a concentrated statement of some of Andrić's central themes: the survival of the imagination in face of the all-engulfing encroachment of time, the notion that stories of all kinds should be heard for every story is 'true', the endurance of essential patterns of experience in new forms in different ages, the arbitrary nature of power and social organisation, and above all the notion of the imagination as providing a means of escape from constraint.

Imprisoned at the outbreak of the First World War for his involvement in the Young Bosnia Movement which was implicated in the assassination of Archduke Franz Ferdinand in Sarajevo in 1914, Andrić returned to the prison as a setting for several stories. In essence, however, the prison emerges as simply a more intense and obvious form of the various kinds and degrees of constraint to which all human beings are subject. And it is the experience of constraint that creates the impulse to escape. For the inmates of the Damned Yard, the only means of escape is through the telling of stories.

The novella is, then, above all a story about story-telling: the kinds of stories people tell, the way they tell them and the reasons for their telling them. There is a hierarchy among the story-tellers of the Damned Yard: some talk to dramatise and glorify their own lives, some to gain vicarious excitement by talking of the more colourful lives of others. Such narrators may be seen as representing the function of popular literature. The more serious story-tellers, Fra Petar and Kamil, are 'professionals'. Kamil is a biographer or historian whose capacity to enter into the life of his chosen subject dominates his sense of self, while Fra Petar is the archetypal self-effacing, reliable, balanced narrator who lets his story speak for itself without comment or intervention. He is the artist who brings a special indefinable quality to his story-telling, a distinct and unrepeatable 'style'. Nevertheless, Andrić the ultimate narrator seems to suggest, all these different kinds of narration should be listened to, for there is something to be learned from everyone and we would know far less about human life if we selected solely according to our personal taste and affinity.

The business of story-telling is the subject also of the volume of short stories published after Andrić's death, *The House on its Own*. Two of them are included here, 'Alipasha' and 'A Story', together with the introduction to the volume which offers a concentrated statement of the strategy of the artist in creating in himself the ideal conditions in which a story may 'tell itself'. The device used to link the various stories in this volume is that they are all the tales of individuals who 'visit' the narrator and draw his attention to themselves in various ways: some are importunate and demanding, some unobtrusive, but all have something to say and should be heeded, each in his own way.

Story-telling is the theme also of 'The Story of the Vizier's Elephant', presented as an illustration of the Bosnian love of story-telling and particularly of stories which are clearly 'untrue' but which nevertheless convey much about the truth of the human condition. The focus of this story is the experience of living under occupation and the abuse, humiliation and severely limited choice of action this entails. This is the essential experience of the South Slavs, under 500 years of foreign rule, expressed in their rich oral tradition as the choice between 'pure' tragic heroism, i.e. martyrdom, or compromise, 'comic survival', embodied in the defiant but ambiguous hero, Marko the Prince. This stark choice is clearly revealed to the character Aljo in this story, as he finds escape from the constraints of occupation through his imagination, in the same way as do the oral singer and the inmates of the Damned Yard.

The kind of 'truth' that can be conveyed by symbols such as the bridge, legend and myth, is distinct from 'fact' and more enduring. 'Fact', indeed, has no reality, unless it is confirmed by others. This proposition is illustrated by the story 'The Climbers' where 'reality' depends on how it is perceived. The power of language is here vividly apparent. The main character, Lekso, performed a remarkable feat in climbing onto the dome of the church, but unless others can be found to say that he did, it is as though he had not done it. In 'The Bridge on the Žepa' the altered perspective of the Grand Vizier's fall from power enables him similarly to understand the power of language for good or evil and therefore to avoid the possibility of misinterpretation or misuse by leaving his creation to 'speak' for itself.

Two other stories in this collection are concerned not so much with the experience they relate, but with the way it is 'processed'. 'In the Guest-House' introduces the engaging character of the Franciscan, Brother Marko. The story is concerned with the potential for conflict between organised religions — here Christianity and Islam — and hints at the destructive power of bigotry. Its focus, however, is the clarity of vision with which the clumsy, awkward Marko cuts through such distortions of the religious impulse to a timeless absolute of communication with divinity. 'Death in Sinan's Tekke' offers a mirror-image of this experience. In Marko's case learning the liturgy did not help him come nearer to his God, while standing in a muddy field planting out cabbages did. The dervish Alidede, on the other hand, led a deeply satisfying spiritual life which was a source of inspiration to many. And yet, at the end, he could not slip as easily as he had thought out of the material world. For all that he had tried to distil his existence into a pure essence of spirituality, at the end he was obliged to acknowledge that he owed his life to the laws of nature and to some extent to repay that debt.

Andrić lived through the turbulent first half of the twentieth century, with its two world wars, and extremes of revolution and totalitarianism. The wisdom that informs his work is tempered from that brutal reality. It was in Bosnia that he experienced the destructive power of the arbitrary divisions between people and their potential for violent conflict. He witnessed the way in which neighbours who had hitherto lived peacefully side by side could turn overnight into deadly enemies and whole communities be wiped out by the irrational power of communal hatred.

At its best, such a mixed society offers the most positive image of conciliation and cooperation: the sense of real peace through the reconciliation of difference communciated by the mixture of styles in the Sarajevo house from the introduction to *The House on its Own*. In many of Andrić's works it is this aspect of Bosnian society that dominates. In others, however, Bosnia stands as a stark image of the violent divisions between human beings. The story 'A Letter from 1920' reads painfully in 1992, the centenary of Andrić's birth, when the hatred stirred up between the different groups in the Yugoslav lands by power-seeking politicians and the media has brought so tragically violent an end to the experiment in consensus and cooperation represented by Yugoslavia, the country which Andrić himself helped bring into being. The success with which the politicians were able to pursue their campaign of division and mutual antagonism depended to a very large extent on the power of language to create a reality people are ready to believe in without reference to fact. The 'truth' of myth as an expression of communal perception and aspiration was a process Andrić understood with singular clarity. It is just this kind of mythic 'truth' that is the material of his art.

In one of his other stories featuring Brother Marko, Andrić uses the image of a coin portraying a saint in a state of beatitude, of which Marko is suddenly reminded as he watches the face of a Turk in the firelight: it seems to him the personification of evil. The narrow edge between the two faces of the coin suggests the thin dividing line between good and evil. If language *may* bring evil, the truly disinterested concentration of the artist described in the introduction to the *House on its Own* works always on the side of good. The Grand Vizier Jusuf's motto, 'In silence is safety' is echoed in the unambiguous commitment of the craftsmen portrayed in the 'Bridge on the Žepa' and 'The Climbers' and in the balanced patience of Fra Petar's narration.

It is precisely this kind of timeless wisdom to which Andrić aspires in his work. In this endeavour, his clear-sighted acknowledgement of the human capacity for evil gives his voice authority and, in the catastrophic conflict afflicting his native Bosnia in his centenary year, a new urgency.

Celia Hawkesworth

Note on the Pronunciation of Serbo-Croatian Names

With the exception of some Turkish words and names (e.g. Cem, the younger son of Sultan Beyazit II, whose story is told in *The Damned Yard*), Serbo-Croatian spellings have been retained. The language may be written in either the Cyrillic or the Latin alphabet. The Latin alphabet includes a number of unfamiliar letters listed below. Serbo-Croat is strictly phonetic, with one letter representing one sound. The stress normally falls on the first syllable.

C, c	—	*ts*, as in ca*ts*
Č, č	—	*ch*, as in *ch*urch
Ć, ć	—	*tj*, close to č, but softer i.e. *t* in fu*t*ure
Dž, dž	—	*j*, as in *j*ust
Đ, đ	—	*dj*, close to *dž*, but softer i.e. *d* in ver*d*ure
J, j	—	*y*, as in *y*ellow (*J*ugoslavi*j*a)
Š, š	—	*sh*, as in *sh*ip
Ž, ž	—	*zh*, as *s* in trea*s*ure

Acknowledgements

Introduction © Celia Hawkesworth, 1992

The Story of the Vizier's Elephant, this English translation © Celia Hawkesworth, 1992. Originally published as 'Priča o vezirovom slonu', *Pripovetke*, Belgrade. (First English translation published as 'The Vizier's Elephant', New York, Harcourt Brace and World, 1962.)

The Bridge on the Žepa, this English translation © Oxford University Press, 1966. Reprinted from *Yugoslav Short Stories* selected and translated by Svetozar Koljević (1966) by permission of Oxford University Press. Originally published as 'Most na Žepi', *Pripovetke*, Belgrade, 1947.

In the Guest-House, this English translation © Joseph Schallert and Ronelle Alexander, 1992. Originally published as 'U musafirhani', *Srpski književni glasnik*, Belgrade, 1923.

Death in Sinan's Tekke, this English translation © Felicity Rosslyn, 1992. Originally published as 'Smrt u Sinanovoj tekiji', *Pripovetke*, Belgrade, 1924.

The Climbers, this English translation © Oxford University Press, 1966. Reprinted from *Yugoslav Short Stories* selected and translated by Svetozar Koljević (1966) by permission of Oxford University Press. Originally published as 'Osatičani', in *Panorama*, Belgrade, 1958.

A Letter from 1920, this English translation © Lenore Grenoble, 1992. Originally published as 'Pismo iz godine 1920.', in *Pregled*, Belgrade, 1920.

Introduction to The House on Its Own, this English translation © Celia Hawkesworth, 1992, *Alipasha* ('Alipaša') and *A Story* ('Priča'), these English translations © Felicity Rosslyn, 1992. Originally published in *Kuća na osami*, Belgrade, 1976.

The Damned Yard, this English translation © Celia Hawkesworth, 1992. Originally published as *Prokleta avlija*, Belgrade, 1954. (First English translation published as *Devil's Yard*, New York, Grove Press, 1962.)

The Story of the Vizier's Elephant

The towns and villages of Bosnia are full of stories. Under
the guise of improbable events masked by invented names,
these tales, which are for the most part imaginary, conceal the
true, unacknowledged history of the region, of living people
and long-vanished generations. These are those Eastern lies
which the Turkish proverb holds to be 'truer than any truth'.

These stories live a strange, hidden life. In this they
resemble the Bosnian trout. There is a particular kind of trout
in the streams and brooks of Bosnia; not large, dark-backed,
with two or three large red spots. It is unusually greedy, but
also unusually cunning and quick, and it will rush blindly
onto a hook in a skilful hand, but cannot be caught or even
seen by those who are not familiar with these waters or this
kind of fish.

It is the same with the stories. You can live for months in a
Bosnian village without hearing one of them properly or to
the end, but it can happen that you chance to spend the night
somewhere and hear three or four stories, of that quite
implausible kind which tell you most about a place and its
people.

It is the people of Travnik, the wisest in Bosnia, who know
the greatest number of such stories, but they rarely tell them
to strangers, just as it is the rich who are most reluctant to
part with their money. But as a result each of their stories is
worth three of anyone else's. According to them, that is.

Such a tale is the story of the Vizier's elephant.

When the former vizier, Mehmed Ruzdi Pasha, was
replaced, the people of Travnik were anxious, and not
without reason. He had been a man who enjoyed life,
carefree, reckless and slovenly in his work, but so easy-going
that neither Travnik nor Bosnia was aware of his presence.
The more discerning and intelligent people had been uneasy
for some time because they had foreseen that this could not
last long. And now they were anxious on two counts, first

that this good man was leaving and secondly that he would be replaced by someone new and unknown. They began immediately to make enquiries about the man who was supposed to be coming.

Foreigners were often surprised at the number of questions Travnik people used to ask about every new vizier as soon as they heard of his appointment, and they would mock them, attributing their behaviour to inquisitiveness and conceit and their habit of involving themselves in weighty matters of state. But they were wrong. (Those who jeer are rarely in the right). What impelled the people of Travnik to ask so many questions about each new vizier and his slightest physical and moral characteristics and habits was neither curiosity nor arrogance, but their long experience and pressing need.

The numerous viziers of Bosnia have included all sorts, wise and humane, negligent and indifferent, comic and sinful, but also some so ruthless and malicious that even the stories told about them would pass over the worst things, just as, out of superstitious fear, people do not like to mention illness and evil things by name. Such viziers were a burden to the whole land, but it was particularly hard for the people of Travnik, for the viziers ruled Bosnia by proxy, but were in Travnik in person, with their escort and servants and their unknown whims.

The people of Travnik made extensive enquiries, bribing informers and buying them drinks, to find out anything they could about the man who was going to be the new vizier. It sometimes happened that they would pay allegedly well-informed people, only to realise later that they were a pack of liars and cheats. But even then they did not think that their money was entirely wasted, for sometimes what *can* be invented about a person will tell you quite a lot about him. Wise and experienced as they were, the people of Travnik were often able to extract from these lies a grain of truth which even the liar had not known lay amongst them. If nothing else, the lie served them as a starting point which they could easily discard when they had discovered the truth.

The oldest inhabitants of Travnik have a point when they say that there are three towns in Bosnia where the people are wise. And they immediately add that one of these, in fact the wisest of them, is Travnik. Only, they usually forget to say which are the other two.

That was how they managed to discover quite a number of

things about the new vizier even before his arrival.

The new vizier was called Seid Ali Dželaludin Pasha.

He was born in Adrianople, an educated man, but when he had completed his education and was to have become an 'Imam' in the poor district of the town, he suddenly abandoned everything, left for Istanbul and entered the military administration. There he distinguished himself by his skill in catching thieves and dishonest suppliers, and punishing them with severe penalties. There was a story told about him at this time: on one occasion he had discovered that a certain Jew, who supplied tar to an army boatyard, was selling thin, unusable tar, and that, having checked the matter and heard the expert opinion of two quartermasters, he ordered that the Jew be drowned in his own tar. In fact that was not quite what had happened. The Jew had been caught cheating and was summoned before a commission which was to investigate the quality of the tar. The Jew had started rushing excitedly around the wooden tank of tar, demonstrating that the accusations were unfounded, while Dželaludin Effendi merely watched him with his unwavering stare. Unable to hide from that stare, or to take his eyes from it, no longer knowing what he was saying or looking where he was standing, the unfortunate supplier slipped, fell into the tank and sank so quickly that it was proved beyond doubt that the tar really was too liquid.

That was what really happened, but Dželaludin Effendi had nothing against those who spread the first, fantastic, terrible version of the incident, like so many other horror stories about his ruthlessness. He calculated that this would earn him the reputation of 'a man with a firm hand' and attract the attention of the Grand Vizier. And he was not mistaken.

Sane and reasonable people who served with him in the army quickly realised that Dželaludin Effendi was not in fact particularly concerned about either justice or the inviolability of the state treasury, but rather that every move he made was provoked by an irresistible instinct and innate need to judge, punish, torture and kill, while the law and state interests served only as a shield and a welcome pretext. The Grand Vizier probably knew this as well, but it is precisely people like that who are required by institutions and authorities which are losing their power.

That is how Dželaludin's rise began, and after that one thing led to another, as required by a declining, out-dated state and a degenerate society, and following the instincts with which he had been born. The peak of his ascent was his appointment to the position of Vizier in Bitolj.

There, several landowning families had become powerful. They ruled quite independently, each on their own estate, feuding among themselves and refusing to acknowledge any authority. Dželaludin Pasha evidently carried out his duties in Bitolj to the satisfaction of his commander and a year later he was appointed to the post of Vizier to the whole of Bosnia, where the declining, degenerate landowner or bey class had long since lost both the power to rule and the ability to obey. That proud and rebellious, powerless yet troublesome class needed to be humbled and brought into line. Dželaludin Pasha was chosen to do it.

'A sharp sabre in a swift and merciless hand is bearing down on you' was the message from the Travnik beys' informer in Istanbul. And he also described to them the way Dželaludin Pasha had dealt with the Bitolj beys and prominent men.

On his arrival in Bitolj he had summoned the leading men to him and ordered each of them to cut an oak stake of at least four metres in length and to bring it to the Vizier's Residence with his name carved on it. As if bewitched, the men carried out this humiliating command. Only one refused, determined to escape, along with a few of his people, into the woods, rather than comply with such a shameful order, but the Vizier's men hacked him to pieces before any of his kinsmen could come to his aid. Afterwards the Pasha ordered that the stakes be driven into the ground of his yard, forming a small forest. Once again he gathered all the leaders in his yard and told them that now each of them knew 'his place' and that if there were even the slightest resistance in the pashalik, he would impale each of them on his own stake, in alphabetical order.

The people of Travnik both believed this story and did not, for in the previous thirty or so years they had heard so many hideous and strange accounts of this kind, and witnessed still more strange and hideous sights, so that even the strongest words lost their persuasive force. They waited to see for themselves with their own eyes. Finally, the day came.

There was nothing particular about the nature of the Vizier's arrival to justify these tales. Other 'terrible' viziers had entered the town with great noise and pomp, intending that their very arrival should strike fear into the people's hearts, but this one came in unnoticed, by night, and Travnik simply awoke one morning to find him. Everyone knew he was there, but no one had yet seen him.

And when the Vizier received the 'leading men' and when they saw and heard him, most of them had another surprise. The Vizier was still a young man, somewhere between thirty-five and forty years old, with red hair and pale skin, and a small head on a long, thin body. His smooth-shaven face, round and somehow childish, had a barely perceptible red moustache and regular patches of reflected light on his rounded cheekbones, like a porcelain doll. And in this face, with its white skin and pale hair, were two dark, almost black, slightly uneven eyes. In the course of conversation these eyes were often covered by long eyelashes, quite pale but with a reddish tinge, which gave his whole face a strange, stiff, almost amused expression, but as soon as his eyelashes were raised, you could see clearly from his dark eyes that this was a mistake and that there was no trace of a smile on his face. His most striking features were his small, pale mouth (a doll's mouth) which barely opened as he spoke, and his upper lip which was never raised and never moved, yet somehow one sensed behind it crooked, rotten teeth.

When the beys met after this first encounter to exchange impressions and ideas, most of them were inclined to judge this once would-be imam less harshly, underestimating him and feeling that the rumours about him had been larger than he was. Most, but not all. There were some more experienced and perceptive people among them, 'good judges of the times', who said nothing but stared straight ahead of them, not daring to form a complete and final judgement about the Vizier even to themselves, but believing that an unusual man had come among them, a scourge of a special, pernicious kind.

Dželaludin Pasha arrived in Travnik at the beginning of February, and it was during the second half of March that the slaughter of the beys and other leading figures was carried out.

On the Sultan's orders, Dželaludin summoned all the prominent Bosnian beys, leaders and town captains to an important discussion in Travnik. There should have been exactly forty of them. Thirteen of them did not reply, some because they were wise and foresaw trouble, others because of their traditional family pride which proved just as useful in this case as cunning. Of the twenty-seven who did come, seventeen were killed immediately in the courtyard of the Residence, the other ten were despatched to Istanbul the following day, chained together with metal collars round their necks.

There were no witnesses and it will never be known how it was possible to lure such experienced, respected men into such a trap and then slaughter them in the middle of Travnik, like sheep, without a sound or hint of resistance. That calculated, cold-blooded slaughter of the beys and leading figures, carried out in the Residence courtyard, before the eyes of the Vizier, without consideration, without any kind of respect for form, in a way in which no vizier had ever carried out a killing before, seemed to the people like a bad dream. From that day all the inhabitants of Travnik were of one mind about Dželaludin, whom they called Dželalija, and that was something which rarely happened. Up to then they had always said of each bad vizier (and even of many who were not so bad) that he was the worst, but they did not say anything about this present one, because from that worst vizier to this Dželalija there was a long and terrible road, and on that road fear made people lose their voices and their memory, and the ability to make comparisons or find words which could possibly convey what and who Dželalija was.

April passed in rigid amazement and silent anticipation of what might happen next, if indeed anything else could happen after this.

It was then, in the first days of May, that the Vizier acquired an elephant.

When people in Turkey rose to high positions and attained power and wealth, they often developed an interest in exotic animals. Something like a hunter's passion, but a distorted passion which avoided both movement and exertion. So it had happened even before now that a vizier would bring some animal which the people had never seen: a monkey, a parrot, or an Angora cat. One had even acquired a young panther, but it seemed that the Travnik climate was unsuitable for big cats of its kind. After its first attempts to demonstrate its blood-thirsty nature, the wild beast stopped growing. Actually, the idle people round the Vizier did tend to give it strong brandy to drink and little cakes made of hashish and opium. In time, the panther's teeth fell out, its coat lost its sheen and began to moult like that of an unhealthy calf. Bloated, undersized, it lay in the yard, unchained and harmless, squinting in the sun, while the cockerels pecked at it and mischievous puppies straddled it indecently. And the following winter the panther died the natural and inglorious death of an ordinary Travnik cat.

Yes, even before this viziers, unusual, cruel and difficult people, had brought strange animals with them, but if the unusual and cruel nature of this Dželalija were to be adequately represented he would have needed to keep a whole herd of the most frightening beasts, such as are seen only in pictures or spoken of in stories. That is why the people of Travnik were not in the least surprised to hear that the Vizier was to be brought an elephant, an animal never before seen in these parts.

It was an African elephant, just two years old, not yet fully grown, and brimming with life. Before the elephant reached Travnik, stories were told about it. Somehow everything was known: how it travelled, how it was tended by an escort, how it was welcomed and fed by the people and local authorities. And it had already been given the nickname 'Fil' which means 'elephant' in Turkish.

The elephant travelled slowly and with difficulty, although it was still a youngster, no bigger than a good Bosnian ox. That capricious baby elephant created hundreds of problems for its attendants. Sometimes it would refuse to eat, it would simply lie down in the grass, close its eyes and begin to hiccup and belch so that its attendants would be petrified with fear that something was the matter with it; and then it would slyly open one eye, look around, get up and, swinging its little tail, set off at a trot so that the youths could hardly catch up with it. At other times it would refuse to move. They tugged it, coaxed it in every language they knew, talked to it gently like a baby and cautiously swore at it, some would even poke it, when no one else was looking, in the soft flesh under its tail, but nothing worked. They had to half-carry it on a special low cart. No one could understand these moods. ('But then, he does belong to the Vizier!'). And the Bosnian attendants just clenched their teeth so as not to let out a word of what they really thought of all the elephants and viziers in the world, cursing the day they had been given the job of accompanying and leading this creature never before seen in Bosnia. Everyone in the entourage, from the most important

7

to the least significant was uneasy and bad-tempered; they all trembled at the thought of what would await them if the task were not carried out correctly, their only source of satisfaction was the unease which they themselves spread wherever they passed, and there was some compensation in the robbery they were able to carry out freely in the name of the Vizier's pet, the Fil.

It was much the same in all the towns and villages they passed through. When the procession with the elephant appeared in some small Bosnian town, the children would run out to meet it laughing and shouting gaily. The older people would gather in the square to see this wondrous sight. But as soon as they saw the dark faces of the soldiers and heard the name of Dželaludin the Vizier, everyone would fall silent, their faces would freeze, and they would all look for the quickest way home, each trying hard to convince himself that he had not been anywhere or seen anything. The officers, clerks, councillors and policemen whose position meant that they could not do otherwise, would go to meet the Vizier's strange animal with fear and respect, and, not daring to ask many questions, they would quickly obtain from the townspeople everything that was asked of them. Most of them approached not only the entourage, but even the young elephant with a winning smile on their faces, looked amicably at this hitherto unseen animal and, not knowing what to say to it, they would stroke their beards and whisper, loudly enough for the guards to hear: 'A fine creature, by Allah! May no ill befall it!'

But they were secretly fearful in case anything should happen to the elephant while it was here, in their own area of authority, and impatiently awaited the moment when this whole company, together its monster, would set off again and cross into the next district, and someone else's jurisdiction. And when the procession did finally leave their town they would breathe a muffled sigh expressing relief and their long-accumulated aversion and hatred for everything, the sort of sigh that officials and 'The Emperor's men' can sometimes breathe, but so quietly that even the black earth cannot hear it, much less any living person, no matter how close.

The people, those insignificant people who are nothing and have nothing, did not dare speak openly or loudly about what they had seen either. Not until the doors were firmly closed behind them did they laugh at the elephant and mock the expense and trouble with which the notorious Vizier's animal was being transported, as though it were some holy object.

Only the children, forgetting all warnings, spoke out loud, making bets and arguing about the length of the elephant's trunk, the thickness of its legs and the size of its ears. In the fields, where the grass had only just begun to grow, the children would play at being the elephant and its escort. How pitiless, candid, fearless and observant children are! One of them is the elephant; he walks on four legs and shakes his head, on which one must imagine a trunk and large floppy ears. Others imitate the escort, the irritable and insolent servants and soldiers. One of the boys would impersonate the official and go up to the pretend elephant with a lot of genuine fear and false amiability and stroking his beard, whisper:

'By Allah, by Allah! A beautiful animal! Yes, yes, a heavenly gift!' .

And he acted so well that all the children roared with laughter, even the one who was playing the elephant.

When the elephant and its escort reached Sarajevo, the same hallowed rules applied to it as to the viziers themselves: that they should not enter the town on their way to Travnik but spend the night on Gorica hill. They could stay two nights at most, and during that time the town of Sarajevo would send them all they needed, food and drink, candles and firewood. The elephant and its escort set up camp in Gorica. None of Sarajevo's 'leading figures' showed the slightest interest in the strange animal. (Many of their families had been bereaved in the recent slaughter carried out by the Vizier). The rich and defiant citizens of Sarajevo, who abhorred the viziers and everything about them, sent only a young man to enquire how large the escort was so that they could despatch what was required. There was nothing for the elephant, because as they said: 'We know what the elephant's vizier eats but we don't know what the vizier's elephant eats, if we knew its nature we would send what was needed.'

And so, going from town to town, the elephant crossed half of Bosnia without any serious difficulty and eventually arrived in Travnik. The manner of the animal's entrance into the town showed clearly what the people thought of the Vizier himself and everything that was his. Some turned their backs and pretended they did not notice anything, some could not decide whether they were frightened or inquisitive, and others wondered how to be attentive to the Vizier's elephant and to be sure that their attention would be noticed and recorded in the appropriate place. And lastly there were many poor people who took no interest whatever in viziers or elephants and who regarded this as they did everything else on earth from one view point only: how a man could have, at least once, and for a short time, everything he and his family needed.

In fact even the most zealous could not decide whether to go out to meet the elephant and so demonstrate their attentiveness towards the Vizier and everything that belonged to him or whether it would be wiser to stay at home. You never know how a thing may turn out in Bosnia, they said to themselves, or what harm or trouble you might land in. (Who can predict the whims and foibles of tyrants?) That was probably the reason why there was not a large crowd to welcome the elephant and why the streets it passed through were more or less empty.

In Travnik's narrow streets, the elephant looked larger than it actually was, and it seemed all the more frightening and the more enormous because all the people looking at it were thinking more of the Vizier than of the animal itself. And many who had just glimpsed it in the procession, among the young green branches surrounding it, vied with each other in spinning yarns in coffee houses, telling amazing tales of the terrible appearance and unusual characteristics of the 'Vizier's wild beast'. No one should be surprised at this, because here, as in every other place in the world, people's eyes easily see whatever fills their hearts. And again, our people are more inclined to prefer their own talk about reality to the reality of which it tells.

Nobody was able to discover how the elephant settled down at the Residence, and how it spent its first few days, for, even if there had been anyone brave enough to ask, there was no one who dared tell. Under this Vizier's rule there was no question, as in the past, of the people in the market-place publicly relating and gossiping about what went on in the Residence.

But what the people of Travnik cannot find out, they are good at inventing, and what they dare not say, they whisper, bravely and persistently. The elephant grew in the people's imagination, and acquired nicknames which sound neither pleasant nor polite when whispered, let alone when written down. But nevertheless, the subject of the elephant was not only discussed but also written about.

The priest of Dolac, Brother Mato Mikić, wrote to his friend, the Guardian of Guča Gora monastery, to inform him of the elephant's arrival, but in a secret, roundabout way and partly in Latin, with the use of quotes from the Apocalypse about the great beast. ('Et vidi bestiam . . .') And in passing also, as was his custom, informed him casually of the general situation in the Residence, in Travnik and in Bosnia as a whole.

'It can happen, as you know,' wrote Bother Mato, 'that some of our people watching the Vizier destroy the Turks and their "prominent people" would comment on how some good would come of it for the rayah, for our fools think that another's trouble must do them good. You can tell them straight, so that they know now at least what they refused to see before: that nothing will come of it. The only news is therefore that "one monster has acquired another monster" and these idle people talk about that and chatter all kinds of nonsense. Meanwhile there are no reforms or improvements and nor will there be any.'

And, cautiously using Latin words here and there like a code, Brother Mato finished his letter: 'Et sic Bosnia ut antea in disorder sine lege vagatur et vagabitur forte until the Day of Judgement.'

And truly, the days passed and there was no word or sign from the Residence, no news about anything, not even the elephant. Since the doors had closed behind the 'Fil', it had been swallowed up by the great building, lost without trace, as though it had become one with the unseen Vizier.

And the people of Travnik really did see the Vizier only occasionally. He hardly ever came out of the Residence. That simple fact, that it was hard to catch sight of the Vizier in the town, was frightening in itself, giving rise to all kinds of speculation, and so became yet another means of inspiring fear. And the people of the market-place were anxious from the beginning somehow to discover some more facts about the Vizier, not only to do with the arrival of the unusual animal, but anything at all about his way of life, his habits, passions, whims, to see whether they might in this way find some little 'aperture' through which he could be reached.

Of that remote, silent and almost motionless Vizier, a well-paid informer from the Residence was able to say only that he

11

gave no sign at all of any strong or obvious passions or whims. He lived modestly, smoked little, drank even less, ate in moderation, was not particularly extravagant with money, and was not conceited, lascivious or greedy.

Like many truths, this was also hard to believe. And the impatient, irreverent people of Travnik wondered when they heard this report, who it was who had slaughtered all those people all over Bosnia, when such a lamb of a man was living shut away inside the Residence? Even so, the report was accurate. The Vizier's one passion, if it could be called that, was that he collected various kinds of pens, fine-quality writing paper and writing cases.

There was paper from every corner of the world, Chinese, Venetian, French, Dutch, German. There were writing cases of varying sizes, made of metal, of jade, of specially prepared leather. The Vizier himself did not write a great deal, nor was he particularly skilled in writing as an art, but he enthusiastically collected examples of calligraphy and kept them rolled up in round boxes of thin wood or in leather portfolios.

The Vizier was particularly proud of his collection of reed pens, the pens they use in the East instead of quills. These pens are made of cane, mostly bamboo, sharpened to a point and split at the end into the shape of a pen.

Motionless and enthralled, the Vizier would sit passing reed pens of every type, colour and size from one hand to the other. There were pale yellow, almost white ones, others ranged from reddish and crimson to completely black, shining like tempered steel; all natural colours, some were slender and completely smooth like metal rods and others were as thick as a man's thumb, with gnarled joints. Many of them, by some trick of nature, came to an end with a shoot in the shape of a human skull, or the knots on the joints of the cane resembled human eyes. This collection, of more than eight hundred reeds included at least one specimen of every kind of pen from the Turkish Empire, Persia and Egypt. And yet not one of them resembled any other. Not one of them was of the cheap kind which you buy by the dozen, but there were unique examples in shape and colour and these the Vizier kept wrapped in cotton in special long Chinese lacquer boxes.

In the large room, which was as quiet as a grave, there would be for hours no other sound than the rustling of paper and the clicking of the pens in the Vizier's hands. He measured them and compared each one with the others, he formed stylised letters and large initials with different coloured inks, then he cleaned them with special sponges and put them back in their places in the great collection.

That was how he passed the long Travnik days.

And while the Vizier was spending hours over his reed pens like this, completely absorbed in this innocent pursuit, people were wondering fearfully throughout Bosnia what the Vizier was concocting. And all were inclined to believe the worst and to see in the unseen Vizier's aloofness and silence unknown danger for them and their families. And each imagined the Vizier in a different way, involved in some other kind of occupation, bloody and all-pervading.

As well as amusing himself with his pens, paper and writing, the Vizier would visit the elephant every day, examine it from all sides, throw it grass or fruit, call it softly by comical names, but he never touched it with his hand.

That was all the townspeople could find out about the unseen Vizier. For the market-place it was simply not enough. A passion for writing-pens or paper did not seem either particularly plausible or comprehensible. The business with the elephant was closer to them. The more so since the elephant began to appear before the eyes of the astonished people.

II

It was not long before attendants began to take the elephant out of the Residence. They had to do this because as soon as it had regained its strength and rested after the long hard journey, the Residence became too small for the young animal. Everyone knew that the young elephant could not be kept in a stable like an obedient bullock, but no one dreamed that the animal would be so restless and capricious. It was easy to take it out, the elephant itself sought wide open spaces and greenery but it was difficult to restrain and keep hold of it. As early as the second day, it suddenly darted across the shallow Lašva, holding its trunk high as a sign of happiness, while the water splashed around it in all directions, tinkling cheerfully. Coming up to some garden fences, it immediately began pushing, in mischievous play, against the stakes of the fence, as though to see whether they were well fixed, and to bend and break branches wherever it could reach with its trunk. The young men ran after it but it went back to the Lašva and sprayed them and itself playfully with water. After a few days the servants decided to take the elephant out tied up, in an attractive, tasteful way of course. They put a strong leather collar round its neck. The leather was covered with red cloth, with little bells and sequins sewn onto it. On either side of this leather necklace there was attached a long chain which the young men held. A tall, broad-shouldered man with dark skin and slanting eyes walked in front of the elephant. He was a kind of trainer and tamer of the young animal, the only person who had any influence over it, with a gesture, a call or a look. The people called him 'Filfil'.

And now various strange things began to be seen around the town. As soon as the elephant and its entourage came into sight at the top of the town, chaos and confusion broke out. The dogs, the numerous town dogs, would run excitedly to and fro. Scenting from a distance this foreign creature which was completely beyond their experience, they would leave their places outside the butcher's shop. Those which had grown old and fat withdrew silently, the younger ones, thinner and more agile, barked through fences or holes in the walls; an ugly, piercing bark, in an attempt to drown their own fear. The cats became uneasy, running across the street and jumping up onto dividing screens in the yards, escaping up pipes onto wooden balconies or even onto roofs. The chickens, which gathered around the market to glean their share from underneath the feed bags of the peasants' horses, fled with a frightened clucking and flapping of their wings, over the high fences. Quacking ducks ran clumsily and threw themselves from the wall into the stream. But it was the village horses which were particularly afraid of the elephant. Those small, brown, shaggy Bosnian horses which peered through the thick tufts of mane falling over their foreheads with velvety eyes, full of some quiet joy, simply lost their senses as soon as they so much as caught sight of the elephant or heard the bells on its harness. They broke their tethers, threw off their loads and their packsaddles and fled, kicking wildly with their hind legs at their unseen opponent. The desperate villagers ran after them, each calling his own frightened horse by name, trying to calm them down and stop them. (There is something very painful in the sight of a peasant who, having reached his terrified horse, stands in front of it, with legs spread wide and arms outstretched, trying with what little understanding he has to be cleverer than both his crazed animal and those madmen whose sheer lunacy makes them lead a monster around the town).

The town children, especially the little gypsies, ran out from side streets and, hiding behind the corners of houses, watched the foreign animal with fear and joyful excitement. From day to day, the children became more and more daring. They began to shout and whistle and, shrieking with laughter, to push one another out into the main street, in front of the elephant.

The women and girls, hidden behind screens, in doorways or windows, observed the elephant in its red vestment, with its entourage of well-dressed, arrogant youths. They gathered together in groups of three or four by a screen, and whispered, making jokes at the expense of the unusual animal, tickling each other and stifling their giggles. Mothers and mothers-in-law forbade their pregnant daughters to go to the window for fear that the unborn child should take after the monster.

Market-day was the worst. Horses, cattle and small livestock would almost break their legs in terror. Peasant women from the surrounding villages in their long white dresses, with white, beautifully tied scarves on their heads, would flee in long strides into side streets, crossing themselves, and shrieking in alarm.

Meanwhile the elephant would pass solemnly by all of this with its rocking, swaying gait, while its entourage would run and skip around it, laughing and shouting, and all of this was so new and strange that at times it seemed as though it was all moving to the beat of some unheard, foreign music and that the elephant's strides were accompanied not by bells and laughter and the shouts of its followers and the gypsy children, but by drums, cymbals, instruments of unknown form and origin.

The elephant strode along on its powerful, cumbersome legs, shifting its weight from one to the other in an effortless, calm rhythm, stepping out like every young creature endowed with far more energy than it needs to carry and move its body, so that all the excess vigour is converted into exuberance and playfulness.

The elephant had already made itself at home in the bazaar, and with each day it showed increasing zest, stamina and ingenuity in carrying out its wishes, and no one could predict these, for there was such devilish cunning and almost human malice in them, at least that is how they appeared to the flustered and indignant bazaar people. One minute it would overturn some poor man's pannier of plums, while the next it would wave its trunk and knock over all the pitchforks and rakes a peasant had arranged, propping them against a wall in the bazaar.

People moved out of the way as in the face of a natural element, stifling their anger and putting up with the damage. Only once did Vejsil the cake-maker try to defend himself. The elephant stretched its trunk towards the round boards on which his cakes were laid out, but Vejsil was faster and waved a wooden lid to ward off the animal, and it did actually draw its trunk back, but then Filfil, who was wiry and strong with the long arms of a monkey, ran up and gave Vejsil a slap in the face such as no one in Travnik had ever seen before. When the cake-maker came round, the elephant and its entourage had already moved on and there were four large bruises on his cheek and a bloody graze made by the ring Filfil wore on his middle finger. And everyone felt that the cake-maker had got off lightly, that it was nothing compared to what might have happened.

In general, the elephant's entourage infuriated the bazaar more than the strange, unreasoning animal itself. Its chief guard and keeper, that Filfil whose real name no one knew, with his long arms and inhuman face, was always there, together with two soldiers, and very often they were joined by some idle servant from the Residence, who simply wanted to enjoy the people's fear and the disruption of the bazaar, the general confusion, comic scenes and the laughter which they provoked. The bazaar people had lengthy experience of the wanton behaviour of these despised and degraded people in a land of shaky laws and bad rulers, for the people of Travnik have long held the view that bad rulers are difficult, but their violent, insolent servants and sycophants are far more so.

So no one restrained the animal, on the contrary, they incited it and provoked it to attacks.

From early morning the idle people and the two gypsies would be ready for the elephant's outing, relishing the prospect of the jokes and mishaps which would occur. And their expectations were always fulfilled. One day the elephant stopped, gave a wriggle, as though it were thinking, and then went up to Avdaga Zlatarević's shop. He was a small-scale merchant, but a prominent and valued citizen (although he valued himself still more highly!). The elephant approached, leant the rear part of its body against the wooden post supporting the front of the shop, and began to scratch energetically and at length. Avdaga disappeared through the small doorway leading into the stone-built store-room at the back of the shop, the entourage stood and waited for the elephant to be satisfied, while the onlookers laughed and the whole wooden shop shook and creaked at its joints.

The next day Avdaga did not even wait for the elephant to reach his shop, but went immediately inside, bitter and angry. The elephant went straight up to his shop, making for that post again, but not to scratch, instead it spread its hind legs a little and began to urinate loudly and abundantly right in front of Avdaga's display counter. Then it shook itself, wriggled the muscles on its back a few times, flapped its ears contentedly and set off again with its slow, solemn gait.

The gypsy children, who were following some dozen paces behind the elephant, giggled and made loud comments, and the entourage tapped the animal's legs to move it on.

There were days when the elephant walked through the bazaar and nothing unusual occurred, there were days when it was taken a different way, but the people had grown so accustomed to the drama and the elephant's attacks that if there were none they invented them.

The idle folk who used to wait for the elephant every day would talk together.

'The "fil" didn't come yesterday,' someone said.

'He wasn't here, but do you know what happened in the Gypsy quarter?' replied a certain Karisik, a heavy-drinking gossip.

'What?' asked two of them in one voice, and at that moment they forgot that this was a man with a well-established reputation as the biggest liar in and around Travnik.

'A gypsy woman gave birth prematurely when she caught sight of the "fil", that's what.'

'Hey, don't say such things!'

'Whether I say it or not, that's how it was! The woman went out, eight months pregnant, to rinse a dish, and just as she was about to pour out the water, something made her look along the lane. The "fil" was coming, making straight for her. The woman gave a cry, dropped the dish, and went out like a light. She started bleeding right away. And they had to carry both her and a male child into the house. The woman still hasn't recovered. But the child is alive and well, only — dumb, it doesn't make a sound. It went dumb with fright! How about that, eh!'

All Karisik's tales ended with these words, they were a kind of hall-mark, a seal on all his stories.

The idle folk began to disperse and went on repeating the tale, and most of them forgot to say that it originated from Karisik. And the bazaar seethed, waiting for the following day and the elephant's visit, or at least for a new story, true or false, about the elephant.

It is not hard to imagine how the shopkeepers and merchants of Travnik felt in all this, the calmest and most dignified traders in Bosnia, serious, inflexible, conceited and proud of the orderliness of their Bazaar and the cleanliness and quiet of the capital.

But the problems with the elephant did not ease, they increased, and no one could see an end to them. Who could know what was going on in the mind of an animal, even our local Bosnian ones, let alone a foreign one, brought from a distant unknown world? Who knows what torment life had inflicted on the elephant? The bazaar people were not in the habit of thinking about the troubles of others, however, but of their own routine and their own interests. While the state was creaking and cracking on all sides and Bosnia stagnated, neglected, in fear and apprehension, while the beys were grieving and dreaming up schemes of revenge, this bazaar knew only of the elephant and saw in it their main enemy. Otherwise, in keeping with their beliefs and customs, these people protect all animals, even harmful ones, they feed dogs, cats and pigeons, they do not kill even pests. But this rule did not apply to the Vizier's elephant. They wished it ill, they hated it as people hate their enemies.

And, as the days and weeks passed, the elephant grew larger and stronger, and became ever more lively and restless.

Sometimes it would run uncontrollably through the Travnik bazaar, just as it used once, as a suckling calf, to race over the high African plain, through the thick sharp grass which whipped it from all sides and aroused its young blood and boundless appetite, it would rush as though seeking something and, not finding what it wanted, would overturn and demolish whatever came its way. Perhaps the 'fil' was pining; it probably wanted to play with its fellow creatures; the 'fil's' tusks were beginning to grow, this made it restless and it felt an insatiable need to bite, to gnaw all that came its way; but the bazaar saw in all its actions the spirit of Dželalija and a hundred infernal plans.

Sometimes the elephant would run by tamely and joyfully, not looking at anyone and not touching anything, as though it were running in a herd of its own kind, knocking its trunk playfully against its head. And sometimes it would stop in the middle of the bazaar and stand motionless, its trunk drooping sadly, its eyelids with their sparse, light-coloured bristly lashes in the corners of its eyes closed, as though it were waiting for something, and it gave the impression of a creature which was lost and discouraged. And the people in the shops would then nudge one another maliciously.

'Do you know who I think this "fil" looks like?' a goldsmith asked his neighbour.

'Who?'

'The Vizier. The spitting image!' announced the goldsmith, who had never dared so much as raise his eyes when the Vizier rode past his shop. And his neighbour, without even looking at the animal, thought that this was quite possible and simply spat, whispering something very unpleasant about both the Vizier and the 'fil's' mother.

Such was their capacity for hatred! And when the hatred of the bazaar attaches itself to an object, it never lets go, but focuses increasingly on it, gradually altering its shape and meaning, superseding it completely and becoming an end in itself. Then the object becomes secondary, only its name remains, and the hatred crystallizes, grows out of itself, according to its own laws and needs, and becomes powerful, inventive and enthralling, like a kind of inverted love; it finds new fuel and impetus, and itself creates motives for ever greater hatred. And whomsoever the bazaar once chooses to hate, deeply and bitterly, will inevitably come to grief, sooner or later, under the invisible but tenacious, perfidious burden of that hatred, there is no hope for him, unless he were to destroy the bazaar to its foundations and wipe out all the future generations of its people.

This hatred of theirs was blind and deaf, but it was not dumb. They did not say much while they were in the bazaar, for Dželalija was Dželalija, but in the evening, when they met in the districts where they lived, their tongues loosened and their imaginations ran riot. And the weather was conducive to this. The autumn was well advanced. The nights were still beautiful. The dark sky richly studded with low stars which kept breaking up, sending sparks shooting over the firmament, and each of them, as it streaked by, made the whole sky sway, like a canvas, in the eyes of those who watched it.

Fires were burning on the steep slopes. The last of the plum jam was being made. People moved or sat beside these fires, working, talking. And everywhere there were jokes and tales, fruit and nuts, coffee and tobacco, and almost everywhere, brandy. And there was not a fire or a meeting where the Vizier and his 'fil' were not discussed, although no one mentioned them by name.

'It's gone on too long!' 'We've had enough!'

Most of these conversations began with these sanctified words. They had been heard in the Travnik bazaar more than once over the last years, over the centuries. There was not a generation which had not been worn down until it reached breaking point, and it could happen several times in a lifetime. You could not discover with any accuracy exactly when some misfortune would exceed all limits and when these words might be truthfully spoken. It was something like a deep sigh or a soft cry through clenched teeth.

Only, the same troubles would be differently expressed and discussed in different ways by different fires. Broadly speaking there were three groups. The first were young men, talking mostly about girls and flirtations, games and their tavern exploits. The second were the bazaar people, the poorer ones, small-scale traders and artisans. The third were the weighty landlords, the wealthy, 'men of business' and people 'of good stock'.

By one of these fires, of the first kind, just two young men were sitting. The host was Šećeragić and his guest Gluhbegović. The host was a young man of not quite twenty, a hunchbacked, sickly, only child, and his guest was his contemporary, a tall, well-built, upright youth with sharp blue eyes beneath thin straight eyebrows, which joined, like a metal rod bent and tapered at the ends. Although they were different in every way, they were inseparable friends and liked to leave the others and talk freely on their own of all that delighted or troubled people of their age.

It was Friday. Their other friends had gone to their various districts to whisper with the girls through fences or half-opened doors.

While some girls moved around the pot of bubbling jam with the boy who was stirring it, the two young men talked quietly, smoking.

Gazing into the fire, somehow withdrawn into himself, the hunchbacked youth said to his friend beside him:

'No one's talking about anything except the Vizier and his elephant.'

'Well, everyone's had enough!'

'I'm sick of hearing the same thing over and over again: the Vizier, the "fil", the "fil" and the Vizier. And if I think about it for a moment, I'm a bit sorry for that young creature. What's it done? It was captured somewhere beyond the seas, chained and sold, and the Vizier brought it here to a foreign land, to suffer, completely alone. And then I go on thinking: the Vizier himself came here by force as well, he too was sent by others who didn't ask him whether he wanted to come or not. But then the one who sent him had to send someone to pacify Bosnia and put it in order. So it seems to me everyone is pushing someone else, no one is where he'd like to be, but instead he's where he doesn't want to be and where no one wants him.'

Gluhbegović interrupted him: 'Hey, watch it, my poor fool! It's a bad idea to think like that. While you wonder who sent whom, the one who's here makes your life a misery. So, stop wondering, and don't let anyone put anything over on you, just lay into whoever's nearest.'

'Ah,' sighed the hunchback, 'if everyone lashes out at everyone who bothers him and happens to be nearest to hand, there'll be no end to it.'

'So what! I don't give a damn!'

Šećeragić didn't say anything, just withdrew still further into himself and stared still more closely at the fire.

There were no consequences from what was said by this fire for either the town or the elephant, nor could there have been, for words achieve nothing.

By another fire, in the same neighbourhood, there were people of a different kind. A whole party had gathered. A dozen of the poorer bazaar people, drinking brandy, some avidly and calmly, others cautiously, hesitantly. The conversation flowed on, grew, filled with jokes, malicious jibes, solemn monologues, elaborate boasts and complicated lies, with brief flashes of truth. Brandy stimulates unexpected feelings and all manner of ideas in people, finds new words and creates daring decisions which, between the cheerful fire and the darkness covering the silent, sleeping world, seem natural and easily realizable.

'Eh, my friends, that beast of the Vizier has got under my skin, mine and the whole bazaar's. It's making my life hell!' Avdaga Zlatarević spoke softly and bitterly.

And straight away a muffled but lively conversation started up, in which everyone joined, each expressing his bitterness in his own way, according to his temperament, his standing and the degree to which the brandy had affected him. Soon, two groups emerged. Some were militant and aggressive, daring in their statements and insolent in their proposals, others were more conciliatory, cautious in what they said and more inclined to roundabout paths and methods which would lead, without noise or speech, invisibly but surely, to their end.

One of the landowners, a small, red-haired, bony, angry and sharp-tongued man, with a short, bristly moustache, approved everything, trembling with the humiliation they were all having to endure. And he cursed Travnik and whoever had buried him in this dump. They ought to burn it down, he said, so there wasn't even a mouse in a woodshed. He cursed the whole of Bosnia in all its length and breadth. Hell, it wasn't like any other country, he said, red with anger, there wasn't a people which hadn't trodden it down; all they had lacked was an elephant and lo and behold, here was one to complete the picture. 'Ah,' he said, 'I feel like taking a rifle, and the next time it comes near my shop I'll fill its head with 20 drams of lead, and then let them cut me down in the market-place!'

Only one hoarse voice, the voice of a man who had not been sober when he arrived, murmured something like approval. None of the others said anything. They knew the man and his threats well. He had often shot those same 20 drams of lead, and everyone he had aimed at continued to this day, alive and well, to eat bread, to be warmed by the sun. But they also knew that Travnik rifles were not fired casually, but if they were aimed, they did not shoot noisily.

The conversation ran on. The landowner continued to make

threats. Others echoed him, only more quietly and less specifically, and for the most part they whispered. There were proposals as well. Many felt that 'something must be done', although they did not know exactly what. Others were in favour of moderate but certain methods, and of waiting patiently until then.

'How long will we wait?' interrupted one of the more militant, 'until the elephant is fully grown and starts breaking into our houses and attacking our families? Do you realise an elephant lives more than 100 years? Well?'

'Maybe an elephant lives that long,' said a pale elderly merchant calmly, 'but his master, the Vizier, doesn't.'

At this all the moderate ones nodded their heads significantly. The more aggressive, recalling suddenly who the elephant's master was, fell silent for a moment, and the conversation subsided to a whisper once more.

Not even by fires like this one, with such loud boasts and whispered complaints, could there be any real conclusions or useful decisions. There were only daring proposals for ridding the bazaar of the elephant's oppression, which delighted their proposer and sometimes those who listened as well, but the next morning, by the light of day, no one even dreamed of putting them into practice. The following evening, again by a fireside like this, the same fantasizing and story-telling would begin once more. If from time to time, exceptionally, it did occur that a conversation would take up the next day a proposal of the night before with the idea of seeing it through, it was never serious and it all usually ended with some new tale. That was how the story of Aljo and the 'fil' came into being.

One warm, clear September night, the people stirring the plum jam were singing, those sitting idle by the fire with coffee, brandy and tobacco, were talking together. Every word a person spoke seemed sweet to him and everything his eyes saw and fingers touched delighted him. Life was not easy, not free, nor secure, but one could dream richly and talk wisely, discerningly and jokingly about it.

There was a particularly lively group round one fire. A dozen shop-keepers had gathered round Aljo Kazaz. They were the least 'significant', but for just that reason, the most radical.

Aljo had a small but good and well-known silk-merchant's shop in the bazaar, where he braided ribbons, plaited trimmings, sold silk bags and cummerbunds. The Kazaz family were descended from the large and powerful Sahbegović family which had now died out. Only this branch had been left by force of circumstance without land and had turned to trade. For more than fifty years now they had had their place in the silk-merchants' guild. That was how they had come by their name, Kazaz, 'silk merchant'. They all had the reputation of being good people and skilled craftsmen. Aljo was no exception, only he was a little eccentric and unpredictable. He was tall and well-built, with a ruddy face overgrown with a sparse and uneven black beard and black eyes, always glistening with a smile. He was known as a great joker, naive, yet wise, a man who was sharp and bold enough to say what others dared not utter, and to do what no one else would ever have done, but of whom you never quite knew when he was poking fun at the whole world, when he was speaking the truth through a joke, or when he was joking with what others called 'the truth'. As a young man he had gone somewhere with the army, under Suleiman-Pasha, to Montenegro, where he had distinguished himself as much for his jokes as for his bravery.

Before Aljo had even sat down, he was greeted with questions.

'Aljo, we've just been wondering: what is the worst and most terrible thing in the world and what is the best and the sweetest?'

'The worst is to spend a windy night on the rocky mountains of Montenegro, with one band of Montenegrins in front of you and another behind.'

Aljo said this quickly, without reflection, like something he knew by heart, but then suddenly gave a start, fell silent, deep in thought. Everyone urged him to answer the other question as well, but he looked at them for a long time with his black shining eyes, defiantly and mischievously, and only then did he say softly: 'What is the sweetest thing? . . . What is the sweetest? . . . Eh, what is the sweetest? Why only an idiot can ask that, anyone with brains knows the answer. Everyone knows, you don't have to ask. Get on with you!'

But after the first innocent jokes the conversation soon turned to the 'fil'. The usual complaints, threats, boasts. Someone suggested that five men from the bazaar should be chosen, to go to the Vizier and openly lodge a complaint about the elephant and its entourage.

The small, sickly Tosun-Aga, a tailor, emptied his little cup of brandy, and breathed out sharply (breath fired by brandy demands strong words!): 'I'll be the first!'

This was the shadow of a man, a sinful person with a shady reputation, but precisely for that reason so vain that his vanity was stronger than anything else in him, even fear. As he spoke, he looked even paler in the strong light of the fire and still more worn out and weak, with little sign of life in him; and if his head had been cut off at that moment, no one would have been able to say he had lost a great deal.

'Get on with you! If you'll be first, then I'll be third, at least,' said Aljo laughing.

But the others drained their cups and queued up to compete:

'I'll go!'

'Me too!'

They bragged and vied with each other like this with defiant words for a long time. They dispersed late that night, with a firm plan and solemn oaths that the chosen five would meet the next morning in front of Tosun-Aga's shop, go to the Residence and seek an audience with the Vizier, tell him the real opinion of the bazaar about the 'fil' and its heartless, unruly keepers and ask him 'to take this misery from their backs.'

That night many of them lay awake, wondering in terror whether it was possible that he, over a drink and in company, had really given his word that he would confront Dželalija in person, or whether it was just a mad dream.

III

When the next day dawned and the appointed time arrived, three out of the five had come to the meeting place. They could not find the other two anywhere. On the way one of the three developed such a cramp in his stomach that he turned off into one of the overgrown gardens by the road, and disappeared without trace. Only Aljo and Tosun-Aga were left. They walked steadily, both with the same thought in their minds: that they must turn back from this dangerous, pointless mission. But as neither wanted to be the first to voice his feelings, they went on. And so, each shrinking from the other, they came right up to the bridge over the Lašva, in front of the Residence. Tosun-Aga had already been lagging behind, while Aljo was preparing to stop at the bridge, and then turn back. He was jolted out of these thoughts by stern voices. From the guard post which stood on the other side of the bridge, two men were shouting something. At first he thought they were driving him away and was about to turn back greatly relieved, but on the contrary, they were calling to him, beckoning:

'Come on!'

'Over here, here!'

The guard had been reinforced, as though they were expecting someone. Two clean-shaven soldiers moved towards him. Aljo shuddered, but there was no way out. So he set off briskly and helpfully towards them. They asked him sternly where he was going and what he wanted round here. He answered in an innocent, natural tone that he was going up to Halilovići for some plums, but had got talking with a neighbour he met on the way, and reached the Residence without even noticing, engrossed in conversation. He smiled at himself and his absent-mindedness, a broad innocent smile, naïve to the point of stupidity. The guards looked at him suspiciously for another moment, and then in a milder tone the older one said: 'Go on, get going!'

Released from his initial fear and already quite calm, in his relief Aljo felt a curious desire to talk to these good young men, to joke with the danger which had passed him by. 'That's right, lads, carry on, guard well! And obey your orders! May God grant a long life to your commander.'

Dželalija's soldiers, hardened professional murderers, watched him with a smirk on their dull faces.

Going up the hill, by the outside wall which enclosed the Vizier's gardens, he turned once more and smiled at the soldiers who were no longer looking at him. At the same time he glanced quickly to the other side of the Lašva, where Tosun-Aga had long since completely disappeared, abandoning his friend and betraying all the oaths of the night before.

When he had climbed really high up the uneven path, between fences, he came across a small piece of level ground under a tall pear-tree from which the fruit had been picked, and whose leaves were already wilting. There he sat down, took out his tobacco and lit a cigarette.

Far below him, out of sight in the valley was the invisible Residence on the right bank of the Lašva, while the whole of Travnik seemed no more than a tightly-packed heap of black and grey roofs, above which blue chimney smoke drifted upwards, two or three wisps joining into one, spreading, thinning and dispersing against the sky.

Only then, with the first smoke of his cigarette, when he had begun to calm down did it occur to him how horribly cheated and let down he had been that morning, and what the bazaar had done to him, driving him alone and helpless to that fearful place to attack something that after all did not bother him in the least, to defend what they themselves did not have the courage to defend.

From that height, he now looked at his home town from a curiously slanted perspective, as if with new eyes. It was so many years since he had left his shop at this hour of the day, or been to this part of town, or climbed to such a height. This district looked strange and unfamiliar, while thoughts kept flooding into his mind, thoughts so new and unusual and so important that they drove out everything else, and the time passed quickly and unnoticed. At that height, and with such thoughts he sat right through lunch time and the whole afternoon. Who could say what was seething that mild September day in that head, in which jokes and facts usually followed one another like high and low tide, replacing each other without trace. He thought about things he had never thought before, about what had happened that morning, about the elephant, about the bazaar, about Bosnia and the Empire, about the government and the people, about life in general. This was not a head accustomed to thinking so keenly and cogently, but today, here, even his mind admitted a weak, brief ray of consciousness about the kind of town, the kind of country, the kind of Empire it was that he, Aljo, and hundreds like him, a few madder, a few cleverer, a few richer, a lot poorer, were living in; the kind of life they lived, a wretched, unworthy life which was insanely loved and dearly paid for, but when one thought about it, it was not worth it, no, it really was not worth it. And in his mind all these thoughts led in the end to one: that people had no courage and no heart.

These damned people are afraid, Aljo kept coming to the same conclusion, afraid and therefore weak. Everyone in this town was, to a greater or lesser extent, afraid, but there were

27

a hundred different ways in which people concealed their fear, or justified it to themselves and others. That was not how a man should be! He should be proud and bold and make sure he never gave anyone cause so much as to glance at him accusingly. Because, were he just once to submit to even the slightest insult, without flaring up (and no one flared up, they had no fire in them), he would be finished, everyone would tread him underfoot, not just the Sultan and Vizier but the Vizier's servants, and the elephants and all the other animals, right down to the fleas! Nothing would ever come of this Bosnia while Dželaludin ruled in it, today Dželaludin and tomorrow God knows who, worse and more terrible than he was. No, you had to stand firm, straight, and not let anyone get the better of you. No one! But how? Was that really possible in a town where you could not get five people together to say one honest meaningful word to the Vizier's face? Nothing, nothing could be done! That was how it had been for a long time here in his country: whoever was bold and proud would quickly lose his livelihood and his freedom, his property and his life, whoever hung his head and gave in to fear, would lose so much of himself as well, that fear would gnaw at him until his life was worth nothing. Anyone who found himself living in this era of Dželaludin had to choose one of those two. Those who could choose, that was. And who was able to choose? In fact, even he who was thinking all this, even he, what could he say for himself? He had always been known for his courage and boasted that he was brave enough for ten people, for half of Travnik, and the bolder half at that. Others had praised him, too. And last night he had been brave, beside the fire, and he was just as brave now, he felt, but where had his boldness been when he was talking to the guards, when everything had left him except his insane fear and his legs had hardly been able to carry his backside over the hill? Was not the truth still the truth and what was right still right even without those four fainthearts? No, no, neither Travnik nor its bazaar people had any more blood or strength left, and what little breath remained to them they spent on jokes and taunts and cunning plans to outwit their neighbours, cheat the peasants and turn one miserable coin into two. That was why they lived as they did and that was why their lives were no good, no good at all.

Aljo though about these things for a long time, and many other unusual things as well, but he left them all, in the end, unresolved, each in its own blind alley.

He was jolted out of his reflections when he heard the bells of the cattle which the cowherds were driving down the hill. At dusk he made his way slowly back to town. And as he went down the hill, the confusion of new and hopelessly tangled thoughts from the little clearing high above town, began to settle down and he gradually became the old Aljo once more, the man of the bazaar, who liked to joke and tease, and with every step the desire grew in him to get his own back on the whole bazaar and in return for their empty bragging and cowardice to make asses of them as they deserved. At the thought of this, his face relaxed back into its old, mischievous smile. As he tried to reach his house unnoticed through side streets, he gleefully thought up a joke with which he could get his revenge and make fun of everyone.

At home his wife and children met him with the tearful joy which comes after anxiety. He ate well and slept still better, and the next morning, when he left home, there was no trace in his head of the previous day's tormenting thoughts, but instead he carried in him the tale, thought out down to the smallest detail, of his visit to the Residence and his audience with the Vizier.

When the market people had opened their shops the day before they immediately noticed that Aljo Kazaz's shop was closed. It soon came to light that Tosun-Aga had returned more dead than alive, and that Aljo had vanished amongst the guards at the Konak. Perturbed, some glanced secretly at Aljo's shop from behind their shutters, others sent their apprentices to take a look, but the boy would always return with the same message, that Aljo Kazaz's shop was not open.

The bazaar closed that evening with this anxiety. And when he walked past in the morning, healthy and smiling, raised his shutters as usual and calmly began to spread out a roll of yellow silk along the length of his shop counter the bazaar people were greatly relieved. While the day before they had been extremely anxious about Aljo's fate (and that meant their own as well) now they were a little angry at their fears and they dismissed them with a cool shrug, saying they had known that it would all end well, because the foolhardy usually stay in one piece. Some of the curious and idle people had already strolled past Aljo's shop. He cheerfully asked after everyone, but apart from his innocent sly smile nobody got anything else out of him. So it went on the whole day. The bazaar was in agonies of curiosity but Aljo was stubbornly silent. It was not until dusk that he told one of his neighbours in the same trade, softly and in confidence, his story of the previous day.

'I can tell you everything,' said Aljo, 'for I know you won't let it go any further. To be honest, when the guards took me and I saw Tosun-Aga disappear round the corner, I was far from happy but I could see there was nothing for it. I tried to make out that I had set out on business and was going to Halilovići by way of Vilenica Hill but they wouldn't buy it. We know everything, they said, you were coming to the Residence, well, here you are, the Residence awaits you. Then they took me into the Residence, through one courtyard, then another and then into a big, dark room. I would have given a lot to be someone else. They left me alone there. I waited and waited: turning all sorts of thoughts over in my mind and wondering the whole time whether I'd ever see home again. I could see two or three doors, but all shut. Through the keyhole of one came lights as bright as sunshine. I tiptoed over and bent down to peep through; but I hadn't even got my eye to the hole when the door opened and, kneeling there on all fours, I fell into a brightly lit and spacious room. When I stood up I really had something to see. Rich carpets and every kind of luxury. The whole room smelt of resin. There were two heavily armed men in dolmans and between them a little further back, Dželaludin-Pasha himself. I recognised him at once. He asked me something, but, confused as I was, I couldn't hear anything. He asked again: who was I and what did I want. His voice was like silk. I began to stammer something as though it were someone else speaking; that we had got together to talk about the elephant and had come here, to ask a favour. Who else is with you? the Vizier asked me in that same faraway voice, looking me straight in the eyes. I was petrified, the blood froze in my veins. I turned around hoping to see at least that weakling Tosun behind me, but knowing there was no one, that everyone had betrayed and deserted me in that fearful place, there was nothing for it but to explain my presence quite alone. And it was at that point that something made me change my mind. I drew myself up, turned my face straight towards the Vizier, bowed my head and laid my hand upon my breast (as though I had been rehearsing this for a long time) and began to speak freely.

"I have been sent, glorious Pasha, on behalf of the whole bazaar, not to make trouble for you (who would even dare think of such a thing) but to ask the Effendi Secretary, as it were, to tell you of our wish and our request; this elephant of yours is, as it were, the glory and adornment of our town, and all the bazaar would be happy to see you order at least one more, so that we may be the envy of the whole of Bosnia, and so that the creature should not be alone and without a mate, as it were. And we have already come to love him even more than than our own animals. And there you have it, that is what they sent me to tell you and ask you on behalf of the whole bazaar, while you of course know best what you intend to do. Only, as far as we in the bazaar are concerned, if you ordered three or four of them, it would not fall heavily on us. And don't believe any other words you might hear, which only deceitful, evil people may say, with whom we in the bazaar have nothing to do. And forgive me for inadvertently appearing before you." That is what I said, not knowing myself where I got all these ideas from. When I had finished I fell to my knees and kissed the Vizier's hems and hands, and he said something to a member of his entourage, what, I did not hear, and then he disappeared somewhere. But he must have said something good, for the two men led me very politely into the dark room, and then into the courtyard. I saw all the Vizier's followers gathered there, about ten or twelve of them all smiling and greeting me as if I were at least a cadi. Two of them came up to me and put an ounce of good tobacco in one of my hands and in the other a bag full of cakes and sherbert, and led me to the gate as if I were a bride.

'And, I can tell you, when I saw the bridge and the Lašva, it was as if I had been born a second time. So there you are, that's how I got out of it in one piece. Oh, if I'd said what the bazaar and the people who set out with me wanted, my shutters would not have opened today, and the sun would not have warmed me this morning. Only don't, please, tell this to anyone, on your life . . . You know how it is.'

'Yes, yes of course, don't worry. What do you think, though, is the Vizier really going to get another elephant?'

Aljo shrugged his shoulders and threw up his hands helplessly. 'God alone knows, and the market-place can worry about that, because after this I don't intend to have any more dealings with Viziers or elephants as long as I live.'

'Hm', grunted the neighbour, wanting at all costs to extract at least another word, but Aljo just smiled and remained relentlessly silent.

When he had finished his story and said goodbye to his listener, Aljo knew that it was just as though he had let a town crier loose in the bazaar. And in actual fact, by the time darkness fell there was not a single shop in which the story of Aljo's visit to the Residence was not known, right down to the smallest details.

During those autumn days Aljo's story was often repeated in the shops and by firesides. Some condemned him as a crazy, deceitful man who had made fun of the whole bazaar, others supported him and blamed those who had started it all and then abandoned the poor fellow at the last minute, a third group kept an injured silence, maintaining that this was all that could be expected, when it was left to a riff-raff of tailors and silk merchants to lead things and prepare complaints to the Vizier, a fourth group shook their heads in embittered perplexity, not knowing what to think about people like this and times such as these. But the silk-merchant's story spread quickly, and passing from one person to another had already changed somewhat, both in form and in content. And Aljo himself would not say anything, black or white, neither 'yes' nor 'no', and when he came in the evening to the fireside, he only smiled in response to the constant questioning, stroking his chin and saying: 'The bazaar has taught me a good lesson, I thank it, here!' And he would bow low, with his hand on his heart. People got angry, regarding him as a clown you could not talk to seriously, and this they would say loudly, when he was not there.

There was also a third sort of fireside. These were the least numerous, around them sat similar figures, but the mood was quite different. These were the 'leading lights' of the bazaar, mostly older people, grey-haired and composed, all, without exception, rich. There was no brandy or laughter or cheerful confused hubbub here, but instead measured conversation, in which long pauses, meaningful glances and silent pursing of lips said more, far more,than words.

Among them too the conversation would regularly turn to the elephant, but all would somehow be expressed in a series of general remarks, mild words which in themselves meant nothing, and which only acquired their real meaning in the looks and facial expressions, which accompanied them, for these signs are the well-tried true language of these men of the bazaar. Even so, it was in fact by these firesides, without complaints or raised voices, without threats or curses, that it was decided how to protect the market-place from the 'fil', how to rid themselves of its weight around their necks once and for all. It was only here, among these old and wealthy bazaar men, that the question could be resolved, if it had a solution at all. For it could only be resolved by cunning, and cunning goes with wealth, preceding it and following it always.

So the bazaar people in their quarters and their gardens and around their fires made jokes and invented stories, either aloud or in a whisper, cursing the elephant and the man who had brought it here. They daydreamed, became bitter and fretful, but also silently dreamed up treacherous plots.

Nowhere do curses and complaints, whispered rumours and plots remain simply words for long and least of all in Bosnia. For a long time it all appears futile; nothing but empty words. People simply raise their hands helplessly and tremble as they clench their teeth unseen. But one day, no one knows when or for what reason, everything crystallizes, takes shape and becomes action. Children or the young and impetuous are always the first to find the strength and resources to begin to act on the grievances and impotent threats of the old.

When the walnuts began to mature on the trees, the elephant proved very partial to the young, ripe Travnik nuts. It would shake them from the branches so that as they hit the ground the dry, dark green shells cracked open and then it would pick them up with its trunk and crush them in its great hidden mouth, neatly spitting out the hard shell, to chew and swallow the milky kernel with evident pleasure.

The boys threw nuts on to the street in front of the elephant and it carefully gathered them up, comically craning its great head on its short neck in the narrow door. And then one of the children hit on an unusual idea. He cut the shell of a nut in half, removed the kernel from one section, and replaced it with a live bee. Then he stuck the two halves together so that the nut appeared whole, and threw it in front of the elephant. The elephant cracked the nut in its mouth and began immediately to shake its head, to trumpet strangely, to pull away from its escort. It was not until it reached the Lašva and began avidly slurping up the cold water that it calmed down a little. The escorts thought it had been stung by a gadfly.

That clever and cruel but naive method proved to be too weak and unreliable for the elephant's mouth. Most of the time the elephant would crush both the nut and the bee and swallow the lot without batting an eyelid. But that was just the beginning. United in their hatred, people became resolute, malicious and resourceful.

The older people began to join in the children's jokes, cautiously and unnoticed. Now they began to throw apples in front of the elephant in the streets, not just any apples, but lovely, big eaters of the most sought after kinds. So that the escorts suspected nothing. However the Travnik people would cut out the core of some of these apples, pour broken glass and powdered arsenic into them and then replace the core so that the apples appeared whole. The glass would be crushed into a fine powder and the arsenic added in small quantities. Then, behind their shutters and closed windows the people would watch the elephant, waiting for the poison to take effect. They had been told it was slow but strong enough to overcome even an elephant. Then the people of Travnik saw how difficult it was to poison so large a creature as the elephant. It continued to wreak havoc in the bazaar. But, nevertheless, as winter closed in, it began to lose weight and show some signs of various disorders of the stomach and intestines. At first the people were forbidden to give it food of any kind and then it stopped coming through the bazaar. It would be taken only for short walks on the slopes around the Residence. Here the elephant recovered a little of its liveliness. It would tread the snow carefully and solemnly, pat it with its trunk, put some in its mouth, and then toss it angrily into the air. But even these walks became increasingly brief as the elephant returned to its stall of its own accord. There it lay on the straw whining softly and searching for liquid in ever greater quantities.

While the elephant was ill the bazaar used all possible means to find out what had happened to it and how it was. There was little to be heard from the Residence, but for a substantial sum of money, they learned from a reliable source, first, that the 'fil' spent the whole time lying down, vomiting and excreting continuously; secondly, that the servants in the Residence were already debating 'how much an elephant skin was worth'; some insisted it was worth a thousand groschen, some refuted that, while others agreed, but added that it would take a year to tan it. For the bazaar, which had an innate and acute concept of what was important, that was enough. They paid as much as that information was worth, and continued to wait without a word, only exchanging brief, silent glances, which conveyed a great deal. And they did not have to wait long. One day a whisper spread through the bazaar that the elephant had died.

'The "fil" is dead'.

And no matter who hard you probed, you would never discover who had first spoken these words. When I say 'spoken' you will, I fear, immediately imagine an actual animated conversation, almost a shout of triumph. To think such a thing, is to misunderstand this town completely. Nobody ever talked in that way, least of all in the time of the 'fil' and 'Dželalija'. They were not even capable of talking like that. They would quite simply not know how to do it. Born and bred in the damp and the draughts of this mountain town, in which for as long as anyone could remember, the Vizier had sat with all his power and his retinue, they were obliged to live in a fear whose cause and name may change, but which always remains the same. They were burdened from birth with dozens of considerations which never went away, while new ones were constantly coming into being. And when something like this happens and their hearts swell with a feeling of victorious exultation, it rises to a certain height, it even reaches the throats of some, and then it returns to where it began, to settle forever beside so many other enthusiasms and bitter protests which had also once risen up in the same way and then settled unexpressed and unheard in that same graveyard.

It was, therefore, in that kind of tone of voice that someone, somewhere had whispered these words, and like invisible water from an unknown spring which can only be sensed by its murmur, the words had flowed through the bazaar, borne from person to person, filling their throats and rising to their mouths: that was how 'the news broke' and that was how it was spread through the whole town from Bosnian throats which could never be properly cleared and mouths which were never sufficiently open.

'The "fil" is dead!'

'Dead?'

'Dead! dead!'

Just like that. The word hissed like a drop of water on a hot dish and everyone knew everything and did not ask or say anything else. One evil had gone under the ground.

But while the bazaar was conjecturing where the elephant might be buried, anxiously waiting at the same time for the Vizier's reaction, another man appeared, more reliable than the other reliable one, and for far less money he sold the Travnik bazaar a different piece of news, true this time, that the elephant was alive. A few days earlier the elephant had indeed 'come close to dying' but then one of the Vizier's men had begun to treat him with a mixture of bran, basil and vegetable oil. And now the animal was better; already it was getting to its feet. In the Residence there was celebration among the servants and clerks, who had been dying of fear along with the elephant at the thought of the Vizier's reaction. There, that was the information brought by the unseen man, whose truth was cheaper than lies.

Even the bazaar can make a mistake.

This unpleasant piece of news passed through the town almost as quickly as the first, but this time unaccompanied by words or whispers. They only looked at one another, and lowered their eyes, slightly pouting their lips. 'Alive?' asked a young, inexperienced man in a tone of bitter amazement. The others did not even answer him, merely waved their hands impatiently and reproachfully and turned their heads away.

And it really was alive. Some time around the beginning of March the elephant was brought out of its large stable for the first time. The bazaar sent a particular man, seemingly unremarkable, but reliable and sharp-witted, to have a look. And he did actually get to see it. The elephant was very thin and had shrunk to half its size; its head had become smaller and more angular, and you could make out its skeleton underneath the skin; its eyes had sunk into their huge sockets, so that they now looked even bigger; and the whole of its skin looked like someone else's clothing that was far too large, its sparse hair had become even thinner and turned a greyish yellow colour in places. Its young keepers were walking all around it excitedly and cautiously, while it behaved as though it did not even notice them, just turning its back towards the sun which was already becoming stronger, and waving its head from left to right, from right to left, sniffing at the pale yellow grass between the thin patches of snow which were fast melting.

With every day that Travnik moved towards spring and spring moved towards Travnik, the elephant's outings became longer. It was slowly but visibly recovering. The disappointed bazaar waited with trepidation and two-fold hatred for the day when the 'fil' would completely recover and when they would again start leading it through the bazaar with God knows what new wild tricks.

The Vizier's young men, and particularly the half-caste who had been entrusted with the care of the 'fil' were convinced that the people of the bazaar had had a treacherous plan to poison it; and because of this they now led the elephant along victoriously, looking murderously around them, thinking up some means of revenge. Already this winter, while the elephant was ill, they had tried to talk the Vizier into punishing the bazaar, really for fear that he might punish them instead. But the Vizier was not interested. For some time his thoughts had been elsewhere. He was not now concerned with the question of the elephant's dying, but rather with losing his own head. He had fulfilled his compelling urge to rule, judge, punish and kill, and if the complex situation in Bosnia and the Turkish Empire of the time could have been resolved merely by force, bloodshed and terror, he might have been able to speak of success; but its solution required far more than that, and this was not to be found anywhere in the Empire, least of all in the methods of those such as Dželaludin. And when violence is shown to be powerless and incapable of resolving the task before it, that violence turns against its perpetrator. That was the way it had always been in Turkey, and particularly now, in the year 1820, when the Empire was breathing with only a third of one lung, and was being attacked on a hundred fronts both from outside and within. This was the case, too, with 'Dželalija'. He was the sort of tyrant who was only a scourge, nothing more, and who could, consequently, be used only once, and if that blow failed, then he himself would perish because of it. 'Dželalija' had not known all this earlier, and even now it was not entirely clear, but it was evident that his blow had not destroyed the beys nor quietened Bosnia, and that he himself, after this blow, did not know what to do or how to continue a task for which violence alone was not enough. A new way of proceeding had to be found, and, therefore, a new Vizier for Bosnia, and this meant, according to the prevailing customs, that there would not be much room on earth for this one, and that nothing but a grave awaited him, or exile, which was like the grave.

Dželalija realised this much, and it was confirmed also by the information he received.

With no roots, and no special connections in Istanbul, a loner and an eccentric, he had no illusions, he could not hope that he would, with time, come out of exile and attain freedom and status once again as had happened to other viziers. In his case exile would mean the end of everything: a slow, ugly, unworthy death. There was no doubt that for him a quick, voluntary death was preferable. In the essence of his being he was a bully and tormentor, he could neither continue to live without inflicting violence on others nor did he have the strength to stand violence against himself.

In March a special delegate arrived from Istanbul with an order from the Sultan: a new Vizier had been appointed to Bosnia, Dželaludin-Pasha was to hand over the administration of the country to the Deputy Vizier, proceed to Adrianople and there await further orders.

The delegate informed him that he was to be appointed governor of Rumelia and sent to put down the rebellion on the island of Morea, and congratulated him on this. He said all this quickly and mechanically like a lecture learnt off by heart. It was not difficult for Dželaludin to discover, with the aid of a little drink, a little bribery, that he had been ordered to say that, that actually a governor had already been appointed to Rumelia, another man with a 'firm hand'. A trap then. Now Dželaludin realised that the crucial moment had come and that this Travnik was the last point on earth to which he had been led by impulses unknown even to himself.

Then it became clear how close the thought of death had been to Dželaludin, he had become quite accustomed to the idea.

He wrote his will scrupulously, dividing all he had amongst his colleagues and assistants, all bullies like himself. He set aside a fair sum of money for the 'turbeh' which was to be built above his grave, he made provision for all the smallest expenses entailed by the burial. He also left an epitaph to be inscribed on his head-stone, which began with the words of the Koran, 'He lives and is eternal'. He himself burned his rich collection of reed pens, throwing them one by one onto the fire which burned in his rooms during those last days of March just as it did in winter. No one in the town knew of this, just as no one knew or could have guessed that he had left his collection of verse, a valuable work of calligraphy, to his scribe Omer-Effendi. There were thirty-two of the most beautiful poems by Arabian and Persian poets copied out in the book. These poems glowed and echoed with roses, hyacinths, wines, girls, fountains, flutes and nightingales in celebration of the black earth and the bright sun, 'which offers all this abundance to man and takes it away again so as to give it to someone else.'

When he had completed all these preparations, the Vizier withdrew into his bedroom, ordering his servant boy to wake him in an hour, when it was time for the midday meal. There he took a teaspoonful of white powder in a glass of cold Travnik water, drank it down as one drinks bitter medicine, and vanished from this world as quietly and imperceptibly as he had once entered Travnik.

When, shortly before noon, the muezzins began to call from the minarets of the Travnik mosques, people quickly realised that this was not the ordinary midday prayer, but the 'Jenaza', the prayer for the dead. And judging by the length of the prayer and the zeal of the muezzins, one could guess that the dead man had been rich and powerful.

The news of the Vizier's death soon spread, and this was the first news to come from Dželalija which was not met with comment from the bazaar. He was buried later that day in that same pervading silence. All the bazaar people were present at the burial, standing devoutly, without a word, speaking neither good nor bad about the Vizier, either then or after the funeral. (It was a victory which needed no exaltation.) None of them had any objection to Dželalija's finding his resting place in their town, four feet down in the earth, motionless and powerless, growing smaller and less like a living man with every day that passed.

The Deputy Vizier arrived at the Residence before the funeral, and Dželalija's companions scattered in all directions, endeavouring to cover their tracks and avoid revenge.

The Vizier had given the elephant to the half-breed who had brought him and looked after him the whole time he had been in Travnik, the one whom the bazaar had named 'Filfil' and whom they resented even more than the animal itself. The Vizier had advised him to take the elephant back to Istanbul and had left him the necessary money to do it. But it was not easy for the half-breed to carry out this testament, since he did not know how to save his own skin. In those times it was hard to take a needle out of Bosnia, let alone an elephant which no longer belonged to the Vizier. So it happened that the hated half-breed fled that same night in an unknown direction, and the bazaar people immediately found a way of getting into the Residence and slipping the 'fil' a stronger and more reliable poison than crushed glass in apples.

On the fourth day after Dželalija's funeral, the elephant died as well. It had left its straw bedding by the door and dragged itself into the furthest corner. They found it there the next day crouching against the wall, lifeless. And they buried it straight away; no one enquired how or where, for when the bazaar frees itself of an evil, it is no longer mentioned, and only later, when it becomes an anecdote, do people begin to talk about it again, as though it were something remote from them which could be spoken of jokingly, with satisfaction, in the midst of new misfortunes.

So the elephant too was laid under the earth, like the Vizier. There is room here beneath the earth for all.

The first spring without Dželalija arrived. Fear altered its form and anxiety its name. The Vizier was replaced. Life went on. The Empire was crumbling. Travnik was wilting, but the bazaar continued to live, like a worm in a windfall apple. People learned that the new Vizier to Bosnia was to be Ornosbeg Zade Sherif Siri Selim-Pasha. The first reports to reach them suggested he was a good and scholarly man, of Bosnian descent. But some of the people were already anxiously shaking their heads:

'If he's such a good man why does he need such a long name?'

'Eh, my friend, who knows what he's like and what he's bringing with him!'

So the bazaar lived in anticipation of new reports and more reliable information. The people suffered, whispered and defended themselves, if in no other way then through stories like this in which they could give life to their vague but indomitable desire for justice, for a different kind of life and better times. Craftsmen were building the 'turbeh' over Dželaludin's grave. A stonemason was carving the inscription on the Vizier's soft headstone and had already written the first sentence. The story of Aljo and the elephant spread through Bosnia, growing as it went.

The Bridge on the Žepa

In the fourth year of his viziership Grand Vizier Jusuf tottered and, victim of a dangerous intrigue, fell suddenly into disfavour. The struggle went on all winter and spring. (It was a wicked, cold spring, stubbornly refusing to let summer shine forth.) The month of May saw Jusuf walk out of prison, in triumph. And life went on, unglamorous, quiet, unchanging. But the winter months, in which life and death, fame and ruin were hardly divided by so much as a dagger's blade, had left a trace of something subdued and wistful in the triumphant man. Something unutterable that experienced men who have known suffering keep in themselves like a hidden treasure and that is reflected, now and then, unawares, in a look, a gesture, a word.

Living confined, alone and in disgrace, the Vizier remembered more vividly his origin and his native land. For disappointment and pain take the mind back to the past. He remembered his father and mother. (They had both died while he was still a humble assistant to the Sultan's Master of the Horse, and he had their graves edged with stone and marked by white tomb-stones.) He remembered Bosnia and the village of Žepa, from which he had been taken when he was nine.

It was pleasant in misfortune to think of the distant land and the scattered village, Žepa, where every house told the story of his fame and success in Constantinople and where no one knew or suspected the seamy side of fame or the price of success.

That same summer he had opportunities for talking to people who came from Bosnia. He asked questions, and they told him what things were like. After the uprisings and wars there were disorders, scarcity, starvation, and all kinds of disease. He ordered substantial aid to be given to all his people, to everyone still living in Žepa, and at the same time he started an inquiry into what was most needed in the way of public buildings. He learned that there were still four households of Šetkićes and that they were among the most prosperous families in the village, but that the village and all the surrounding country was impoverished, the mosque dilapidated and partly burnt, the fountain dried up; and, worst of all, there was no bridge over the Žepa river. The village was situated on a hill right above the confluence of the Žepa and the Drina, and the only road to Višegrad crossed the Žepa about fifty paces further upstream. Whatever bridge they made of logs, water carried it away. For either the Žepa swelled suddenly like all mountain streams, undermined the bridge, and washed the logs away; or the Drina rose and blocked the Žepa, overflowing into its channel, so that the Žepa also rose and swept the bridge away as if it had never been there. And in winter slippery ice covered the logs, and both men and cattle were in danger of breaking their necks. Were someone to build a bridge there he would do them the greatest service.

The Vizier gave six carpets for the mosque and enough money to have a fountain with three pipes erected in front of it. And at the same time he decided to have a bridge built for them.

At that time there was a man living in Constantinople, an Italian master-mason who had built several bridges in the vicinity and so made his reputation. He was engaged by the Vizier's treasurer and sent with two of the Vizier's men to Bosnia.

There was still snow in Višegrad when they arrived. For several days the surprised townspeople watched the master-mason, bowed and grey, but with a ruddy young face, pacing about the big stone bridge, pounding the mortar from the joints, crumbling it between his fingers and tasting it with his tongue, and pacing out the span of the arches. Then for a few days he kept visiting Banja and its quarry, from which the stone for the Višegrad bridge had come. He brought workers and had the quarry cleared; it had been covered with earth and overgrown with brushwood and young pines. They kept digging until they found a wide, deep vein of stone which was denser and whiter than that used for the Višegrad bridge. Then he went down the Drina, as far as the Žepa, and designated the place to ferry the stone. Then one of the Vizier's two men returned to Constantinople with the estimate and plans.

The mason remained and waited, but he did not want to live either at Višegrad or in any of the Christian houses above the Žepa. On a plateau, in the corner formed by the confluence of the Drina and the Žepa, he made a log-cabin — the Vizier's man and a Višegrad clerk were his interpreters — and he lodged there. He prepared his own meals, buying eggs, cream, onions, and dried fruit from peasants. As to meat, people said he never bought any. He spent most of his time hewing, making sketches, examining various kinds of stone, or watching the course of the Žepa.

One day the clerk who had gone to Constantinople came back with the Vizier's approval and the first third of the money needed for the bridge.

Work started. People stood agape wondering what was going on. It did not look like a bridge. First, heavy pine beams were driven into the river bed obliquely across the Žepa, then two rows of stakes were set between them, and everything was wattled together with brushwood and stuffed with clay, like a trench. So the course of the river was diverted and half its bed left dry. The work was just finished when, one day, there was a cloudburst in the mountain, and at once the Žepa became troubled and swollen. On the following night the newly-finished dam gave way in the middle. And when the next day dawned the water had already withdrawn, but the wattle had been broken in many places, the stakes plucked out, the beams bent. Among the workers and peasants there were rumours that the Žepa would not let itself be bridged. But by the third day the master-mason had ordered new stakes to be driven in, deeper than before, and the remaining beams to be straightened and brought into line. And again, from deep down, the rocky river-bed echoed with mallets, workers' voices, and rhythmic blows.

Stone-dressers and masons, from Herzegovina and Dalmatia, arrived only after everything had been prepared, and the stone from Banja brought in. Sheds were put up for them, and they chipped stone in front of the sheds, white with stone-dust like millers. The master-mason walked among them, leaning down and measuring their work with a yellow try-square and a lead plummet on a green thread. Both steep, craggy banks had been cut through when the money ran out. The workers grumbled and the people muttered that nothing would come of the bridge. Some of those who came from Constantinople reported rumours that the Vizier had greatly changed. No one knew what was the matter with him, whether it was illness or anxiety, but he was more unapproachable each day, forgetting and abandoning work he had begun in Constantinople itself. But a few days later one of his men arrived with the rest of the money, and the building went on.

A fortnight before St. Demetrius's Day, people crossing the Žepa over the logs, a little upstream from the works, noticed for the first time that from the dark grey slate on both banks a white, smooth wall of dressed stone was beginning to appear, plaited all over with cobwebs of scaffolding. It grew every day. But then the first frosts came and work was halted. The stone-dressers went home, and the master-mason spent the winter in his log-cabin which he hardly ever left, bowed all the time over his plans and calculations. But he often visited the building site. When spring was approaching and the ice began to crack, he would pace anxiously around the scaffolding and the dams; sometimes even by night, with a link in his hand.

Before St. George's Day the masons came back and the work went on. And just at midsummer the work was finished. The workers pulled down the scaffolding merrily, and from the criss-cross of beams and planks the bridge appeared, slender and white, a single arch spanning the space between two rocks.

Nothing could have been harder to imagine than such a marvellous structure in this desolate split landscape. It seemed as though a spurt of foam had gushed out from one bank to the other, and the two spurts had collided, joined into an arch, and remained like that for a moment, floating above the abyss. Through the arch, in the background, a stretch of the blue Drina could be seen, and deep below it the foamy Žepa, now tamed, gurgled on. It took a long time for the eye to adjust to the arch of well-designed, slender outlines; the arch seemed to have been arrested in flight, only for a moment, caught on the rugged dark rocks with their hellebore and clematis, always on the point of taking off again and disappearing.

From the neighbouring villages people bustled to see the bridge. The townspeople of Višegrad and Rogatica also came and admired it, regretting that it was built in such a rocky wilderness and not in their own town.

'It isn't easy to give birth to a vizier!' the inhabitants of Žepa would answer, patting the parapet of the bridge, straight and sharp-edged, as if cut from cheese and not hewn from stone.

While the first travellers, stopping in surprise, were crossing the bridge, the master-mason paid off the workers, loaded and fastened his chests full of instruments and papers, and set off with the Vizier's men for Constantinople.

It was only then that the townspeople and villagers began to talk about him. Selim, the gypsy, who had brought him things from Višegrad on his horse, and was the only man who had visited his log-cabin, would sit in shops and tell, God knows how many times, everything he knew about the stranger.

'Indeed, he is not a man like other people are. When the work stopped in winter, I wouldn't go to see him sometimes for ten or fifteen days. But whenever I came everything was in a mess, just as I had left it. In the cold log-cabin he sat with a bear-skin cap on his head, wrapped up to his arm-pits, only his hands showing free, livid with cold, while he chipped at his stones and wrote something down; chipped and wrote. The whole time. I would unload my horse and he would look at me with his green eyes, his eyebrows raised — you'd think he was going to devour you. But he never said a word. I've never seen anything like it. And, my friends, you wouldn't believe how hard he was at it for a year and half, and when he finished his work, he set off for Constantinople and we took him across on the ferry, and he hurried away on his horse; but do you think that he turned back one single time to look at us or the bridge? No!'

And the shopkeepers asked more and more questions about the mason and his life, marvelled more and more at what they heard, regretting that they had not watched him more closely when he walked in the streets of Višegrad.

Meanwhile the master-mason travelled and, two stages before Višegrad, he fell ill of the plague. In a fever, hardly able to cling on to his horse, he reached the town. He was taken immediately to the hospital of the Italian Franciscans. And at the same hour the next day he breathed his last in the arms of a monk.

The next morning the Vizier had already learned of the mason's death, and the remaining bills and plans of the bridge were brought to him. The mason had received only a quarter of his wages. He had left behind him no debts and no cash, no will and no heirs. The Vizier thought it over for a while and ordered one of the remaining three-quarters of the wages to be paid to the hospital and the other two given for the paupers' bread and broth.

As he was giving his orders — it was a quiet morning in late summer — a petition from a young, learned Constantinople mullah was brought to him. The man had been born in Bosnia, wrote smooth verses, and the Vizier had sometimes supported him. He had heard, he said, of the bridge which the Vizier had built in Bosnia and hoped that an inscription would be carved on it, as on any other public edifice, telling the world when it was built and who had built it. As always, his services were at the Vizier's disposal and he begged the Vizier to deign to accept the enclosed chronogram which he had composed with great difficulty. On the enclosed sheet of stout paper there was a finely copied chronogram with a red and gold initial:

> When Good Rule and Noble Skill
> Offered each other a friendly hand
> This beautiful bridge was born,
> To the delight of the subjects and Jusuf's pride
> In both worlds.

Underneath was the Vizier's oval seal, divided into two unequal fields; on the larger one was written: *Jusuf Ibrahim — God's true slave*, and on the smaller one was the Vizier's motto: *In silence is safety*.

The Vizier sat for a long time with the petition, his hands apart, one of his palms pressing the verse inscription and the other the mason's bills and plans. He spent more and more time lately reflecting over petitions and papers.

This summer it was two years since his fall and imprisonment. At first, after his return to power, he had not noticed any changes in himself. He was in his best years — when a man knows and feels the full value of living; he had triumphed over all his opponents and was more powerful than before; he could measure the height of his power by the depths of his recent fall. But as time went on, instead of forgetting, he was more and more haunted by the thought of prison. And if he sometimes found enough strength to drive away such thoughts, he could not stop his dreams. The prison began to obsess his dreams, and from the dreams of night, like a vague horror, it passed into his waking life, poisoning his days.

He became more sensitive to the objects around him. He was irritated by things which he had not even noticed before. He gave orders to have all the velvet in the palace replaced by bright cloth, soft and smooth, which did not rustle under the touch. He came to hate mother-of-pearl, for it was suggestive of some cold, desolate loneliness. The touch of mother-of-pearl, the mere sight of it, set his teeth on edge and made his flesh creep with horror. All furniture and weapons which had mother-of-pearl on them were removed from his rooms.

He began to regard everything with secret but deep mistrust. Without any apparent origin one thought was firmly rooted in his mind: every human action, every word *may* bring evil. And this *possibility* linked itself to everything he heard, saw, said or thought. The triumphant Vizier had come to know the fear of life. So, unawares, he entered the stage which is the first phase of dying, when a man comes to be absorbed more in the shadows of things than in the things themselves.

This evil gnawed at him, tearing him from within; he could not even think of confiding it to anyone; and by the time it had completed its work and burst through the surface, no one would be able to recognise it; people would simply say: death. For people did not suspect how many of the powerful and the great were silently, invisibly, but rapidly, dying like this from within.

This morning the Vizier was again weary, not having slept, but calm and cool-headed; his eyelids were heavy, and his face as if frozen in the freshness of the morning. He thought of the foreign mason who had died and of the poor who would eat his earnings. He thought of the distant, mountainous, gloomy land of Bosnia (there had always been gloom in his thoughts of Bosnia!) which even the light of Islam could only partially illuminate and where life, lacking lofty conduct and gentleness, was miserable, niggardly, harsh. And how many such lands there were in Allah's world? How many rivers without a bridge or ford? How many places without drinking water, how many mosques without decoration or beauty?

Before his mind's eye a world appeared, full of various needs, misery, and fear in different shapes.

The small green tiles of the summer house blazed in the sun. The Vizier looked down on the mullah's verses, raised his hand slowly, and crossed out twice the whole inscription. He stopped a moment, and then crossed out also the first part of the seal with his name. Only the motto remained: *In silence is safety.* He stopped for a while, looking at the motto, and then raised his hand again and in a resolute stroke wiped that out, as well.

So the bridge was left nameless, without any sign.

Over there, in Bosnia, it shone in the sun and glistened in the light of the moon, taking men and cattle from one bank to another. Little by little the circle of dug-out earth and scattered things which surrounds every new erection, disappeared; people carried off and the water swept away broken stakes, pieces of scaffolding and the rest of the timber, and the rains washed off the traces of stone-dressing. But the landscape could not accept the bridge and the bridge could not accept the landscape. Seen from the side, the bold span of its white arch always looked isolated and lonely and took the traveller by surprise like a strange thought, gone astray and caught among the crags, in the wilderness.

The teller of this story was the first man to whom it occurred to examine and find out how it came to be there. This happened one evening when he was coming back from the mountains and sat down wearily by its parapet. It was the season of hot summer days and cool nights. When he leaned his back against the stone, it was still warm with the heat of day. The man was sweaty, and a cold wind was blowing from the Drina; pleasant and strange was the touch of the warm, hewn stone. They understood each other at once. Then he decided to write its history.

In The Guest-House

Ever since the abbot had rebuilt the guest-house in the spring of last year and separated it more clearly from the monastery, he had entrusted Brother Marko entirely with keeping it in order and managing it.

Brother Marko Krneta was the nephew of the late Bishop, Brother Marijan Bogdanović. Because he was the only male offspring in his family, he was taken while still a boy by the Bishop into the monastery, to study and serve. But in spite of the Bishop's favours and attention, the youth made no progress at all. He was headstrong and dull-witted, he stammered and spat when he spoke, had no ear for music, beat up the younger boys and disobeyed his elders. And no one could stop him from swearing like a shepherd. The only 'progress' was that his habit grew shorter and shorter and its cotton fabric tighter and tighter.

'You can't drive a forked stake into the ground, nor our Brother Marko into the holy order,' the Bishop informed his sister, who died grieving that her son would not also become a bishop.

The exasperated Bishop decided that as a last resort he would send him to Rome, in the hope that he might come to his senses once he was abroad. As he struggled with his uneducated and stubborn brethren, the difficult and uncertain Bosnian roads, and the arbitrary and ever-hungry Turkish authorities, he remembered as if in a dream his own years as a youth in Rome. Now he was sending his sister's son to the same red-tiled Franciscan monastery where he had spent three years, young and full of knowledge and grand plans. It seemed to him that his own life was being renewed.

But here too he was disappointed. Entrusting the boy to his old friends proved useless.

'He shows no aptitude for anything. All he does is grow inexorably taller and broader. And his behaviour — it is like anything but that of a monk, if I may dare say so, most Reverend Father,' came the letter from Rome. 'He is pure and modest, and pious in his own way: he truly does not show the least desire for worldly pleasures and vanities. But unfortunately he is totally devoid of any sense of learning and contemplation, or of holy penitences towards his superiors and tolerance for others,' wrote the director of the institution.

And from Brother Marko himself there came letters written in an uneven, gnarled hand, full of errors, in which he implored his uncle desperately to have him recalled to Kreševo.

'Deliver me from this! I can't go on living with these people!' If only he could see Kreševo again, even if — like the bandit Ivan Roša, who did not dare enter his native town but climbed the mountain to satisfy his longing — only to look at it from afar.

He wrote constantly in this vein.

The Bishop was going to wait a year, thinking that by then if the boy had not adjusted or reformed, he would bring him back to Kreševo. But that very winter the Bishop caught cold and suddenly died. Brother Marko was immediately called back from Rome. In his place they sent Brother Mija Subašić, an ambitious and sickly youth.

And now Brother Marko was already in his second year as steward of this monastery. He took care of the livestock and the wine, supervised and paid the workers, and welcomed even Turkish guests in the guest-house.

Spending all his time with the peasants in heavy toil, he lost even that little discipline he had, and forgot all that he had learned. His hands grew coarse and his voice husky. Tall and broad-shouldered already, he became even larger and heavier. He grew a bristly moustache and became ruddy in the face. Swear words crept more and more frequently into his speech.

He was unsuccessful in learning, grumpy and obstinate. Without his uncle's protection life in the monastery was not easy for him. The worst was that he never knew when the brothers were making fun of him and when they were being serious, so that he would sometimes blow up for no reason and look even more ridiculous, while on other occasions he would throw himself into a conversation, not noticing that in the far corner of the refectory they were laughing at him.

He cut himself off more and more from the other monks. Absolved of the obligation of communal dining and prayer, he would spend his days off in the fields or in the guest-house. He haggled and squabbled with the peasants, and himself took up a hoe and dug in front of everyone until he was bathed in sweat, and then stood steaming in the cool of early evening like a hill after a rainfall. Or he would decant wine in the damp cellar, rolling barrels about and smoking them with sulphur. Or he would spend an entire day pouring grain in the granary and then be unable for two days afterwards to wash the dust out of his throat and ears.

But with all that he had his moments of 'bliss' which no one knew of or even suspected. And he himself did not know either how this came about or when it would happen.

After some heavy work, he would sit down on a log, wipe the sweat from his face and breathe hard, then suddenly he felt the blood roaring in his shoulders, his neck and his head, louder and louder, until his head spun and the noise filled him completely and carried him away. He sat with his head in his hands, his eyes open, but it seemed as though he were flying swiftly away somewhere. And then he, who did not know how to write nicely or to speak cleverly, was somehow able to understand everything and to speak clearly and freely with God Himself.

On other occasions too, whatever job he was doing, he prayed under his breath to God. Sometimes he even settled accounts with the Almighty, after his own fashion.

He would be planting out cabbages after a day of rain. He bent down, bored little holes in the soft soil of the garden patch and pressed the earth together around the new plant with his fingers. At each stalk he whispered a prayer, repeating over and over again: Good luck to you, in God's name, good luck to you.'

The sweat dripped from his face. When he finished one row, he stood up groaning (his back was killing him!), wiped off the sweat with the back of his dirty hand, and muttered with a sigh: 'Well, I've planted it — now send the caterpillars to eat it, just like You did last year!'

Sometimes the blissful sensation would fill him for no apparent reason. He would touch a knot on a tree or the seam on his clothing and the same ecstasy would stream through his fingers and engulf him; and he stood there numb, his mouth agape, a lost look in his eyes. A long time would pass like this, and when he came to he wouldn't remember having seen or heard anything specific.

For the last three days not a single Turk had stopped at the guest-house. Every day Brother Marko aired and censed it to drive out the smell of suet, onion, rakija and sweat left behind by the previous guests. But on the third day, early on Saturday evening during Vespers, some Turks showed up again.

At the moment of their arrival Brother Marko was at the hearth pouring coals into the censer, which a young boy was holding. When he saw the Turks coming up the hill, he poured half the coals past the censer and singed the child, who ran away. He opened his mouth to swear, but restrained himself and merely pulled his cap down over his eyes.

The Turks were climbing slowly up the hill. Brother Marko took half the sugar and coffee and went off to hide them. He came back to the guest-house out of breath, placed himself athwart the door and looked down the track. There were three Turks all told; two of them were leading a third, holding him under the arms. He recognised one of them — it was Kezmo the janissary. The other two must be strangers. The sick one was still quite young.

As soon as they entered they asked for a blanket and some pillows, and put their sick friend to bed. Then they asked for some lemons. Brother Marko was sorry: he would look, but feared there were none.

'Take a good hard look, old man! Don't make *me* start looking for them!' shouted Kezmo to him.

This Kezmo had already terrified the monastery and caused them to be fined several times.

Brother Marko returned with the lemons and they gave the sick man lemonade.

'Now take down the frying pan, so I can hang up my rifle,' joked Kezmo.

Brother Marko took down the frying pan and began to cook some eggs. The Turks sat down and started smoking. The sick man rested and drank the lemonade, and when he felt better stretched out on the pillows and joined in the conversation, although he was trembling and his eyes glittered with fever. Brother Marko served them rakija and eggs, and put on water for coffee. They ate their food noisily and offered some to the sick man, who declined it. Then they stretched out, belching.

'Hey, you didn't have any pork in that pan, did you?' asked Kezmo, bringing the empty pan up to his nose.

Bent over the coals and busy with the coffee, Brother Marko mumbled to himself, Hmph, now you think of it, after you've eaten your fill.

'What's that you said?'

'Nothing, Aga, nothing. There's no pork here.'

He served them coffee. Kezmo watched him with his large green eyes.

'I hear the judge fined you twenty groschen when he found a chicken's head in the pilaff. By Allah, if you gave that swine twenty, you'll have reason to give me forty.'

'Money's something I don't know about.'

'Ha, ha ,you're all the same: "I don't know", "I don't have any"' but you're as full of money as a pomegranate, you just have to be squeezed a bit.'

But then everything turned into a joke again.

Night fell. The Turks started talking about war, janissaries' wages, and kept on drinking. The sick man would doze off, then wake up and listen. Brother Marko sat down in the corner, propped his elbows on his knees and his head on his palms, fell silent and listened. From their conversation he gradually made out that the sick Turk was Osmo Mameledžija from Sarajevo. Now they were killing time roaming about, waiting for their pay to arrive so they could leave for Vidin.

Kezmo was telling stories with gusto — how big Mustapha Pasha's bridge was, how big the caravanseray in Adrianople was, and what the brothels in Istanbul were like, with their Greek and Armenian girls.

'I tell you, girls like that could even take in Brother Marko. Eh, Brother Marko?'

'Tss, I don't know about such things.'

'Oh, come on!'

'We don't go in for that. In fact we would blow up every one of those places if we could.'

The Turks laughed. The sick man groaned lightly in his sleep. The others were drowsy too, with the journey and the rakija. Brother Marko got up and doused the coals that remained in the hearth.

The next day the sick man was worse. After eating another dozen eggs, the Turks deliberated what to do. The Abbot would have liked to be rid of them. He told them through Brother Marko how hard it would be on the sick man to have to stay in the guest-house. In turn they asked for horses. Knowing that they would never return them, the Abbot made the excuse that there were none, but offered them five groschen apiece. So it was concluded that the Turks would be given the money and the friars would care for the sick man only until the following day, when they would return for him with a horse. They set off.

Brother Marko was angry that they had left the Turk in his care.

'He had to come here to lie around! As if I hadn't enough of healthy Muslim swine!'

The Abbot tried to soothe him, scolding him.

The first day he did not even look at the Turk. He put some bread and cheese down beside him and then left.

Three days passed, and the Turks did not return for the sick man, who groaned all day long and asked more and more often for water. Brother Marko got used to bringing him water, and serving him milk and sweets. Several times a day he would leave his work and run into the guest-house to see the sick man. He quarrelled with the cook because he kept picking out the best pieces and taking them to the sick man. The friars noticed his concern for the Turk and began to tease him.

'How's your patient doing, Brother Marko?'

He would just retort sharply in passing: 'He's over there, croaking his last. Come and see him if you're so interested.'

In fact, the weaker the Turk grew, the more Brother Marko worried about him, although he tried to hide this from the others and did not want to admit it even to himself.

The Turk was mostly silent. One evening Brother Marko had made a fire to bake the communion wafers. While waiting for the baking mould to heat up among the coals, he sat next to the hearth, blinking from the heat.

'Brother Marko,' came the voice of Mameledžija from his bed in the dark corner of the room.

'Eh?'

'No sign of Kezmo?'

'No sign.'

Both were silent.

'Ah, if only they'd just take me to Sarajevo, and then . . . '

The logs on the bottom burned through and fell to pieces, the fire came together and crackled, and sparks flew around Brother Marko. Then the flames settled down and the room was filled with a dark red glow.

'Well, don't you bother thinking about Sarajevo and such nonsense . . . '

And suddenly (he himself was surprised), he continued calmly, without his usual stuttering: 'Instead, why don't you get baptised, my poor Osmo? Then if it is your fate to die you can die like a good Christian soul and if you stay alive than you can live as a man and not some mindless animal.'

The Turk said nothing in response. He lay mute and immobile, his eyes tightly shut.

From that time on Brother Marko spoke to him about it every day, not even thinking of the danger should the Turks return and Mameledžija tell them he had been trying to baptise him. He even concealed his efforts from the friars, lest they make fun of him. But he wanted to save Osmo Mameledžija's soul, at all costs.

Silence was the Turk's response to every attempt at persuasion, nor could one get any idea from his face what he was thinking.

Sometimes it seemed to Brother Marko that his heart was softening, and other times the Turk seemed hard and incorrigible.

One morning one of the women working at the harvest went into the guest-house to get some coals of fire. As she squatted down by the hearth to scrape up the embers, her pantaloons billowed out and settled down around her in a wavy circle. Mameledžija had been feverish and up to a moment before had been listening without any expression on his face to Brother Marko, who was speaking of the sweet pleasures of repentance and the beauty of a Christian death. All of a sudden he tried to raise himself up from the pillow, stretched out his hand from under the blanket and, trembling, tried to reach the woman's pantaloons. Brother Marko, who had stepped out for a moment, came back in just then. He saw the change in Mameledžija: his eyes shone, his hand trembled, the blanket had fallen away from him, and he was stretched out on the bare floor.

Brother Marko wanted to shout out, but first his voice failed him completely and then it would only gurgle and hiss. He seized a broken axe handle from the corner and threatened the woman: 'Get out, daughter of the devil!'

The woman leaped up and tried to take away the embers she had come for, but he would not let her, driving her out instead. Not knowing why he was chasng her out, she turned and protested in vain that she had been sent to get some fire. But he hurled the handle after her.

'Get the hell out, you bitch! I'll break this over your head if you ever come back to shake out your skirts in my room.'

He made no attempt to look at Mameledžija who was once again lying peacefully in bed. Only when the noon bells sounded did he heat up some milk and place it beside him. Then he left the room immediately, muttering: 'Pffooo, you dirty dog, you'll never see the face of God.'

But by morning he was in a good mood again. He nursed Mameledžija and spoke to him again and again about baptism and faith. And at night he dreamed that he was fighting with devils who had gathered around his patient. He scattered them with the same broken axe handle, but like a person fighting in a dream, he could not swing it with his full strength. And there were more and more of them all the time, all shaggy, and only under their joints could you see their grey, sinewy skin.

He woke up. He was standing in the middle of the room. He lit the light. His arm ached. He pulled the Book of Rites down from the shelf, and the porcelain angel as well, breaking off the top of

55

its left wing. He crossed himself and lay down once more.

Mameledžija grew ever weaker. He ate nothing. All day long he groaned, his eyes closed. Kezmo had not returned. The Abbot was worried that the Turk was going to die in his monastery.

One evening Mameledžija felt better. He brightened up and became lively, and he kept striking up conversations with Brother Marko, who was twisting wicks for candles. Listening to his feverish assertions that he was better, Brother Marko thought that he might be nearing death. And so he came up to the bed and began to persuade him eagerly.

He grew more heated by the minute. And he himself wondered how he could speak with such ease. One minute he would be speaking from memory according to the prophets and Scripture, and the next he would forget himself again and speak to him in his own way.

'Poor fellow, do you really want to be with that slimy Kezmo in the next world too? Can't you see he's all swollen with drink and filth? He's still on this earth and already he's like the devil. He walks on the lid of Hell wherever he goes, and one day it'll open up and he'll be in the midst of the burning pit. And you with him!'

Here he got angry and was about to say something unpleasant, but then quickly regained control of himself and begged him to remember 'dear sweet Jesus and his mother Mary'. Still choosing his words, he described to Osmo how a Christian dies and how they greet the soul of a Christian in the next world with trumpets, splendour and glory beside which all earthly pleasure is nothing.

The Turk had fallen silent; his closed eyelids occasionally twitched. Brother Marko had leaned right over him. He was observing him closely but was unable to make out what he was thinking. His face was just as it always was — thin and oval, with pouting lips like a defiant boy's.

'Just say: Saviour be a help unto us. Say it, Osmo,' whispered Brother Marko to him as softly and sweetly as he could. The Turk was silent. From him came only heavy breathing and the bobbing of his Adam's apple.

Thinking that perhaps he was unable to speak, Brother Marko took the little crucifix on the rosary which hung at his waist and brought it to the Turk's lips.

'Kiss it, Osmo, this is your Saviour and mine. Kiss it and He will forgive your sins and receive you unto Him.'

The Turk's face moved almost imperceptibly, his eyelids began to tremble and he moved his lips as if he wanted to say something. Then he pursed his lips tightly and with a great effort

— he spat. The spittle filtered down through his beard.

Swiftly Brother Marko pulled away the cross, leapt up, and ran outside growling.

The vast monotonous hum of a summer night. Only towards the end of summer are the stars so big and the sky so low. He gripped the fence with his hands, clenching his fingers. The blood rushed to his head from anger and would not quiet down but rather kept throbbing up again. He gazed though the dark tree trunks, far away into the depths of the sky where the stars were starting to appear and spoke as usual, to himself: 'There's not a brother who's worse than me, nor a Turk that's filthier than that Osmo. I try to baptise him, and he — oooohh!'

He shook the fence in torment.

But gradually he calmed down. He began to lose himself in the quiet night, in the gaze of innumerable stars. He slowly forgot himself. Waves from his trembling body carried over onto everything around him and he felt as though he were sailing swiftly over an ocean in the dark. The sky above him rocked perceptibly. There were sounds all around. He clasped the railings tightly.

Everything was on this great moving ship of God's: the village and the fields, the monastery and the guest-house.

'I know that You do not forget anyone, not even stuttering Marko or that sinful Osmo Mameledžija. If someone does spit on Your cross, it is only like a bad dream. There is still room for everyone on Your ship. Even for that crazy Kezmo, if he hadn't gone away ...'

In his ecstasy, he did not know whether he was speaking out loud or only thinking to himself. But he could see: there was room on God's ship for everything and everyone, because He measured neither by the yardstick nor by the scale. Now he understood how it was that 'the Lord is awesome', how He could move worlds, now he understood everything, although he had no words for it, only he could not understand how it was that he, Brother Marko Krneta, a clumsy and disobedient monk, was standing here holding the tiller of that ship of the Lord's. — And then he forgot himself again. He knew only that everything that existed was moving and travelling, and that it was all going towards salvation.

Hours passed in this way.

A cool night breeze. His blood was quieting down. First he felt his numbed hands wrapped around the railings, and slowly he began to detach himself and come to his senses. He felt cold and sore, as he had during his novitiate when he would be awakened, still sleepy, before dawn. Barely managing to let go of the fence, he passed his hand over his habit and returned to the guest-house with unsteady steps.

The candle had burnt down and was melting and sputtering. The Turk was lying with his face to the wall and the covers up to his eyes. Brother Marko put out the candle, heated up some milk and came over to the sick man. He called his name twice, and when there was no answer, he went to uncover him, but Mameledžija was already cold and stiff.

He put the pot of steaming milk down next to the dead man's head and went out to call the Abbot. It was already quite light.

He ran through the refectory and the courtyard, banging on the doors, and entered the sacristy. The Abbot had just pulled his chasuble over his head. When he heard the door slam, he stopped with his arms outstretched and stared at Brother Marko through his spectacles: 'Now what is it?'

Waving his arms about in agitation, Brother Marko nearly shouted: 'He's gone, that one! The Turk, in the guest-house.'

'Why are you shouting? Hush!' scolded the Abbot in a whisper, pointing towards the altar.

The Abbot was concerned. As soon as he had finished saying Mass and drunk some coffee, he went down to the village to inform the authorities of Mameledžija's death and to summon the Turks to take him and bury him according to their law. He knew that suspicion would fall on them and that they would not get off without a fine.

Brother Marko did not want to return to the guest-house. Instead he sent the novice Martin to sit with the dead man, while he went out to the field with the workers who were digging the beet patch.

Sleepless and distraught, he trudged heavily across the furrows.

The young men and girls of the village had begun to dig. Brother Marko went out ahead of them and started to break off the lower leaves so that the beets would grow stronger. Standing astride the rows he bent down and tore off of the leaves, and as he broke off handfuls of leaves, he would put them to one side. Behind him the little piles of leaves mounted up. And whenever he would straighten up, he looked back along the fields to the large, dark monastery and beside it the small, white guest-house. In it lay the dead man whose soul he had been unable to save.

Then he bent down quickly and broke off the leaves, and after he had trimmed each stalk he shook his hands so that the torn-off leaves fell through them.

'Grow now, God speed you on your way . . . He guzzled our rakija and ate our cheese, but the cross and repentance he wouldn't take . . . Grow now, God speed!'

Somewhat later he saw the Abbot coming, along with the Muslim Imam and two other Turks, black as flies. When he saw them carry the dead man out, he bent down again and began breaking off the leaves even faster: 'Good luck to you, God speed you on your way,' he repeated mechanically, but his thoughts kept returning to the departed one: saved or not, he had cared for him and loved him as a brother!

As he stood, bent over, the blood pounded in his head. Hissing and panting, he prayed for the soul of Osmo Mameledžija, 'let it be where it may!'

But from time to time he would raise his head and shout at the young men who were teasing the girls: 'Dig, you loafers! What are you fooling around for? Just look at him! . . .'

And then he would return to his work again, breaking off leaves and praying.

Death in Sinan's Tekke

From the time Alidede came back to Sarajevo, Sinan's tekke, the dervish monastery, became the place where the best and most intelligent people gathered.

This famous man had spent forty-five years in Istanbul. He was known afar for his learning and sanctity, and for good works done not only among his Order but for individuals and the statesmen who had wanted to listen to him.

Destiny had bestowed on him not only knowledge and discernment, and an outlook wider than other men's, but also such a perfect harmony between body and soul that to everyone who knew him, either personally or by reputation, he figured as a paragon of all perfections whom they despaired of imitating. Restlessness, and the human need for restlessness, seemed quite unknown to him. People said he did not know what a woman's body was, or fleshly pleasures at all. He had never tasted any kind of intoxicating drink, nor a cup of Turkish coffee, or a breath of tobacco smoke. But he did not condemn the people who do use such God-given gifts in this brief life of ours. In general, he passed through this world like a man who noticed nothing in it either evil or ugly.

Everything that Alidede did or spoke has been written down, but nowhere has it been recorded, nor will it ever be explained, how or from where such a pure and sublimely religious man appeared. In the times into which he was born, and the world in which he lived, he remains an inexplicable exception, a marvel.

In his sixty-fifth year Alidede suddenly decided to leave the head-tekke from which he had spread the fame of the Order, to bid farewell to Istanbul, his admirers, disciples and the brethren with whom he had grown old, and to return to Bosnia. No one dared oppose his decision, though all were dissatisfied with it. Because he had never said a word in his life to pain or disparage another person, he did not like to tell them the real reason — that death and his homeland were calling him. On the contrary, even from parting, which is the most painful thing in the world, he was able to draw beauty and a moral lesson. He spoke to those who expressed astonishment and regret at his leaving them about the breadth and the uniformity of the created world. What is far to a believer? And what can be strange to him? All over the wide world, a little shade can be found, in which a man may stretch out in prayer; everywhere men know which direction is East; everywhere a little water can be found that has passed over at least forty pebbles, and is therefore pure for ablution. And where even that does not exist, the man who lives in the true faith can never be confounded. Even in the regions where for weeks, the sun does not appear — and there are such — the heart of the believer will direct him to the East, towards which he must pray. Even in the desert where there is not a drop of water, sand can be used for ablution; and where there is no sand either, the true believer can wash in thought alone, for thought is stronger and purer than anything else. So why should they mourn his leaving for Bosnia, from whence he sprang, and which was as full of God's beauty as any other country on earth? A man owes something to his native country.

That is how Alidede came to Sarajevo this spring. He was grey-haired, bent and half-blind from much reading, but his blue eyes were clear and gay, with a perpetual smile reflected in his silver beard, and his hands were peaceful, pale and ageless, like the hands of all people who live spotless lives.

Once a week, on the evening of Friday, learned men, respected citizens and pious travellers on their way through Sarajevo came to Sinan's tekke, as did all the friends of the tekke and the Order who wanted to hear Alidede's words.

Thus they had gathered this evening too. As the night was warm and clear, the meeting took place in the courtyard of the building. It was a rectangular space, entirely of stone. On all four sides grew yellow flowers and up the wall climbed a vine which in summertime made a green roof over the yard. In the centre was a low fountain whose jet did not shoot into the air, but merely spurted up to flow down again around a ball of marble and then trickle into a round basin. Thus it did not offend the eye with that repeated drama of fatigue and failure according to the implacable law that when water shoots upward as high as it can, it must collapse impotently back on itself, but looked like a large tropical flower which opens at the top to show its silver centre but never blooms or fades. In the basin, green with moss, the water was dark; inside were two red fish, like two secret, incomprehensible letters. A large rush carpet was spread on the stone flags for the guests and on the dais, by the wall, was a cushion for Alidede.

They had all assembled by now. Alidede was sitting in his place. A little before he began to speak, the old man abstractedly broke off a vine-leaf and held it between his teeth. Biting lightly on the young stalk, he tasted the sharpness of the vine on his tongue and it astonished him by its bitterness. At the same time something gripped him in the chest. He felt he had lost his breath and would not be able to say a word, yet he began. With his first words he choked several times as if from a strange childish cough, but each time he continued to speak, though ever more weakly. Suddenly his voice broke in the middle of a word, his head dropped a little and his right hand sought his heart. At first his listeners, who were mostly looking in front of them, did not pay any attention to the silence; they supposed him to be carried away by some idea, as often happened. When the silence became too prolonged, the dervishes and disciples began to wonder and exchange glances, for they knew the dervish rule Alidede had recommended to them, and followed himself — that it was wrong for a man to dwell in his ecstasy, lest he grow proud and draw on himself the envy of others. When at last they looked up and saw the movements of his right hand, they ran towards him. Alidede was in his death-throes. Under his half-closed lashes was a glassy gleam. Leaning against the wall, he merely waved his hand feebly, and just managed to whisper in his kindly voice: 'It's nothing . . . nothing!'

They carried him to his room, unbuttoned his clothing and laid him down on the floor, supporting his head with a cushion from the sofa. They sprinkled him with water and rubbed him with ointment. Without opening his eyes, which seemed all at once to have sunk, he sought to pull out the cushion from under his head with his hand. Thus he lay on the ground, with the vine-leaf trembling on his chest and his perturbed disciples moving around him. He lived only two or three minutes more.

His memory worked rapidly and vividly. Only twice in his life had he been moved by the appearance of a woman, and these were inconspicuous events, meaningless and unimportant, the sort which take place in secret, unknown and unseen by anyone else, and are eventually forgotten even by ourselves. But now, out of his whole long and industrious life, only those two incidents confronted him: two small and senseless anxieties which had filled a few days of his boyhood and youth, now grown into two distinct ghosts, which swept aside all the rest, his life, body and thought, and merged into one single feeling of pain which filled him entirely. Yet all of this was less than the point of the sharpest needle — the last trace of consciousness and the last proof of his existence.

He was ten or eleven years old. Their house was outside the town, isolated among fields and plum orchards in the place where the river Bosna takes a sharp bend, and skirts Zenica. In spring and autumn when the water rose, the Bosna grew muddy and swollen and came up to the house itself, sweeping their garden fence away and carrying along the fences of other people, broken off from God knows where. It rolled down logs and roots, depositing a thick sediment of mud, branches, rags, broken barrels and sawn wood. For children it was a new world to delight in, foreign and mysterious, which they spent days exploring after every flood.

That spring the water was unusually capricious, subsiding suddenly and suddenly rising again on the same day. Early one evening the water had subsided after a startling and muddy inundation which had swept through their garden that morning. The sky was low and cloudy, and from the mountains came a distant, muffled roar announcing a new flood. The child was wandering by himself and, with a long stick, drawing patterns at random in the soft reddish mud left behind by the water. Right by the fence he noticed a short, round beam half buried in mud, leaves and pebbles. He was as pleased with it as with an unexpected toy and immediately climbed onto it; carefully, for it was still wet and slippery. He was supported by his stick against the fence and his feet on the log, and so he wavered, losing and then quickly regaining his balance, wholly taken up with those peculiar movements which adults think so senseless and dangerous, but which for children are imposed by the demands of their growing bodies and awakening imaginations. But children's bodies tire easily and their imaginations are quickly satisfied. The child threw away his stick, let himself down and sat astride the beam, feeling the deposit of sand and dry boughs with his left hand. Then his glance fell on something strange and puzzling. In the sand and branches he seemed to see a human ear and a lock of hair. He turned around, and behind him he saw a naked female body caught between the beam and the fence, more than half buried in mud; but a shoulder protruded clearly from the sediment, and a little lower down a white hip stuck out. The knee was hidden in mud, but then a calf emerged and the toes. The child went suddenly still. After he had passed a second glance along the whole length of this body the flood had brought, he got slowly down from the beam and began to retreat through the garden, moving backwards without taking his eyes off the place where the drowned woman lay. When he reached the firm, dry ground where the beehives were, he stopped; it was only there that he was seized by fear. Running towards the house, he was suddenly overwhelmed by a sense of shame he had never known before. Although he was tormented by fear and the need to speak, he could not have found a single word in which to tell them of what he had seen. He wandered around the courtyard and they could scarcely draw him into the house. All the time he looked at his father, mother and brothers, he was thinking, 'Well, now I have to speak, now I shall tell them what I saw.' But when he tried to find the first word and begin, his throat closed up and his lips were sealed. As long as it was light, he was in dread lest one of his brothers go into the garden and discover the secret.

As there were numerous children in the house, no one noticed that the little boy ate nothing. The evening passed and bed-time approached. The memory of the corpse he had seen grew and turned into a confused kind of guilt which tormented him and made him want to tell his mother everything immediately, to sob it out and find an explanation. But at the same time, he was aware of the impossibility of his saying anything at all about it. He approached his mother several times, trying to draw her attention, but she did not notice anything strange about the child and he did not have the strength to start a conversation. Finally he went to bed. It was only then that the play of childish fancies and nerves began, with his first experience of insomnia.

In his thoughts he climbed onto the beam a thousand times, approached the drowned woman, looked her over, ran, calling his mother's name and, finding no solution or comfort at home, returned to the garden. He stirred and turned over beside his brothers, who were sleeping soundly. He resolved endlessly: now he would get up, call out and beg his mother to go into the garden with a burning torch to see. But he remained nailed to the mattress, while the feeling of fear went on growing and the incomprehensible guilt grew deeper.

Morning found him in a fever. He got up before anyone else, and ran into the garden. He saw that it was half-covered in water, which had risen in the course of the night. There was no trace of the beam or of the drowned woman. The water had risen to the height of the fence, the mainstream was sweeping though the centre of the garden and the river went on rising all day. The rain cleared up and a weak spring sun shone, but the mountains sent down those noisy torrents which flow only one day a year, and all that day boil, rage and carry everything before them.

It seemed to the child that these new inundations of muddy water were carrying away everything that had tormented him. He spent the day in confused anticipation, and the next night he slept without dreams or wakefulness, worn out by the insomnia of the night before. When he went down to the garden the following morning, the water had subsided considerably. In the course of the day it fell enough for the whole fence to emerge; great puddles of muddy water lay all around it, but it was clear that the water had carried both the beam and the drowned woman further on.

All that spring the child was tormented by his secret. Every day the thought repeated itself that, now it was all over, he would tell his mother all about it. He felt it would make it easier for him; but he never found the courage to begin, or the words to express it. As well as the shame that had restrained him right from the start, the fear overtook him that no one would believe him now, they would make fun of him, or they might punish him for not speaking out immediately. It was only with the hot summer and invigorating autumn that he began to forget; and even so, for long afterwards, especially in the late afternoon, he was liable to be surprised by this fear of the unknown corpse — along with an inexplicable feeling of guilt, the need to confess and tell someone about it and the impossibility of his doing so.

A year or two later the child was taken away by one of his uncles, an eccentric, affluent man who lived in Sarajevo. There he went into Sinan's tekke and learnt to love the rules and teaching of his Order. That led him on to Istanbul.

He was around twenty-five years old. He had already been five or six years in Istanbul, the youngest of the teachers, highly respected, and unusually mature for his age.

The building he was living in had two aspects. The longer, main one looked onto the sea; the other onto a steep hillside with gardens and graveyards with a solitary road leading down it.

One night, the young man stirred and woke up just at midnight. He got up, opened the window and, leaning his head against the wooden bars, breathed in the cold air of early spring. The night was moonless, but clear and starlit.

The cobblestones of the street ahead of him gleamed as the road mounted the hill, bounded on both sides by a high wall and dark gardens. His eyes began to close slowly from the fresh night air; he was about to shut the window and go back to bed when a

white figure appeared at the top of the street, making its way
rapidly down it. He opened his eyes wide in a daze between
sleeping and waking. The figure was approaching at great speed:
it was a woman in a white dress, or perhaps just a shift. A little
later two dark male figures appeared from a corner at the top of
the street; they were running too. The heavy thudding of their feet
soon made itself heard. The woman was running straight towards
the gate, which was right under the window; she was racing,
sparing no effort, evidently mad with fear like a hunted animal.
As she came close, she could be clearly seen to be dishevelled,
half-naked, her clothes torn.

The dull, weak sound of her body could be heard thudding
against the heavy, locked gate. The young man leaned out and
saw the woman as clearly as before, lying on the broad
flagstones. Her head was resting on the threshold itself, and her
hand stretched up vainly for the knocker, which she did not have
the strength to reach.

Her pursuers, who were only twenty paces away from the
building, stopped suddenly when they saw that the woman had
managed to reach the gate, and swiftly lost themselves in a narrow
alley between the garden walls.

The young man did not dare glance down to the gate again. As
if he too were playing his part in this strange nocturnal drama, he
let go of the bar he was holding. Stepping backwards, he began
slowly to retreat to his bed and quickly lay down.

He was utterly numbed, stiff, without a single thought, as if
what he had seen just now had not pierced his consciousness at
all. The bed quickly warmed beneath him, and he fell into sleep as
rapidly as a faint. He slept five minutes, possibly ten; then
something painful and violent awoke him. Like someone else's
rough hand, his own stomach roused him from sleep; and,
immediately, before he opened his eyes, there flooded through
him the painful twilight consciousness of some complicated
misfortune. He had experienced something dreadful and terrible.
Perhaps he had dreamt it? How wonderful that there is such a
thing as consciousness — that a man can wake up and shake off
his dreams! Or perhaps he had really experienced something
painful, which would be waiting for him as soon as he opened his
eyes? So he wavered between sleeping and waking for a while,
until at last the heavy conviction grew in him that it had not been a
dream, but reality. Awake, he clearly saw the dark, armed men
once again chasing the half-naked woman, clearly heard her fall,
and once again saw her arm stretched out for the knocker, which

was too high. And her knocking might ring out at any moment.

His first thought was not to carry on suffering this painful uncertainty, but to get up, go to the window and verify it for himself. That thought existed in his mind, but it had no power over him; not letting it go, he lay unmoving, while his imagination grew ever more active. Just to avoid getting up and perhaps seeing something more of the night's events, he deliberately deluded himself that it might have been a dream after all: that there was no point in getting up and looking, for his action itself would lend the thing a semblance of reality. The delusion then began to work in him, speeding to and fro like a shuttle on a loom.

'Well, then, if there really isn't anything there, if nothing did happen to you, why don't you get up and take a look at the gate from the window? What are you afraid of?'

And then the same thought would rush by in the other direction: 'Why get up and look when I know there's nothing, when I know it was all a dream and illusion?'

So it went on endlessly, like a crazy see-saw, with little intermissions of a minute or two's sleep after which the see-saw began again: 'Why not get up?' And beyond all that, the unbearable terror that any second her knocking might ring out.

At dawn, all his uncertainty was suddenly at an end. He no longer asked himself what had happened in the night, or whether it had happened; he just dressed quickly and went downstairs like a guilty, convicted man, expecting that the daylight would pitilessly expose the night's events in which, although he did not know exactly how, he too was implicated. He moved around cautiously, awaiting the first words and questions like blows. But the servants, disciples and dervishes went past him with everyday expressions and the usual greetings. How was this? Had no one found the unconscious woman at the gate, then, or her corpse? The joyful thought that there had been nothing there, that it had all been just a dream, shot through him like the sun. Let his night's vain torment be forgotten, then, which now seemed almost pleasant and grateful to him. But immediately he had another thought: to ask some of the dervishes whether they had heard anything in the night or noticed anything in the morning. Immediately he felt powerless to do it. And just as he had been helpless in the night with his inner decision — 'I ought to get up and find out what is happening' — so now he approached the dervishes, intending to question them or to say something himself about the night's events; but stopped, frightened, before the first word, and fell silent or turned the conversation to another subject.

When the evening of that day fell, he no longer wondered whether anything had happened or not, or whether or not to speak, but escaped to his room with a vague yet profound sensation of guilt and a fear there was no escaping. He lay down without supper or prayers, not to sleep, but to agonize and not just on the first evening, either. He tormented himself for days and days. He did not question any longer where this had come from, when it began, how or why it had come, and whether there was any real reason for it; he only knew he carried within himself something secret and dark. For many nights more he awoke from the rapping of a knocker which only he could hear, and kept vigil with the feeling that the body of an unconscious woman was lying by the gate beneath his window; he consoled himself immediately then that it was not so, that it would be sufficient to get up and go to the window to assure himself that there was nothing there; but he never did get up. In his insomnia and the treacherous darkness he asked himself, 'Who was that woman? Why were they chasing her? What happened to her? And how did she disappear from in front of the gate?' He reproached himself bitterly for not having gone down to the courtyard immediately that night, for not waking up the others, opening the gate, and helping the hunted woman — but he felt that now, too, if it were to happen all over again tonight, he would behave in the same way he had done then: he would not have the strength to do otherwise.

For months he did not dare go near the window or take a closer look at the upper gateway. Finally the baseless torment passed, like a kind of illness. The memory of it first lost its strength and then disappeared, leaving no trace.

After that he lived forty years in Istanbul without ever knowing disquiet or pain; nothing but work, and prayer. This was that life of Alidede's we spoke of before, of which stories were told wherever there were Muslim ears to hear them.

And here, now, was his last minute, and with it this memory, the last gleam of his consciousness.

He tried in vain not to think of it, or to remember something else, anything. Nothing but these two dark memories and a pain which tears, groans or howls could not express. In an anguish hitherto unknown and unsuspected, his last strength was converted into a prayer such as no true believer, learned or simple, had ever made. This is how Alidede prayed under the unbearable pressure of his pain, while his lips moved simply from habit, for there were no longer any words upon them:

'Keeper of all things, Great and Only One, I have been Thine from my beginning, and held so firmly in Thy grasp that no harm could befall me. This knowledge, this peace which Thou givest those who forsake all else and give themselves wholly into Thy care — this is true Paradise. I have lived without hardship, floating like a little grain of dust that dances in the sun's rays; without weight it floats on upward, filled with sunshine, like a little sun itself. I did not know that this kind of bitterness could fill a man's soul. I had forgotten that at the exit from this world, as at the entry, stands woman like a gate. And now comes this bitterness which cleaves my heart in two to remind me of what, with my eyes on heaven, I had forgotten: that the bread which we eat is in fact stolen; that for the life which is given us we are indebted to *takdirat*, evil destiny, and sin; and that we cannot pass from this world to that better one until we have broken off like ripe fruit, fallen headlong in a painful drop and hit the hard ground. We probably bear the bruise from that fall even in Paradise. This is my thought, O gracious one, and Thou seest it, whether I speak it or not: it is a bitterer and harder thing than I knew to be enslaved to the laws of Thy world.'

Seeing Alidede moving his lips, his disciples thought he was speaking his dying prayer and stopped wherever they happened to be, motionless and sad.

So he breathed his last. It was Friday evening, the night of a new moon; and by general agreement, his death was miraculous and holy and filled men with wonder, like his life itself.

The Climbers

Osatica. A town on a plateau, but the plateau is surrounded on all sides by high mountains and their bare, karst slopes. So both parties are right: those Osaticans who claim that their town is on a hill, as well as those who say that it is in a hole. But in spite of conflicting opinions they all have one thing in common: all Osaticans are born with an aspiration for heights and even the most unassuming and the humblest of them want to climb at least a span higher than they are. To climb higher and to have it seen and known. Those who are no good for anything else at least dream of climbing and tell stories about it. And this desire for climbing of all sorts and at all costs, for the illusion of height, never leaves them until their death — which is the end of all desires and, for the Osaticans, a kind of last and very special climbing. This craving is handed down from old to young, from one generation to the next.

And as regards this Osatican 'climbing urge' there is no difference between Muslim and Christian — although there is little else in which the two Osatican denominations agree: they even live in separate parts of town. The Christian part is on karst, on a hill, clustered round the church which is situated at the highest point, whereas the Muslim part is on the slopes of the hill, where everything is 'within reach' as they used to say, and where the soil, easier to cultivate, yields better crops.

In the days of Turkish power in Bosnia, the inhabitants of the lower part of the town climbed more frequently and were more ambitious climbers. They could well afford it, for indeed they were the Sultan's sons, looking down upon this world from horseback. Although, of course, there were poor men among them too: more men leading other people's horses than rich and noble riders. But even when the Turks' power was gone, their riches no more, their fame and their reputation remained, together with great self-esteem and a hundred stories about the good old days. Each story was told in rapture and heard with delight, and if you hear one of them, you will understand why — for instance, the story of Hasim Glibo who was so much talked about during the last Russo-Turkish war on account of his great, truly Osatican, exploit.

When the Turkish power was recruiting Muslims all over Bosnia for the war against Russia, every soul tried to avoid enlistment as best it knew how. The greater your reputation, your riches, your ingenuity, the more successfully and easily you could break away from the yoke of service. And yet somebody had to go, at least one or two men from every village and town — and they were usually young, poor men, day-labourers who had no influential relatives, no connections, and no reputations to lose. To serve in the Sultan's army and to put on the Western 'tight uniform' was not to climb up but rather to fall down; this is why only a single soldier set out from Osatica — Hasim Glibo, a humble-looking, dwarfish youngster who could not pay the ransom and had nobody to protect or defend him. But one single man from Osatica achieved greater fame than all the rest of the Sultan's army and, at least in the Osatican story, climbed higher than anybody else. To be sure, he never came back to his little town but was left behind on a camp site, where, wrapped in his thin blanket, he died of utter exhaustion and dysentery and was buried in black soil and quicklime, together with several dozen nameless askars like himself, felled by the same illness. But in Osatica a story sprang up about his glorious death; this story was not only more beautiful than the unbeautiful reality, but it was also bound to last longer than Hasim would have lasted had he stayed in the town, and for his fellow townsmen it was much more valuable than he himself could have been, there and living.

Every child knew it. The Russians had shut themselves in a craggy castle, they had stuck their flag on top of it so that it fluttered among the clouds. The Turkish army stared at the flag, but there was nothing they could do about it. And our Hasim, he also stared, he stared until he could no longer resist his heart's desire. He asked the commander to let him climb up and take down the giaours' flag. The commander refused to hear of it. Hasim told him who he was and where he came from and tried to make him see that for a man from Osatica, going up and down all his life anyway, there was no precipice which could not be climbed. At last the commander drove him away, rejecting his foolhardy plan. But Hasim set out alone, on his own account.

He set out at the break of day. Day was parting from night. The daily gun-fire, the usual trench fighting, the skirmishes and manoeuvres at the foot of the fortress had not yet begun. Barefoot, his trousers rolled up to the knees, his sleeves up to the elbows, with just a knife at his belt, Hasim began to climb up the precipice, which was not protected, because the Russians thought it inaccessible. At first nobody saw him, because it never occurred to anyone that a man could climb that side of the fortress. Finally both armies noticed him, the Turkish and Muscovite, but nobody fired. People could hardly recover from the first fit of wonder and surprise. Everybody stood motionless, as if petrified, just staring upwards. Whispers spread through the Turkish army: 'Ah, what's that?' 'An acrobat?' Until somebody said: 'Hasim of Osatica!' 'Yes, it's Hasim, no, it isn't Hasim!' And while they went on guessing, the Muscovites, after a long time, recovered and started shooting. But the Osatican moved from one boulder to the next, from one dead angle to another, climbing higher and higher, though nobody could see a foothold in the rock, though nobody could see even him clearly. Now he appeared, the next moment he was gone.

The armies watched what Hasim was doing. Commanders spotted him with their binoculars, gunmen with their sighting slits, but he climbed the highest bulwark and appeared on the plateau below the flag. From below the Russian army fired at him with everything that could yield fire. Bullets showered like hail, but Hasim's commander, a traitor jaundiced with envy, gave orders to some of his men to shoot. And so our Hasim was shot dead by a Turkish bullet — he was not destined to take down the Muscovite flag to the glory both of himself and of his town Osatica in Bosnia.

So the Osatican Turks buried Hasim Glibo in glory at the top of a Russian fortress, Hasim Glibo who had served in the Turkish army in their stead and perished, poor devil, heaven knows where.

But, as it was said before, it was not only the Mohammedan Osaticans who were possessed by the 'climbing urge', but also those who lived up the slope, gathered round their church; to be sure, they never climbed quite as high as they wanted to, but certainly as high as they possibly could. And here is a story about them.

The Climbers

When the Turkish askars left Bosnia and the Austrian administration took over, the Osaticans realised that their church ('The Temple of the Holy Ascension of the Town of Osatica') was degradingly small, low, humble-looking, that they had no bells and no bell-tower. Their eyes, it seemed, were suddenly opened to this. They were ashamed and tried to do their best to change it and put things right.

First they built a bell-tower, as strong and as high as they possibly could, and then, without letting their godly rapture cool off, they got the bells from as far away as Vršac — two at once, a small one and a big one. This cost the whole parish a great deal of money, but their joy and their glory were also great, and great were the opportunities of defying their infidel neighbours down in the valley.

The bells were driven in with great pomp, on a cart which was decorated with green leaves and boughs, with flowers and tricolour ribbons. Every male, even if just a span tall, helped to raise the bells. There were so many helping and making themselves useful that the job could hardly be done at all; there was almost an accident. And when the bells were at last hung, a true orgy of metallic noises began. The big one, Our Lady's, boomed, and the small one, Michael the Archangel's, tinkled. Without stopping. Old and young worked in shifts at the bell-tower, swinging on the ropes and trying to climb them, their eyes bright, their palms numb, their mouths open, singing with full breasts something that was lost in the ringing of the bells. For two days people danced the round dance in the churchyard. The bells never stopped. It seemed that they never would and that from now onwards people would spend their lives in incessant roaring and ringing.

Those of the lower part of the town came to hate life because they had to listen to this loathsome noise and crazy clanging. This was a kind of nemesis for their drums and trumpets which, from time immemorial, used to wake up their Christian fellow-citizens in the upper part of the town, before sunrise, for a whole month at a time, during the Ramadan fast.

So both sides had their way.

The bells were not yet fully paid for, and a lawsuit was in progress because of the expense of transporting them, when a new collection of money and material was started — this time for the expansion of the church and for the erection of a dome.

The old church, clinging to the ground, with its ordinary, low shingle roof, black with age, could no longer satisfy the needs of the parish of Osatica and meet the exalted idea it cherished of its power and its reputation. This evidently became clear to everybody at the same moment. Once uttered, the word 'dome' became a bee in everyone's bonnet. To be sure, none of them had ever seen a dome, with the exception of the domes on their church icon representing 'Heavenly Jerusalem', a fantastic city full of strange, high towers and domes. No one could quite tell or imagine what would be better or more beautiful at Osatica when their church acquired a dome, or why this should be so, but everybody dreamed and talked about it, convinced that a dome was indispensable for the future life of the town and for the happiness of the generations to come, almost the same as air, bread and water. And whenever people begin to dream and to talk about something in this way, sooner or later it is bound to come.

Men who travelled on business and who had seen the world found a master craftsman, Rista of Niš, at Nova Varoš — he was repairing the church there. They invited him to Osatica, and he came, considered the project, and agreed to undertake the work. He said straight away that the church could not be greatly expanded if a dome was to be put on it and that the dome could not be put too high, if they wanted it to last and to be pleasant to the eye. The Osaticans agreed. Because, to tell the truth, the church was not too small for them as it was — their main objective was, in any case, to have their wish and see the dome raised, such as could be had. Finally, an approximate estimate of expenses was worked out, a contract was made, and the work began at once.

The work was finished exactly as stipulated. The church of Osatica acquired a dome. The dome, to be sure, was not, either in shape or in size, such as many had imagined it was going to be, it was not in the middle of the church building like the domes on the icon of 'Heavenly Jerusalem' but in front, just above the door, narrow and pointed, and an ordinary saddle-roof, the same as before, was left behind it; and the dome was not covered with tin plates or even copper, as some had dreamed, but with small, fine shingles, specially cut, which peasants had given free as their contribution to the temple, and which were shaped according to the master's design. Things did not quite come up to their expectations, but the dome was there and the Osaticans were too excited about it, such as it was, to go on thinking for long of the one they had dreamed about. And after all, they consoled themselves, who could tell if the other domes in bigger cities and on famous churches had met all desires and expectations, if, in fact, anybody in the world had the dome he desired and imagined. Not everybody could have a dome like those on the icon of Heavenly Jerusalem. Besides, who could tell what those looked like in reality, for the icon is one thing and reality another. What mattered was that their church was rising to great heights, as high as it possibly could, that it was no longer stuck to the ground pretending to be smaller than it was, and . . . that those down there, in the lower part of the town, could see it so beautifully.

There was a great deal of talk about the cross which should be put on top of the dome. The master craftsman from Niš suggested that the cross should be wooden and just plated with tin; this opinion was shared by some people on the parish council, but a great majority of townsmen thought that they could put only a golden cross on the top of their church — a golden one or none. As they did not have enough money, they put up, provisionally, an ordinary wooden cross, and then they applied themselves to collecting the necessary sum. They organised collections in neighbouring villages, went as far as Sarajevo for contributions, exerted pressure on the well-to-do, changed the last wills of some old women. At last the order for the cross was placed with a firm at Novi Sad, to be paid off in instalments, and the cross came at the best time of the year. Together with the cross the firm sent one of its men to put it up and fix it on the top.

These were great days for upper Osatica. A golden cross was to be fixed high up, a master craftsman was among them, a stranger, exciting preparations were going on for the dangerous ascent. All of which were proper subjects for endless, lively arguing and for the great day-dreaming which Osaticans like so much.

As to the master craftsman, called Jakov Bodnar, his appearance and bearing failed to come up to the idea which people cherished here about that particular kind of artisan. He was, in their opinion, too small, humble-looking, and simple, not sufficiently eloquent and dignified for the lofty work he was doing. He put up at the tin-smith Lekso's house.

Aleksa Janković, called Lekso, was the only master of that craft in the town. A sturdy, blond lad with a pair of bright, radiant eyes which changed colour and flickered all the time. He had been at Višegrad and worked as apprentice to an Austrian craftsman, of whom he talked a good deal. His master had not smiled for four years, but he had never slapped him in the face either. That is what he was like. After obtaining journeyman's status Lekso came back to Osatica and he started a shop, as a branch of his master's firm, for small-scale tin work. When he achieved the full rights of a master, he changed the name of the firm to his own, having first done his military service. Business was good, considering modest Osatican needs, and his earnings were adequate. He drank as much as everybody else and behaved in drink like any other Osatican. He was over twenty-five and still a bachelor. He lived with his father and mother. It was only in this respect that he differed from his fellow townsmen.

Lekso spent the whole time with the craftsman from Novi Sad, he helped him in everything and served as a kind of liaison-officer between him and curious townsmen. He told them everything, as they went on asking questions about the craftsman who had come from far away. Was he quite strong and competent enough? Was he skilled especially in the raising of crosses? Was he a pork-eater? Could he belong to some other faith?

In the meantime the craftsman, quiet and unnoticed, made all the preparations for raising the cross. Several ladders were made according to his design of good, light wood, varying in length and thickness, pegs were hammered into the roof of the dome, and a rope-ladder was set up; a scaffolding of short, solid planks was put together and fastened round the top and the master walked on it shouting orders from above like a *hodja* on a minaret. Lekso helped him in everything and was seen everywhere. Also the workers who were helping them were instructed and assigned positions.

The churchyard was closed, as the master wanted it, but people gathered around all the time and watched what was going on from outside: children never left the top of the fence for a moment. Everybody watched, slightly disappointed, the monotonous, routine work with no apparent objective, waiting all the time for what was most important: the moment when the 'gold' cross would flash up above Osatica. And indeed, one day Bodnar, with Lekso's help, raised the cross to the top of the dome, soldered it there, secured its bottom with iron rails, and tied it on all sides with strong, but thin, almost imperceptible, steel wire. All this was done more quickly and seemed easier than the townsmen had expected, so that they felt, as it were, somehow taken in, as if tricked out of the most important and the most exciting moment: the moment when the cross flashed up above Osatica for the first time. It was too late now. The cross was already shining with every ray of sunlight and for every eye, as if this was the commonest thing in the world, as if it had always been there. And the master craftsman was preparing to go away; Lekso never left him for a moment, and when he set out on his journey, Lekso accompanied him all the way to the Good Waters, an hour's walk from the town, as far as the Osaticans used to go when accompanying their nearest of kin as they set off into the great world.

Standing by the drinking-fountain, rich with water which fell in four heavy, silvery jets into a long trough, Lekso watched the car which was carrying Bodnar away.

He was a true master of his trade, a man who applied himself to his work and completed his task in the same way whether doing it in a dark cellar or on top of a church dome — without an evil thought and without deceit, neither half-hearted nor vain. This was the opposite of the Osatican 'climbing urge' and the desire for a conspicuous, high place.

To be a craftsman is to be able to separate the work one is doing at the time from everything else, to know exactly and to hold before one's eyes one thing only: what should be done and how; to disregard whatever has no connection with this; not to care about success, not to think of failure; not to fear anything and not to leave anything to chance; to be always completely absorbed in the particular work one is doing at the moment. If you work like this, everything works with you and everything helps you, every tool is your friend, every change a sign-post and the material obedient under your hands; everything runs without an error or a hitch, or rather every error is set right, every hitch made up for. Then your work must progress, the further — the better; it gains vigour and beauty along the way, because it grows out of itself like a plant from a seed which was selected, properly sown, tended.

To be a master of one's work, a maker of things! Nothing better or more certain in this life in which there is little good and nothing certain.

Lekso understood it all without being told a word about it and he understood it better and better after every day spent

with Bodnar at work. He understood it and could not forget it
even now as he was standing by the drinking-fountain, but as
soon as he turned and started walking back to the town on the
hill, he felt it all going misty and dim within him. And with
every step a little of the master's wordless lesson was being
lost to him. He would stop for a moment and turn back, but in
the distance he could see only the dark mass of an oak forest
devouring the white road on which the car carrying the master
had disappeared.

Bewildered and empty, Lekso came back to town. The
cross on the dome was shining from high up in the early
morning sunlight. He looked at the cross and, as if seeing it
with new eyes, for the first time, he thought: 'I put it up there!
Yes, I was standing by its side, up there on top of the dome,
touching it with my hand, sharing the care and the effort all
the time till it was fixed and secured where it is now. Me!'
The thought of the master craftsman also came to his mind,
but now that thought was, surprisingly, weak and fading in
the distance, like a point becoming smaller and smaller as it
moved away.

Walking thus through the town he kept his eyes open —
now looking up at the cross, now at the people passing by.
Nobody raised his head. They were all bent on their own
business or just wandering idly, as if neither the cross nor the
dome were rising above them. He went back to his shop,
which now seemed to him bleak and empty, he began to work
but he was unable to go on for long. He rose up and stood on
the threshold of the shop, leaning on the door-post. People
went on passing in front of him, going up and down the
street; he watched askance the expressions of their faces,
trying to catch everyone's look. It was quite clear that after a
few days of wonder and admiration people had forgotten
about the cross on the church and about those who had put it
up. At first this surprised him, then gave him pain, and at last
he was embittered. It was only then that a living and full
consciousness of his own exploit touched him to the quick.

There is not one among them, he thought, offended and
angry, the crown of whose head I did not see, and see it from
a high and dangerous place — but now they are passing me
as they would pass by a Turkish graveyard, pretending not to
know, or to have forgotten, as if something like this could be
forgotten so easily. Who among them knows what this place
called Osatica looks like when seen from *above*? No one.

Until this morning there were only two of us — Bodnar and myself. And now there is only myself. The only one in the whole town.

That day on his way home for lunch he walked through the town, in the middle of the street, his arms hanging away from his body, his waistcoat unbuttoned, and sticking out his chest. His looks lashed all around him and tried to read in other men's eyes the true significance of his exploit, but he did not find it. Not a trace of anything. Just harsh indifference or personal worries reaching no further than the ridge-beams of their homes.

In the evening, at the inn, people went on talking about what was and what was not, what could be and what could never be, but nobody said a word about the cross. And the next day and the day after. Lekso sat silent and sullen, but nobody took any notice of his scowling silence. Smothering his rage and anger he asked himself it if were possible to forget in a few days what was dreamed of for years and talked about for months. Was it possible that these people who could have seen him helping Bodnar, standing on the scaffolding just below the cross itself, high above them, had lost their memory and had nothing to say to him, no way of showing that he had accomplished an extraordinary achievement and performed a great deed? Restraining his anger he tried himself to bring up the topic of the raising of the cross, of the master craftsman from Novi Sad, of the great work which had been brought to its end. Without mentioning himself or his own example he talked, casually as it were, of how such achievements were esteemed in the great world. He knew that newspapers wrote — Vienna newspapers! — about people who had climbed towers, and they also printed their pictures, both of the man and of the tower. He had seen this when he was apprenticed to his master, at Višegrad. This was how things were over there, in the great world.

(To be sure, Lekso never mentioned what those towers were like compared with this one at Osatica, how those people had climbed, and how high. But one's own height is the highest for everybody. And when this intoxication, this intoxication with height, turns a man's brains, then there is no sense of proportion, there are no distinctions. There are no higher and lower towers. Every giddiness is as good as another.)

People would listen to him with indifference and then

change the subject. And when he got hold of an inveterate drunkard, he would treat him to half a glass of plum-brandy and begin, beating about the bush, to ask questions about the raising of the cross, but the man would just blink, remembering with difficulty:

'The cross? . . . Yes, they put it up, didn't they — so what?'

And the drunkard would begin a story about one of his own achievements, invented and incredible, compared to which the raising of the cross seemed hardly worth mentioning; and he went on, absorbed, for a long time — forever looking at the brandy before him, as if reading from its opalescent shades. So Lekso listened now to another man's lies and swallowed his own truth, as if the liar had paid for his brandy, and not he for the liar's. He listened and pondered. Well, this was what his Osaticans are like! They liked to make much of themselves and rise high, and when they could not do this, they tried at least to pull down the man who had risen above them, to bring him back to their own level, or a little below it.

Embittered and numbed, he would go back home with the desire to pull his blankets over his head as soon as possible, to wipe out, even from his own mind, all he had done, to sleep — a sound, deep sleep without memory and without dreams. But things were happening now which had never happened before — he woke up suddenly in the middle of the night: the thought from which he wanted to escape by sleeping was alive and whole before his eyes. Indeed it seemed that nobody thought that it was he, Lekso, who had put up the cross.

Wide awake and quite conscious, even he began to ask the question in the darkness — was it really himself who had climbed the dome and taken part in the raising of the cross? (He was not thinking of the craftsman any more.) Yes, of course it was — and that in broad daylight, before the eyes of all the world. So he answered his own question, and a slight shudder shook his body because he had to ask himself such questions in the night and answer them himself again. And other questions followed immediately. Yes, he had done a great deed, but was it possible that nobody was willing to recognise it, not by a word or a look of acknowledgment, was it possible that such an achievement could be forgotten so quickly? It could be that they even thought him a swaggerer, and that instead of fame and recognition, he had gained the reputation of a liar. This was Osatica, after all.

He swore in the dark that next day, as soon as it was dawn, he would ask the first man he met in town a plain, straightforward question — what he thought of him and his achievement. But the next day he realized that it was not possible to carry out the decision which had seemed so easy and simple in the night. He went into a shop, sat down and began: well, he'd come to a good friend, just to ask him a question, to ask him about something which mattered to him very much indeed . . . and then, suddenly, he started back as if facing an abyss, frightened by his own decision, by his question and by the answer he might get, and also afraid of the man he wanted to ask. And then, faltering, beating about the bush, he changed the subject, he thought up something else, something unimportant, something he had apparently come to ask. After several attempts of this kind he dared no longer to hint at his question. Only, as he met somebody in the street, he would think: Here, I could ask him! And with this thought he passed by.

The whole summer was for Lekso one long, ridiculous, and inexplicable, but still very real torture. And this summer was suddenly interrupted: before it had fully matured it began to change into a rainy, early autumn. The weather was no good for anybody or anything: either for work in the fields or for the mood of the people. And the Osaticans have always depended so much on their weather and on their mood. They all now drank more than they usually did, and gathered in the inn before it was time for it — the inn usually being their refuge only in winter. Everybody complained of the damp and of the south wind and of this autumn snatching away the days from summer.

'It's come early . . . ' said one.

'It's not so much that it's come early, but look what it's like.'

'Yes, it's just . . . just like . . . '

So everybody blamed the autumn which had pressed down heavily upon the end of summer; nobody could say what it was like, but they all knew quite well what they meant when they were saying that it was 'just . . . '

Indeed, everything was going wrong somehow in Osatica in those days of late summer and precocious autumn. Something morose and heavy had crept in among the mountains with the damp south-westerly wind, it had come down upon the houses and the gardens and the streets and was never to leave them.

On a night like this — the autumn had already set in and the first kettles of plum-brandy were simmering — some junior clerks and young craftsmen were sitting late in the inn. They had sat down not meaning any harm; on the contrary, they were unanimous in their inviolable decision to go home for dinner after the third glass. However as it sometimes happens, the course of the evening changed unexpectedly and they did not see either their homes or their dinners, but eating a little with their drink they stayed deep into the night. They quarrelled and made friends again and kissed each other, shouted and sang, swaggered and boasted of their exploits. The weather was such that one felt dim in the head even with no drinks at all. And since dusk they had been drinking the early autumn plum-brandy which does not affect the drunkard's legs but his head, depriving him of reason and giving him great strength and volubility, so that little remains that he would not be able to say and do. They sat singing and disputing about things which would never occur to a sober mind.

Petar Stanković, the teacher, called 'Drumstick', was among them that evening — a tall broad-shouldered, slightly squint-eyed man in his thirties, with a devastating sense of humour that knew no mercy, a joker who never smiled. He was a teacher in a small village only about six miles from the town, so he used to spend more time in Osatica than in the village where he worked.

Lekso tried, as always to bring the conversation round to his achievement, but nobody wanted to take it up. At last he came out with it himself. At that moment Petar the Drumstick, absent-mindedly scornful, looked at him askance with his large squinting eyes. What dome? What cross? When was that? — and he turned his back on him.

Lekso stopped, motionless, astonished by such insolence, and looking at this man who was such a bad teacher, who knew only how to drain glasses and shuffle cards in inns, he asked himself how it was possible that such people who had never undertaken anything themselves had such a great, terrible power of denying everything that their betters, people of greater abilities than themselves, had undertaken and achieved.

Then he started from his thoughts, jumped furiously towards the teacher, and caught him by the breast of his coat.

'"What dome?" Have you never heard of Bodnar, at least, the master craftsman?'

'So what?' said Drumstick coolly, casually as it were. 'What have you got to do with him?'

'What? What have I, what have I got to do with him? What I *have* got to do with him is that I stood by his side at the top of the dome and helped him all the time till we secured the cross. I was less than a span below him and I was the last one to come down.'

So Lekso shouted, as if wanting to convince the whole of Osatica, which kept silent and pretended not to understand what it was all about; and shouting, he spread his arms as far as he could to show the height which he had attained and the vastness of the views he had seen from up there.

Drumstick waved his hand from the heights of his own scorn — which were above all towers and heights.

'You've never climbed anything, mate — not more than the grandfather climbs up the grandmother.'

'Who? What! I haven't ... I haven't?' stuttered Lekso in rage and surprise, glancing at all the faces around him — faces which contracted with malice or smiled at him with mockery. 'Here, here! So I haven't climbed, haven't I?

He was shouting these words as if being skinned alive, despairing because a lie could be so shameless and speak with such authority, because among so many people here there was not a grain of reason or honesty, not one witness to confirm the obvious truth which everybody knew.

And then he fell silent. Standing there with his head bowed, he simply felt himself decreasing in stature. Not only that he had never climbed higher than any of them, but he did not come up even to their ankles as he stood there before that cruel teacher like a confused pupil.

And the people around him began to talk about something else, to sing, while he stood scowling, amazed, his arms hanging loose, his eyes burning. He stood like that for a while, and then all at once he spread his arms again.

'So I haven't climbed, haven't I?'

He shouted and waved his arms like a drowning man.

'Perhaps you have, in your dreams,' answered Drumstick quietly, and their voices were completely lost in the noise and the song.

Nobody turned his head towards the despairing tin-smith, but as soon as Lekso found a moment of silence, he jumped towards the teacher.

'I have, I have! And I will climb again, tomorrow, tonight if needs be. I bet you anything you like!'

So a short September night went by, seeming even shorter to the men who were drinking. In the smoke and the dim light of the lamp hanging from the ceiling one could feel at one moment a new restlessness, that painful foreboding so well known to all drunkards, that the peak had been reached, that the night was coming to its end and the morning approaching, bringing with it sobering and hangovers, and then every rapture and charm would come to its end and they would all, like ghosts, have to go their different ways, to retreat. It was at just such a moment that the dispute between Lekso and the cynically cool, unyielding teacher warmed up again.

From the very beginning of this night's dispute Lekso had suggested that he should perform his exploit again before them all. Nobody took any notice of this and the teacher only waved his large, pale hand. But now, with the night so advanced and the effect of the drinks so strong, they were no longer the same people who had sat down at those tables the evening before. Nothing seemed impossible or pointless any more. The teacher and Lekso wagered five florins. And those new people, moved by the special kind of alcohol, rose up and, as if following a previous arrangement went to look for ropes, for a ladder, and the other things which were necessary for climbing. They did all this as if it were the most natural and common thing in the world. And everything was found, as if by a miracle.

The last cocks were outcrowing each other and the day was parting from night when they came to the church. Lekso placed his ladder carefully and disentangled the rope ladder. The drunken men helped him and stood in his way, but in spite of all the intoxication he was carried away by a new force directing his work straight to its aim. He neither saw nor heard anything that people said and did around him, he was not quite aware who, what, or where he was, and had somebody called him by his Christian name, he would have stopped in surprise and, perhaps, fallen over like a sleepwalker, but he did his job quietly and carefully, fully absorbed in it. Using the iron hooks and rungs which had been hammered into the roof of the dome for the first climbing, Lekso went up quickly and safely. More easily and more safely than the first time when he had climbed it sober, together with the sober master craftsman Bodnar.

The moon had not yet faded away at one end of the sky when something appeared at the other end: between the dark mountains and thin, greyish clouds a cold, yellow light, the vanguard of the sun, was bursting through like a pale germ from a dark membrane. And between them — Lekso, tall and upright, with his left hand holding the cross, with the right one high up and waving, waving, not to the people down there whom he seemed to have forgotten, but waving to the sun and the moon, to the left and to the right, to the landscapes and the vast spaces and everything that he, from his height, could see, and that those looking at him from below would never see, at least not in this way and not from this point.

And Lekso climbed down and removed all the traces of his exploit — the most conscientious and sober craftsman could not have done it more thoroughly. Some of the people who had come with him had already begun to disperse before this; they were driven away by the breaking of day, and the thing which had brought them here had no longer any significance or importance for them, for drunken people give up their pastimes quickly and easily, as children cast away their toys.

The drunkards slept it off and sobered up, and the Osatican days followed their usual course, people pursued their everyday work. One cannot go on drinking every night till the break of day and one cannot do something great and absurd after every evening of drinking and sitting at the inn. Lekso rid himself of his strange thoughts and doubts, he was no longer tortured by the painful question of whether people acknowledged his climbing; he did not think about it at all, he did not even ask for the money due to him as the winner of the bet. And everybody else held his tongue about it. In all probability the whole event would be forgotten and would remain hidden in the wanton fantasy of a drunken night, buried somewhere between daylight and darkness, where things were and were not according to your ability to look and your will to see them, and where they remained forever unknown, without explanation, without social consequences.

This had happened before. Warmed up by drink, people used to seek an opportunity for an exploit, not stopping until they found one. And this usually occurred when dawn was approaching, when it seemed to drunkards that one had to do something extraordinary at all costs, climb high up or pull something down while everybody else in the town was sleeping, when it seemed that there was no authority, no law, nothing to stop the follies of the night. It happened on such occasions that they took down the tiles from the roof of the gauging office in the market-place, carried them away to the Town Hall, and laid them down carefully in a heap in front of it. They also used to dig out young, small pines which had been planted the year before in front of the Bey's House, transplanting them in front of the inn at the other end of the town. And having done the work like the best of gardeners, they would tread the earth with their feet, water the transplanted trees, and dance in a ring around them. And, of course, next day the Magistrate would punish them all with fines and imprisonment, make them dig up the pines and plant them under the supervision of the police in front of the Bey's House again.

Sometimes there were even worse follies, but nobody said a word about them and they were forgotten. So it seemed now that Lekso's climbing for a bet would be over in the same way, without the interference of the authorities. True enough, rumours went through the town that drunken people had bustled about the church that night, but the rumours soon died out. It all happened by night, when the town was sleeping. The only witness was Mile the cowherd, who always got up before everybody else and who was just passing by the church at that time. But what is a witness if he is a poor devil without a home and family, a crack-brained, good-natured bandy-legged dwarf talking only in rhymes and maxims? And as to those who had taken part in the adventure, when they sobered up and their heads cleared, they had no reason and it was not in their interest to go on talking about it and spreading the story further. On the contrary. All this seemed to suggest that everything was going to remain unnoticed and passed over in silence. And this was how it would have been — had it not been a question of the church.

A month had passed from the night which Lekso and company had begun to forget when all of a sudden the highest ecclesiastical authority from Sarajevo spoke up. Informed about the grave and sacrilegious offence against the holy sanctuary, the Metropolitan See sharply reprimanded Parson Stojan for not having let them know about it in person, urging him to send his report immediately, threatening with heavy punishments and fines, both ecclesiastic and secular, not only

those who had transgressed but also the parish, not excepting
the Parson himself. To understand this development better,
one should know what follows.

The Metropolitan hated the Parson of Osatica with a monk's
hatred — a hatred which had become proverbial long ago.
Parson Stojan inherited this hatred together with the parish.
His father, Parson Arso, a small, bony man, well-known for
his quarrels and his lawsuits against all the world, had a long
dispute with the Metropolitan. The dispute in which the
Osatican Parson embittered the life of the head of the church
came to an end only when Parson Arso died; this was the end
of the dispute but not the end of the Metropolitan's hatred.

The prematurely aged Metropolitan was not only as
quarrelsome and pedantic as a spinster but a genuinely evil
and vindictive man to whom old age brought a weakening and
drying up of all his abilities except the ability to hate. He
always kept the map of his diocese before his mind's eye and
on this map fiery circles marked the parishes of the parsons
with whom the Metropolitan had quarrelled and who
accordingly ought to be hated and persecuted — all the time,
by all possible means, and on all occasions. Those blazing
points glittered incessantly before his eyes, even during
church services, even in his dreams. On this map, Osatica, an
out-of-the-way place in the mountains of Eastern Bosnia, was
marked by such a fiery circle. The only difference after
Parson Arso's death was that the Metropolitan transferred his
hatred to Arso's son who was the very opposite of his father
— a good-natured, mild and obliging man. But the
Metropolitan, who had sworn never to leave even Arso's
grave alone, saw in Parson Stojan always and only his father
and so he persecuted him wherever and whenever he could
with a hatred which the years could only poison and inflame.

The Metropolitan was very friendly with the civil
authorities; besides, in every town, particularly in those
marked with fiery circles, he had men in his confidence, his
secret agents, invariably chosen among those who hated and
envied the Parson. The story of drunks who, after a night of
revelling had climbed the church for a bet and fiddled with the
cross spread from town to town and soon reached the
Metropolitan's ears. At once he initiated proceedings against
the parish of Osatica and its Parson, one of those legal and
ruthless proceedings in which ecclesiastical canons, paper,
and ink are used to ruin somebody's reputation and poison his

life. The Parson defended himself. Some drunken men had bustled about the church of Osatica on the 'self-same' night, but this was not so uncommon in Osatica, particularly in autumn when the plum-brandy came in, because that was what the people here were like, wilful and wanton — you could expect anything from them. But it was not true that anybody had climbed the roof of the church and that the recently sanctified cross on the dome had been 'polluted and sacrileged', because drunken men can hardly stand on their feet when walking on the ground, and as to one of them, in such a state, being able to climb the dome, no man in his senses could believe that. Anyway, it had all happened by night, without a sober witness, and the drunkards themselves did not remember anything. It was all just another Osatican story, their way of teasing each other when drunk or hungover. In these stories they had even climbed the clouds, but nobody had ever taken that for truth and fact. Therefore this denunication should not be considered, but rejected as an unfounded, ridiculous, and malevolent libel by which somebody wanted to slander the parish.

The Metropolitan See was merciless and stood firmly by its accusations and its demands. First of all, it reproached Parson Stojan because his parishioners were like that, such drunkards and atheists that nothing was sacred to them. And then it demanded, in its official and impersonal way, that the cross should be taken down from the dome, sanctified in front of the church, and put back in its place. If they failed to do this, the Metropolitan would pronounce an anathema on the parish, so that they would not be authorised to read the liturgy and perform the marriage and christening rites in their church. Both Parson and townsmen were put in a difficult position. To have the cross removed from the dome, sanctified and put up again — that would involve enormous expense and even greater disgrace, and was simply not possible. And, what was most important, neither Parson Stojan nor anybody alive at Osatica would acknowledge his mistake and let the Metropolitan have his way for anything in the world.

This was one of those insane and insoluble Bosnian disputes for which only time could, perhaps, bring a solution. The correspondence went on for a long time. The civil authorities interfered in the dispute. The Metropolitan himself asked for their interference. The Magistrate was given orders to investigate the case and submit a report.

This was not the first time that Magistrate Đuro Pavlas had investigated one of the Osatican leaps in the dark, one of their offences that were so difficult to understand.

After the Austrian occupation, when the military authorities handed over the administrative rule to the civil ones, Osatica was a 'district post', and the first commander of the post was a clean-shaven young Austrian, born in Koruška, and he behaved as if he had come to a colony right off the map. An aristocrat and an eccentric, carried away by the unswerving self-confidence of his class, full of good intentions and abstruse projects, he wanted to order and make happy the little area of his administrative authority without regard to the rest of the country and without regard to the circumstances he had happened to find there. He communicated with people through an interpreter. Tragi-comic misunderstandings and conflicts kept cropping up between him and the townspeople. When he was, at last, withdrawn to Sarajevo, he left Osatica firmly convinced that all the Osaticans were hysterics and maniacs, brutal and ungrateful savages, whereas the general and settled opinion remained at Osatica that the town had been run for two long years by an insane, utterly insane, and deranged man. Then Osatica was raised to the rank of a district centre and Đuro Pavlas, from Lika, was appointed its Magistrate.

He was a different man. He had a large family with four children, all boys. Simple and reasonable, restrained and deliberate, diligent and helpful, a good magistrate in so far as that was possible within the limitations of the outdated and essentially inhuman régime which he served. A tall, frowning, sturdy man with a high-pitched voice and large, grey eyes, his hair always cut short, he spoke little, seldom laughed, and when laughing he would turn his head aside, as if hiding his smile. A harsh and rigid master of the border type, but humane by nature and sufficiently close to these people by origin, he had been governing this district for eight years. He was used to the Osaticans and they were used to him. There was only one thing which this sober and dry man could by no means accept or handle. He was disturbed and continually bewildered and annoyed by what he called the 'Osatican fantasy'. They drank a lot and in drink they were never quite sober. They did not see, so it seemed to him, they could not and did not want to see the difference between words and deeds, between what each thing was and what, in their opinion, it had to be. In the commonest and plainest dealings they would often go off the beaten track suddenly and unexpectedly, they would try to take off foolishly and vainly, and the next moment they would fall down with disgrace and damage to themselves and others. And in that respect you could never be quite sure of or sufficiently careful with the soberest of the Osaticans. This had often brought the Magistrate to rage and cold despair. As soon as it seemed to him, that he had grasped at long last all, even the finest threads of their motives, and that he had come to understand their hidden impulses, unknown even to themselves, that he had mastered the abstruse logic of their conduct, which had little to do with the common logic of other people, they would suddenly do something which would bewilder and discourage him for a long time to come.

Talking to the head of the Tax Office, his personal and family friend Ladević, he often used to discuss this.

'Yes, yes, with these people here twice two never makes four,' the tax-collector would say with a sigh which spoke of experience.

'Never,' the Magistrate would reply, 'but worst of it is that nobody could tell you what it does make — considering that it never makes four.'

And then a long and detailed exposition would follow, making clear certain proceedings or ideas of these Osatican people in their everyday life and their dealings with the administrative authorities.

The case of Lekso, the tin-smith, was a particularly difficult one for the Magistrate. He heard, of course, as early as the next day, about the heavy drinking-bout and the night promenade around the church. The story also reached him, rather like an incredible hint, that there was some climbing for a bet. But as the sobered participants held their tongues about it all, Parson Stojan was not to be seen anywhere, the Magistrate decided that the best course to take was to pretend not to have noticed anything and to leave the whole thing to the oblivion which had already covered up so many Osatican disgraces, large and small. Experience had taught him that the ruling administration should be watchful and conscientious, but not too zealous. A wise administration, in his opinion, should have both eyes in their place, two sharp and always wide-open eyes, but it should also be able to blink one of them for a moment and to pretend not to have noticed what it saw. It should do this, of course, only in exceptional cases, only from time to time — when and how, the administration itself ought to know if it is really wise. The Magistrate would have followed this rule in this case, had not the Metropolitan See submitted its accusations and grave demands requiring the investigation of the administrative authorities.

When he received orders to begin investigating and had to answer why he had not done so before, the Magistrate was aware that all this had originated in the Metropolitan's hatred of the Parson, and he was also well aware that in this case he had to protect his Osatica and his Osaticans, whatever his personal opinion of them and their misdoings might be.

First of all the Magistrate consulted, in their official capacities, district judge Turković, a passionate hunter and a merrymaker, then his friend Lađević, and finally Parson Stojan, without disclosing his intention. Without wasting too many words and without calling anything by its full name, they agreed silently that there was only one way out of this trouble: to carry out the investigation which would prove in the end that the act of which the drunken people were accused had not been committed and that there was no ground for a verdict or punishment.

The investigation began with every formality and strictness. First the Magistrate demanded officially a written statement, to be submitted by Parson Stojan. The Parson repeated the same things he had said in his reply to the Metropolitan See — rejecting the accusation as unfounded. Then several townsmen who had taken part in the drinking-bout were interrogated. The Magistrate examined them in person and most of them were brought in by a patrol of two gendarmes with bayonets on their rifles.

They denied everything resolutely and unanimously. Would they ever do a thing like that? Climb up the church? No man in his senses would ever try it. Even foolish children would never do that. It might have been mentioned in jest, we all know how people talk over a glass of brandy, and somebody must have taken it in earnest. It was true that they had sat up fairly late that night and had a glass more than they usually did, but as to the church and climbing it . . . heaven forbid! At last Drumstick, the teacher, Mile, the cowherd, and Lekso, the accused, were examined. Drumstick was more resolute and insolent than anybody else.

As a member of the civil service and an educator he came

unaccompanied by gendarmes one afternoon when there was no school. Taller even than tall Pavlas, he moved towards the Magistrate as he spoke, leaning towards his face and talking confidentially, as if supplying the evidence of his own free will. The Magistrate did not want to accept such a familiar tone, he drew back and raised his voice in order to give the whole procedure the brand of officialdom and to enable the clerk, who was keeping the record of the proceedings at a small table, to hear him properly.

Drumstick said that the night had 'caught' him at Osatica and so he went to sit for a while at the inn, against his will. People were drinking, talking about one thing and another, and after a time they set off for their homes. On the way they stopped at the church. There Lekso the tin-smith talked about the raising of the cross and pointed with his hands to the place where the ladder had been put. That was all. And they parted there.

In Drumstick's story everything seemed simple and innocent, reduced to a joke without importance.

The Magistrate looked the teacher straight in the eyes, into the wide, greenish and white surfaces of those eyes that never looked down or blinked — even when telling obvious lies. In his dealings with people Pavlas had come to know that type of man who was never bewildered and who lied spontaneously and boldly with the whole mass of his vigorous body, with all the weight of his physical strength. Such were the most difficult to shake and expose. But this time he did not want to to do that.

'So, according to you, there was no sacrilege at the church at all?'

'Nor could there be any,' added Drumstick insolently, 'because I would never have tolerated anything of the kind in my presence.'

'And Aleksa Janković, the tin-smith, did not climb the church?'

'No more than the Metropolitan of Sarajevo.'

Pavlas began to cough, showing that he neither permitted nor approved of this line, and Drumstick changed his tone at once.

'If babbling about climbing were the same thing as climbing, eh, then one might think that he did climb. But as it is — no. The idea of climbing turned Lekso's brain as soon as the cross was raised, and he has been unable to talk of anything else ever since. And it's out of his babbling that this whole story has been cooked up. And the Metropolitan See should know and understand this, instead of cultivating rancour against our parish . . . '

'This has nothing to do with the matter in hand!'

'Still, the whole town will confirm it, Your Honour.'

'All right. So you stand by your evidence?'

'Absolutely!'

'And you are prepared, if necessary, to swear to it?'

'At any time of day or night!'

Drumstick signed the record of the proceedings and went to the inn, quietly and self-confidently, as a man who had discharged the duty of a citizen.

The examination of Mile the cowherd, the only sober Osatican who had witnessed the scene at the church, demanded more effort, but it too was brought to a successful end. The weak-headed little man, brought into the room by the uniformed messenger of the District Office, was more dead than alive with fear. His bright, childish eyes glanced round the room, he smiled from time to time with a desire to soften the hearts of these people around him and to dispel his own fears. The examination began with difficulty. Mile answered every question by saying that he was not guilty at all and that he had never been in a law-court before.

When he was told that he ought to tell the truth and nothing but the truth, otherwise he would be punished, the blinking of his tiny, smiling eyes quickened. Bewildered, he looked above himself, through his smile, up to the Magistrate's face, like a man asking himself what else but the truth he could say, and why he shouldn't tell the truth here and now, considering that all his life he had never told anything but the truth.

But Mile's truth was neither clear nor definite because it consisted of innumerable little truths and verisimilitudes.

Well, this is how it was, he went out that morning, as he always did, at the very break of day, or rather, a little before the break of day, and he saw some people near the church shouting and waving their hands. How many of them? Who were they? Eh, this is rather difficult to say — well, you know, it had dawned on the one hand, and it hadn't really dawned on the other. But they were men or at least that is what they were most like. He looked and looked and it seemed to him that he saw, or perhaps he didn't quite see it, because his eyes were usually dazzled when he looked up like that: on the dome, by the cross, somebody was standing — a man.

'How did you "see it or perhaps didn't quite see it?" What man? Who saw him? Speak up!'

'Well, both the sun and the moon saw him — as, you know, day was parting from night, so that in a way . . . '

'Leave the sun and the moon out of it, the day and the night! Those are no witnesses. I am not asking you about *them.*'

The Magistrate interrupted him sharply, rose up and walked right up to him, and leaning towards him began to shout from above:

'I am asking you whether you have seen the above-mentioned Aleksa Janković standing at the top of the church and holding the cross, and can you swear to it here, on this Holy Bible?'

The cowherd's little eyes were rolling in all directions at once, searching where to hide from this thing that was threatening him like a storm and asking for the terrible oath. If the question had been put to him in the same way in which everybody talked to him in the town, in the ordinary way, half in jest, he would have told everything as it was and as he had seen it, but this: a certain 'above-mentioned' Aleksa, and the Holy Bible, God and the oath! No! No, he didn't want to have anything to do with that, he couldn't possibly know, he wasn't able to say anything about that.

'Yes or no?' thundered the Magistrate from high above him.

'No . . . no, I can't.'

'I am asking you again — did you or did you not see it, and can you swear to it?'

'I didn't . . . I can't,' replied Mile in a wailing voice.

'Did you at least see the ladder and the ropes?'

'No, no . . . I didn't see a thing.'

Then the Magistrate turned to the clerk, and having angrily muttered to himself: 'The sun and the moon indeed!' he dictated the witness's statement to him.

Lekso the tin-smith was brought in by two gendarmes and confined for a whole day in the Bey's House. In fact, his examination was short and simple, and during the greater part of the day he just sat locked in an empty office, smoking one cigarette after another. It was only at dusk that he was released to go home.

On the preceding day, after his conversation with the Magistrate, Parson Stojan had asked Lekso to come to his house and they had a long, confidential talk there.

The enormous, quiet Parson, whom otherwise nothing could rouse or move, was now worried and spoke in a new, decisive voice.

The Metropolitan had swooped upon their parish and he was prepared to go to any lengths. He was able to make them pull down their cross and have it sanctified again. And there was no need to tell Lekso what that would mean. Let alone the disgrace and the confusion of the people and the severe punishment which would reach 'the perpetrators of the sacrilege'! Therefore there was only one thing to do: they should all unanimously deny the accusation and stand firmly by their evidence to the end.

Parson Stojan did not say a word which would have implied that he knew who 'the perpetrator' was and he talked to Lekso as if taking counsel with him in order to avert a danger threatening Osatica and his parish. Bewildered and frightened, Lekso found this soothing. It dawned on him suddenly that there was a lot of horse sense in this slack, drowsing Parson of theirs.

'We must deny it, yes!' he said readily.

And Parson Stojan went on. Yes, it should be denied, but it was important to deny that there had been any climbing — by day as well as by night.

'What?'

All of a sudden Lekso's old suspicions and pains re-awoke in him, whole and unchanged, although they had disappeared after the night of drinking. What did this mean — 'by day as well'?

And the Parson went on explaining. The higher administrative authorities must be convinced of how unfounded and how absurd the accusation was, and they must be convinced thoroughly. A man was charged with having climbed the dome of the church — by night and drunk, whereas he had not been able to do it sober, by day, when he should have climbed there to do his work. If you put it this way, it was worth something.

'But there are people who saw me when I climbed it . . . together with Bodnar!'

'No Christian soul will bear witness to that.'

'No?' Lekso said blankly, feeling a coldness creeping further and further into his veins.

And the Parson went on justifying himself both in his own and in Lekso's eyes. This had to be done, because this was a time of great trial. And God would forgive. The Metropolitan was — what was the point of disguising it? — an old perjurer, a man without a heart or a soul, and he would be able to bring this whole parish to ruin, just to satisfy his spite.

Lekso came to realise all this and Parson Stojan seemed to him more and more sensible, but he could not feel the divan on which he was sitting, he could not feel even his own body, which was falling apart in cold shivers. 'By day as well as by night!' he thought to himself, and with a colourless, as it were with somebody else's, voice he agreed that this was the only way out, and with a resoluteness which he himself found surprising he declared that he would deny everything as everybody else was going to do, come what might.

His resoluteness kept him in a state of cold excitement both during the night and on the following day when he was taken to the Bey's House. When Magistrate Pavlas, frowning and severe, asked him the first questions about the climbing of the church, he had ready-made answers to hand.

He had never climbed the church, never, and he was not able to do it either, because not only as a good Christian would he not want to, but he was not capable of doing it by day, let alone by night. The only one who had climbed it was the master craftsman from Novi Sad. And as to that night in the inn, yes, climbing was mentioned, but just in drink and in jest, and it was true that, when parting, he and his friends had stopped near the church, and it was also true that he had shown them, from rather far away, how the master craftsman had climbed while he himself was passing him what he needed from below. But nobody had touched the church that night, let alone anything else.

The Magistrate asked new questions, but Lekso stood firmly by what he had said. No and no, and he was ready to swear to it on the cross and on the Holy Bible, and if a . witness were to be found who could prove the opposite, let them cut him where he was thinnest.

He spoke coolly as if all this had nothing to do with him personally, and his look was absent-minded.

While the interrogation was in progress, Osatica began to 'reel'. The townspeople were seething with excitement, the temperature was rapidly rising. All were determined to defend their church, their Parson, and the reputation of the town. All were ready to swear that the statements of the witnesses and of the accused were true, and that the charge was false. Not a single man could be found who was prepared to witness to the contrary. Older people remembered and enunciated the instances of malice of the hated Metropolitan towards the late Parson Arso. Everybody was talking, some were threatening bitterly. And this bitterness, like a godsend, satisfied their need for big and violent words. Their eyes flashed, they beat their chests, they whispered in rage or shouted, without choosing their words or caring about their meaning, unaware of the contradictory things they were saying.

'We aren't going to submit to the Turkish or Kraut toadies even if we knew we'd all be killed.'

'What — has the time come when a man is no longer allowed to drink a glass of brandy and pass by the church? And who was it that saved the church in the hard Turkish times but us?'

'What does that wretched newcomer want? The church is ours, we keep it and repair it — we can set fire to it if we want.'

'We'll all become Turks if it comes to that — but we won't let the cross be removed from our church!'

So the town remonstrated and defended itself for a long time — until it was exhausted, because months went by and no verdict came. The bitterness had already rather spent itself when about the middle of the following summer the District Office was informed that owing to the lack of evidence further proceedings were suspended and the whole case of 'the sacrilege at the church of Osatica' should be put into the archives. Osatica had won. The Metropolitan had to give up the idea of full revenge and wait for the next opportunity.

Everything had settled and cooled off and everybody was, at long last, satisfied. The Osaticans triumphed because they had outwitted and overshadowed the hated Metropolitan. Parson Stojan was happy because he had got out of trouble. The Magistrate was at ease because he had justified his action to the higher authorities and saved the peace and reputation of the town.

At dusk he sat drinking a glass of beer. Tax-collector Ladević and the judge of the District Court, Turković, were with him. They were talking about the behaviour of the local people before the judicial and police authorities in the course of the interrogation.

'I've been here for three years, but I can't boast that I've come to understand these people and their strange behaviour in the court. They will confess what they don't have to confess and tell the truth which nobody else would tell, but at the same time they will deny in an absurd way and try to cover up with all sorts of lies some unimportant details. Why? They don't know themselves. The most important thing is that you can never be quite sure when they're lying, when they're telling the truth, and why they're doing it.'

'It may be difficult to determine when they lie and when they don't, but as to the whole and the factual truth, I know that they never tell it,' said the tax-collector softly and pensively.

The Magistrate was silent.

Everybody was satisfied and in all probability, far away from there, the Metropolitan himself was also satisfied, because he had caused so much trouble to Parson Arso's son and heir. The only one who could not be satisfied and who had come out of this confusion even more bewildered and troubled than before was Lekso the tin-smith. All the old restlessness and all the strange suspicions had revived in him again.

He had climbed to the top of the church twice, both sober and drunk, both by day, to work on it, and by night, unlawfully, wantonly. And everybody knew that. And still nobody ever said a word about it and everybody pretended not to know anything about it; nobody gave him credit for it and nobody could, because he himself had denied it all, officially and in writing, like all the rest of them. Well, so it had to be and so it was. But if only just one of them would show, just by a smile, that he was aware of his double exploit and that he believed him. A wink of the eye — in jest, that would be sufficient. But no! It may well have been that they considered he was not to be taken seriously, as a man who says what is not so. He looked other people in the eye and they turned their eyes away. So it happened more and more frequently now that he himself did not know what had really happened. And again he began to doubt what he had done and lived through himself, and he felt as though he was going mad. And again he was possessed by the need to talk about it all, to hear, just once, from one single mouth, a confirmation and an acknowledgment, and then, so it seemed to him, he would find peace till the end of his life. And when he really tried once in his own shop, with his next-door neighbour, a cobbler, to bring the subject up, timidly and in a roundabout way, the man dragged him deeper into the shop and leaning towards him and whispering angrily said to his face:

'Listen to me, Lekso, we've had enough of that! Because of that bee in your bonnet and your swaggering about it, we were in great trouble and were almost left ashamed and disgraced, both without our cross and without our church. Shut up, I'm telling you, and never mention that again!'

A foul smell spread from the cobbler's mouth, and as soon as he said this, he went out.

And teacher Drumstick, when they happened to meet in the street, just looked at him sharply, without blinking, and Lekso could hardly endure it, this stare from Drumstick's hard, cruel eyes. And Lekso, whenever he could, kept out of his way.

Sometimes when he began to feel the stabs of doubt and mortification, he thought that it would have been better if he had disobeyed Parson Stojan and admitted at the interrogation that he had climbed the church, come what might. He would have paid the fine and served his term in prison, but now he would have peace of mind and the certainty of what had happened. And at the same instant he realised himself that it was impossible to do that, to inflict such damage and bring such disgrace to his church and fellow-townsmen. He realised this and calmed down, but after a short while the mad whirlpool in his head began to work anew, by day as well as by night: I have climbed as none of them has, and proved it again, drunk, in the darkness, and then I have denied it all, and the others have denied it; and everybody knows as well as I do that I have climbed and nobody can acknowledge it, nobody dares to speak abut it, and it's going to be like this till the end of time, always the same circle: it has happened and it ought to be proved, and it has not happened although it has been proved that it has . . .

And now one had to find his bearings and live in this devilish circle, alone, without talking and without explanation. By day one could, somehow, manage, because at least from time to time it was clear what is and what is not. He could tell himself half-audibly: 'Yes, I've climbed, of course I've climbed!' But by night! When he fell asleep, he had bad dreams. He dreamed that he as walking between two cordons of scornful looks and mocking Osatican smiles which told him in their dumb way: 'This is the one who *says* that he has put the cross on the church!' He was walking, as it were, between two rows of whips, and he was unable to stop and he could not resist them, because a man is defenceless in his dreams. Or he would dream, for instance, that he was climbing a dome, steep and slippery; all the time tottering and feeling that he was going to fall down, that he had to fall, that he was falling. Then, falling with all the weight of his body, he flew with his head down, with a full consciousness of falling, and this went on for ever. To strike against the ground and fall to pieces — that would be the end and salvation. But there was no end.

And when he woke up with a blow coming, as it were, from within and found himself in the doughy darkness which had not been there when he was falling asleep, but which was kneaded while he was sleeping, then it was terrible and hard and everything was utterly vague. You did not know your own name. You did not feel in what position your body really was. And what you should do was ask somebody a question, just in order to hear a human voice, like a ray of light in the darkness. And then it might be easier. But who could he ask? His father and his mother slept in the other part of the house and he could not think of going there and waking them up. Night winds rustled outside in the top of the high mulberry tree which covered the greater part of the courtyard. He felt that sleep had abandoned him completely, and the fiery wheel turned in his head more and more quickly: yes, he has climbed, and no, he hasn't, and it is a glory, and it is a shame.

Then one had to wait for day to come and bring relief, but it was so incomplete.

Not knowing in his trouble what to do or where to go, Lekso thought of marriage. That was the only thing left in life which could be done, and which he had not done. And he took a girl from the neighbourhood, with whom he had grown up, and who was, without any reason, on the threshold of spinsterhood. Her name was Darinka.

Their marriage was a difficult one, its burdens invisible and unknown to the world. (And when it is said here that a marriage is a difficult one, it invariably means that it is difficult for the wife.) When the first days were over, days which are always over quickly, Lekso began to start up in his sleep at night as he had done before his marriage, always woken by the same questions. At first he held back and was silent by the side of his sleeping wife, but soon all consideration disappeared. Troubled by his uncertainties, he would wake up his wife to ask her what was the matter. He wanted to hear from her mouth an acknowledgement of the fact that he really had performed what he had performed and that sensible, sober people did not doubt it, that the world was not ridiculing him.

The young wife, who had heard various and contradictory stories about connubial nights and marital relations, never suspected that anything like that came into it.

After her first sleep she would be shaken and woken up ruthlessly. In the dark, checkered by the irregular reflections of the bright night outside, she could just make out his eyes below a frowning forehead and dishevelled hair. He was sitting by her side, holding on to her arm, as if drowning, and gazing questioningly into her face.

'Darinka, tell me honestly . . . . '

These were the moments of great trial. What did the man want of her? If she could understand him, she would do anything to help him. As it was, she could only tremble in silence. Her jaws contracted with fear, and even if she had been able to speak, she would not have had anything to say, because she could not find a single word and she could not find it even if they were to skin her alive. But he was insistent.

'What do the people say? What is the truth? I want to know it, you could have heard it and you can tell me. You must!'

What could she tell him when she could not understand either his question or what he wanted of her? She wept with fear, with a strange sense of shame because of all that her husband did to her. Through her tears she made weak and clumsy efforts to calm him down with kind words and fondling, but he would break away, abusing and reproaching her, saying she was insincere, false, and alien. Unable to defend herself against these mysterious and unjust accusations, she would cry more bitterly and more desperately. Sometimes it happened that after furious reproaches and harsh words he also began to cry. And so he would fall asleep again.

At moments of evening affection she would beg him, caressing him timidly, not to wake her up, to promise that he would never do it again. And he would promise, himself believing at the moment that he would keep his promise, swearing to it. But two or three days later the same thing would happen again, the same torture, the same mysterious fears.

This was repeated so many times that the man's appeal no longer expressed itself in clearly shaped, definite questions. He would just clutch her by the arm and say in a painful voice:

'Darinka! Tell me, please!'

And when she began, through her tears, to calm him down in whispers and to try to persuade him to lie down and sleep, his grip would tighten and he would shake her sharply:

'Speak up!'

And she would writhe on the mattress and weep with her face in her hands.

Sometimes it happened that the man would rise up and, like a somnambulist, in his sleep, start for the door, probably determined to go out and climb the church once more and so prove what he had already done twice, what nobody gave him credit for, and what he himself had denied. His wife would then run after him, stop him with great difficulty, and hang round his neck, shouting:

'Where are you heading for, my poor devil?'

Awakened, he would come back to bed and go to sleep, but now she herself would wait in vain for sleep to come.

She tried to ask him about it by day and to have it out with him, but he refused resolutely to talk about it. He would steer clear of the subject in all possible ways — by a joke, by a man's superior wave of the hand, by roughness when he had no other course. It seemed that he did not really know by day what he was doing by night. And when it got dark and sleep came to him — the scene was repeated. If not that night, then the following one.

The fear of these pointless night scenes spoilt every joy for the young woman. Sometimes he did not wake her up at all for several nights running, but this did not help either because her sleep was haunted now by the foreboding that she might be awakened. She slept with one eye open and sometimes not at all. She often lay down and closed her eyes and then, as she would begin to dose, it suddenly seemed to her that somebody was shaking her and waking her up. She would start up and look around in fear. Nothing. Darkness and silence. By her side the man was sleeping like a log, peacefully. But now *she* could not go to sleep, and *she* was troubled with questions. Dumb and immovable, she would ask herself and her mate who had sunk to sleep and all the people in the world, the wakeful and the sleeping, what it was

that gave rise, out of nothing, to misunderstandings among
people, to conflicts and fears, what it was that made them
spoil their own and each other's lives, disturb their sleep, and
poison the pleasures which were anyway not too many.

How could she, alone and frightened, find an answer to
this? She thought of telling her mother everything, of
complaining to her closest friend, but she soon realised that
those were troubles which did not bear telling. For such
questions answers were not to be found in other people, but
in oneself, here, by the side of the man to whom she was tied
by all possible ties and, the most difficult of all, by sharing a
bed. And she looked for a long time for a way out and a
solution, and she was tortured by the feeling that she would
not find them.

The first child had come, a girl, but the gratuitous wakings
were repeated. The child was weak and tearful, and so it
wanted much care and nursing, by day as well as by night.
The woman grew weak and noticeably thinner. But it was
about this time that she began, little by little, to defend herself.
When he woke her up at the most awkward hour, she would
say sharply and bitterly:

'Why did you wake me up? Have you got a heart, man?
Don't you see that the child doesn't give me a wink of sleep.
And what little sleep I get, you come to break it.'

A little ashamed, he would draw back, but as soon as the
next day she might be awakened again and tortured by an
interrogation of one kind or another.

However, the woman found now not only more and more
courage to defend herself but also strength and a way to
answer his questions. The second child came, this time a boy.
Her strength and her art seemed to grow with the growing of
the child.

It seemed to her natural, she was taking it for granted now,
that one should answer the questions of one's fellow human
being, and particularly of the fellow human being with whom
one was sharing everything in life, however unjustified and
unintelligible the questions might seem. One ought to find
sufficient patience and strength for it and at least try to come
to an understanding. This was a duty — because what many
of us need sometimes is just a friendly word from somebody
close to us. One should talk because silence is sloth and
cowardice, and it poisons human relations. And so she began
to answer him. In a calm voice and quite naturally.

It happened more and more frequently now that the husband and his wakened wife talked a little, and talked intimately in the darkness. She was not afraid and she did not weep any more, but calmed him down, indulging him in everything he said. Her words were quite ordinary and they did not provide answers to his questions; but still, they were spoken by a sane, familiar human being, in that hour of the night when they had the power to calm and to lull to sleep just because they were so ordinary. And the man would soon stop asking questions and, after a little silence, lie down obediently and fall asleep.

And the woman would watch for a time, sitting up like the guardian of her family. Her daughter and her son sleeping on her left, and her husband, like a third child, on the right. And then she would lie down among them too, to try to get a little sleep.

It was not only better like this, but the crazy wakings became less and less frequent and with time they dropped off altogether. The trouble was over — the trouble in which Darinka, a woman as good and as ordinary as bread, had borne the heaviest burden. But this was mentioned no more. Everything was forgotten; this made life so good. Lekso had calmed down, put on flesh and become slightly heavier. He ate well, slept like a log. The old unintelligible thoughts and insomnias were forgotten like the diseases of childhood. Business was good. There was a journeyman in the shop and two apprentices with him. They made pots, watering cans, and Austrian tin gutters. Ordinary work, but good earnings. When there was a tin roof to be put on a house or mended, Lekso sent his journeyman. He no longer felt like climbing.

In the course of the next four years two more children came to Lekso's home, both boys.

Years went by, the new generation was coming up, with new exploits and a new climbing urge.

Magistrate Pavlas, after long service at Osatica, was appointed District High Commissioner and moved to Sarajevo.

'Our Magistrate has climbed high!' the townsmen of Osatica used to say.

The following summer the District High Commissioner, on his official tour, called at Osatica and stayed with his friend the tax-collector Lađević, who was going to wait at Osatica, so it seemed, for his pension and his death.

Early in the morning Pavlas went for a walk, alone, along the steep Osatican streets, as he used to do when he was living here and worrying only Osatican worries. He passed by the church with its strange dome and its golden cross, by the inn, by the well-known houses and shops. He recollected various incidents and mishaps, but no longer with anxiety and anger as before, but viewing it all from a height of his present position from which such things seemed less important and smaller, almost insignificant trifles.

He was at the end of his walk, in the oldest part of the town, and he was just passing by a house sunk deep into an orchard, when the tearful shouting and screams of children and the cries and wailing of women suddenly broke out from down there. Pavlas stopped, looking into the courtyard below. On the waving top of a high mulberry tree, lost in the leaves, a small boy was screaming, a boy who could not, obviously, go further up and did not dare or know how to get down. Below him boys and girls were running in a circle, all calling with one voice:

'Mama, mama! Jovica has climbed the mulberry-tree and can't get down. Look, he's right at the top. Oh, Mama, he'll break his neck!'

A lean woman, with her blouse unbuttoned, her hands dusty with flour, rushed from the house. Frightened out of her wits she shouted, calling the boy in her shrill voice, cursing him and cajoling him, encouraging him and warning him:

'What are you doing so high, devil take you! . . . Wait, my dear, don't budge, Mama'll bring a ladder in no time . . . Eh, may you break your neck, brave boy, as you're bound to if you go on climbing like this! . . . Wait, don't move, hold fast and mind you don't put your foot on a thin branch! . . . Mama'll bring a ladder now.'

'A ladder, get a ladder!' cried another female voice, while the boy went on howling up there and calling for help, the other children answering him by screaming and wailing under the mulberry-tree.

The District High Commissioner turned the other way, downhill. The shouts from the courtyard were slowly lost behind him.

A Letter from 1920

March 1920. The railway station at Slavonski Brod. Gone midnight. From somewhere a wind was blowing, and it seemed colder than it really was to the weary travellers, longing for sleep. High above, stars slipped between the clouds. In the distance, yellow and red signal lights travelled faster or slower along invisible tracks, with the piercing sound of conductors' whistles and the long drawn-out howling of the locomotive, which we travellers invest with the melancholy of our fatigue, and the tedium of our long, bad-tempered waiting.

In front of the station by the first track, we sat on our suitcases and waited for the train. We didn't know when it would come, when it would leave. All we knew was that it would be overcrowded, crammed with travellers and luggage.

The man sitting next to me was an old friend I'd lost track of for the last five or six years. Max Levenfeld, a doctor and a doctor's son. Born and raised in Sarajevo, where he had built up a large practice. Jewish in origin, long ago converted. His mother was born in Trieste, the daughter of an Italian baroness and an Austrian naval officer, himself the descendant of French emigrés. In Sarajevo, two generations remembered her figure, her bearing, and her elegant style of dress. She was marked by the kind of beauty respected and appreciated by people otherwise quite impudent and vulgar.

Max and I went to high school together in Sarajevo, only he was three years ahead of me, which at that age was a lot. I vaguely remember that I noticed him as soon as I came to high school. He had just entered the fourth class, but still dressed as a child. He was a strong boy, 'The little Kraut', in a navy blue sailor suit with anchors embroidered at the corners of the wide collar. He was still in shorts. And on his feet, perfectly shaped black shoes. Between his little white socks and shorts — powerful bare calves, ruddy and already sprinkled with light hairs.

Then, there wasn't and couldn't be any contact between us. Everything divided us — age, appearance, customs and habits, our parents' financial position and their social status.

But I remembered him much better at a later point, when I was in the fifth and he in the eighth class. Then he was already a lanky young man with light eyes that betrayed unusual sensitivity and a very lively mind; well, but carelessly dressed, with thick blond hair that fell in heavy slicks, now to one, now to the other side of his face. We met and came closer during a discussion with some senior boys in the park on a bench.

Such schoolboy arguments acknowledged no limits and showed no respect for anything: all principles suffered, and entire philosophical worlds were mined to their very foundations by our bombast. Afterwards, of course, everything remained in place; but those passionate words were significant for us and the fate awaiting us, as a foreshadowing of the great achievements and painful perplexities of the combative times that were yet to come.

After one such lively discussion, when I started for home still trembling with excitement and convinced of my triumph (just as my opponent was of his), Max joined me. This was the first time that the two of us had been alone together. This flattered me and intensified my sense of triumph and high opinion of myself. He asked what I was reading and looked at me carefully, as if seeing me for the first time in his life. I was answering excitedly. All at once he stopped, looked me straight in his eyes and said in a strangely calm way: 'You know, I wanted to tell you that you didn't quote Ernst Haeckel correctly.'

I felt myself blushing and the earth slowly moving from under my feet, and then back again into its place. Of course I had quoted him wrongly — my quotation was from a cheap pamphlet, uncertainly remembered and, most likely, badly translated. All my former triumph turned into a pang of conscience and feeling of shame. His light blue eyes watched me without sympathy, but also with no trace of malice or superiority. And then Max repeated my ill-fated quotation in the correct form. And when we got to his beautiful house on the bank of the Miljacka, he firmly shook my hand and invited me to come the following afternoon to look at his books.

That afternoon was an experience for me. I saw the first real library of my life, and it was clear to me that I was seeing my own destiny. Max had many German and some Italian and French books which belonged to his mother. He showed me all this with a calm that I envied him more than the books. It wasn't really envy, but rather a sense of limitless contentment and a strong desire that one day I too would move so freely in this world of books from which, it seemed to me, streamed light and warmth. He spoke just as if reading from books, freely, and moved without boasting in this world of glorious names and great ideas. And I trembled with excitement, with vanity, as I shyly entered this world of great men, fearing the world I had left outside to which I had to return.

These afternoon visits to my old friend's house became more and more frequent. I improved quickly in German and began to read Italian. I even brought those beautifully bound foreign books home to my wretched apartment. I fell behind in my school work. Everything I read seemed to me to be the sacred truth and my sublime duty, which I couldn't escape if I didn't want to lose my self-respect and faith in myself. I knew only one thing: I had to read it all, and try to write the same or similar things. I couldn't envision anything else in my life.

I remember one day in particular. It was May. Max was getting ready for his final examinations, but without any fuss or noticeable effort. He led me to a small, separate bookcase with *Helios Klassiker-Ausgabe* engraved on it in gold. And I remember being told that the bookcase was bought together with the books. The bookcase seemed to me a holy object, its wood imbued with light. Max took out a volume of Goethe and started to read *Prometheus* to me.

> Cover thy spacious heavens, Zeus,
> With clouds of mist,
> And, like the boy who lops
> The thistles' heads,
> Disport with oaks and mountain-peaks;
> Yet thou must leave
> My earth still standing;
> My cottage too, which was not raised by thee;
> Leave me my hearth,
> Whose kindly glow
> By thee is envied.

At the end, he rhythmically but powerfully pounded the arm

of the chair he was sitting in with his fist, his hair falling down on both sides of his flushed face.

> Here sit I, forming mortals
> After my image;
> A race resembling me,
> To suffer, to weep,
> To enjoy, to be glad,
> And thee to scorn,
> As I do!

That was the first time I had seen him like that. I listened to him with awe and slight fear. Then we went outside and continued our conversation about the poem in the warm dusk. Max saw me to my steep street, and then I saw him to the river bank, then back we went to the street, and back again to the bank.

Night was falling and the people had begun to thin out, but we continued to measure that path pondering the meaning of life and the origin of gods and men. I remember one moment particularly well. The first time we reached my nondescript street and stopped at some grey wooden fences, Max stretched out his left hand in a strange way and said to me in a sort of warm, confidential voice, 'You know, I'm an atheist.'

A thick clump of elder was blooming above the tumbled down fence and spreading a powerful, heavy scent which came over to me as the scent of life itself. The evening was solemn, everything around us was quiet, and the dome of heaven above me, full of stars, seemed brand-new. I was so excited I couldn't say anything, I just felt that something important had happened between me and my older friend, that now we couldn't just separate and each go our own way home. And so we went on walking until late into the night.

Max's graduation separated us. He left for Vienna to study medicine. For a short while we wrote to one another, but the correspondence petered out. We sometimes saw one another on vacations, but without our former intimacy. And then came the war, which separated us completely.

And now, after several years, here we were, meeting again on this ugly and boring station. We had travelled from Sarajevo on the same train, but we didn't know it, and only saw one another here; and now we were waiting for the uncertain arrival of the Belgrade train.

In a few words we told one another how we had spent the war. He graduated in the first year, and then worked as a doctor on all the Austrian fronts, always serving in Bosnian regiments. His father died of typhus fever during the war, and his mother left Sarajevo and moved to her relatives in Trieste. Max had spent the last few months in Sarajevo, just as long as he needed to put his affairs in order. By agreement with his mother, he had sold his father's house on the Miljacka and most of his things. Now he was on his way to his mother in Trieste, and then he might go to Argentina, or maybe even Bolivia. He didn't say it explicitly, but it was clear that he was leaving Europe for ever.

Max had grown larger during his life on the front, had roughened; he was dressed like a businessman, as far as I could tell. In the darkness I could just make out his strong head with its thick blond hair and hear his voice, which had become deeper and more masculine over the years, and his Sarajevo dialect in which the consonants are softened and the vowels slurred and drawn out. There was a certain feeling of insecurity in his speech.

Even now he spoke as if he were reading from a book, using many strange, bookish, learned phrases. But that was the only thing that remained of the former Max. Otherwise there was no reminder of either poetry or books. (Nobody remembered Prometheus any more.) First, he spoke about the war in general, with a great bitterness revealed more in the tone than in the words — a bitterness that did not expect to be understood. There were not, so to speak, any opposing fronts for him in this great war; they had mixed, flowed into one another, and utterly merged. The general suffering had blinkered his vision and deprived him of an understanding of everything else. I remember how shocked I was when he said he congratulated the victors — and that he pitied them deeply, for the conquered see what they're up against and what needs to be done, while the conquerors can hardly suspect what is in store for them. He spoke in the caustic and hopeless tone of a man who has lost a great deal, and can now say what he likes, well aware both that no one can do him much harm for what he says, and that it cannot do him any good. After the great war, there were many of these embittered people among the intelligentsia, embittered in a peculiar way, about something indefinable in life. These people couldn't either manage to reconcile themselves and adapt, or find the strength for firm decisions in the opposite direction. He was, it seemed to me at that moment, one of them.

But the conversation quickly ran aground, because neither he nor I wanted to quarrel that night, after so many years, at this strange place for a reunion. So we talked about other things. Actually, he did the talking. Even now, he spoke in carefully chosen words and complicated sentences, like a man who spends more time with books than people, in a cold, matter-of-fact manner — with no beating about the bush, just as when we open a medical textbook, and find the symptoms of our illness inside.

I offered him a cigarette, but he said he didn't smoke, stating that hastily, almost with fear and distrust. And while I lit one cigarette after another, he spoke with somewhat forced nonchalance, as if driving away other, heavier thoughts.

'You see, the two of us have just come to the first main-line station. That means, we've taken hold of the latch of the door that opens onto the wide world. We're leaving Bosnia. And I will never go back, although you will.'

'Who knows?' I interrupted, pensively, spurred by that peculiar conceit that makes young people want to see their own fate in distant lands and along unusual paths.

'No, no, you'll come back for sure,' my fellow traveller said with certainty, as if making a diagnosis, 'while all my life long I'll be struggling with the memory of Bosnia, as if with some Bosnian disease. What the cause of it is — the fact that I was born and grew up in Bosnia, or that I'll never be coming back again, I don't even know myself. Not that it matters.'

In a strange place, at a strange hour, even conversation becomes strange, a little like a dream. I looked sideways at the large, hunched silhouette of my former friend next to me and wondered; I thought how little he resembled that young man who pounded with his fist and recited, 'Cover thy spacious heavens, Zeus! . . . ' I thought, what will become of us if life continues to change so quickly and profoundly for us; I thought that only the changes I noticed in myself were good and right. And while I was thinking all this, I suddenly noticed that this friend was talking to me again. Rousing myself from my thoughts, I listened to him carefully, so carefully that it seemed to me that the station noises around me had fallen silent and his voice alone murmured in the windy night.

'Yes, for a long time I really did think that I should spend my life treating children in Sarajevo just like my father, and that my bones, like his, would rest in the graveyard at Koševo. This conviction was already shaken by what I saw and experienced in the Bosnian regiments during the war, but when I left the army this summer and spent three whole months in Sarajevo, it became clear to me that I could not go on living there. And the mere thought of living in Vienna, Trieste, or some other Austrian city revolts me, revolts me to the point of nausea. And so I began to think of South America.'

'Fine, but may one ask what it is you're running away from in Bosnia?' I asked, with the recklessness at that time typical of people my age asking questions.

'Well, "one may ask", but one isn't likely to get a concise answer in transit at a railway station. But if I still had to say in one word what is driving me out of Bosnia, I would say: hatred.'

Max suddenly stood up, as if he had unexpectedly run into an invisible fence in his speech. And I emerged to the reality of a cold night at the railway station in Slavonski Brod. The wind was beating stronger and stronger, colder and colder, signal lights were winking in the distance, tiny locomotives were whistling. Above us, even that diminished sky with sparse stars had disappeared, and just fog and smoke made a blanket worthy of this plain where, it seemed to me man sank up to his eyes in rich, black soil.

At that moment we heard the roar of an express train, immediately followed by its heavy whistle, muffled, as if coming out of a concrete tunnel. The entire station instantly came to life. Hundreds of previously invisible figures moved about in the darkness and began to run to meet the train. And the two of us jumped up, but the crowd we were caught up in separated us even further. I only managed to shout out my Belgrade address.

About three weeks later, I received a rather long letter in Belgrade. I couldn't guess who it was from by the large handwriting. Max had written it to me from Trieste, in German:

'My dear old friend,

When we ran into one another in Slavonski Brod our conversation was disjointed and difficult. And even had we had a far better occasion and more time, I don't believe we would have understood one another and got to the bottom of everything. The unexpected meeting and abrupt departure made that quite impossible. I'm getting ready to leave Trieste where my mother is living. I'm going to Paris, where I have some relatives on my mother's side. If they'll allow me, as a foreigner, to practise medicine there, I'll stay in Paris; if not, I'm truly going to South America.

I don't believe that these few disjointed paragraphs I am writing in haste will be able to explain the matter fully, or justify in your eyes my "running away" from Bosnia. But I send them anyway, because I feel I owe you an answer, and remembering our school-days, I don't want you to misunderstand me and see in me an ordinary Kraut and "carpetbagger" who lightly leaves the country he was born in, the moment she is beginning a free life and needs every ounce of her strength.

But let me come straight to the point. Bosnia is a wonderful country, fascinating, with nothing ordinary in the habitat or people. And just as there are mineral riches under the earth in Bosnia, so undoubtedly are Bosnians rich in hidden moral values, which are more rarely found in their compatriots in other Yugoslav lands. But, you see, there's one thing that the people of Bosnia, at least people of your kind, must realise and never lose sight of — Bosnia is a country of hatred and fear.

But leaving fear aside, which is only a correlative of hatred, the natural result of it, let us talk about hatred. Yes, about hatred. And instinctively you recoil and protest when you hear that word (I saw it that night at the station), just as every one of you refuses to hear, grasp, and understand it. But it is precisely this that needs to be recognised, confirmed, and analysed. And the real harm lies in the fact that no one either wants or knows how to do it. For the fatal characteristic of this hatred is that the Bosnian man is unaware of the hatred that lives in him, shrinks from analysing it and — hates everyone who tries to do so. And yet it's a fact that in Bosnia and Herzegovina there are more people ready in fits of this subconscious hatred to kill and be killed, for different reasons, and under different pretexts, than in other much bigger Slav and non-Slav lands.

I know that hatred, like anger, has its function in the development of society, because hatred gives strength, and anger provokes action. I know that there are ancient and deeply rooted injustices and abuses which only torrents of hatred and anger can uproot and wash away. And when these torrents dwindle and dry up, room for freedom remains, for the creation of a better life. The people living at the time see the hatred and anger far better, because they are the sufferers by them, but their descendants see only the fruits of this strength and action. That I know well. But what I have seen in Bosnia — that is something different. It is hatred, but not limited just to a moment in the course of social change, or an inevitable part of the historical process; rather, it is hatred acting as an independent force, as an end in itself. Hatred which sets man against man and casts both alike into misery and misfortune, or drives both opponents to the grave; hatred like a cancer in an organism, consuming and eating up everything around it, only to die itself at the last; because this kind of hatred, like a flame, has neither one constant form, nor a life of its own: it is simply the agent of the instinct of destruction or self destruction. It exists only in this form, and only until its task of total destruction has been completed.

Yes, Bosnia is a country of hatred. That is Bosnia. And by a strange contrast, which in fact isn't so strange, and could perhaps be easily explained by careful analysis, it can also be said that there are a few countries with such firm belief, elevated strength of character, so much tenderness and loving passion, such depth of feeling, of loyalty and unshakeable devotion, or with such a thirst for justice. But in secret depths underneath all this hide burning hatreds, entire hurricanes of tethered and compressed hatreds maturing and awaiting their hour. The relationship between your loves and your hatred is the same as between your high mountains and the invisible geological strata underlying them, a thousand times larger and heavier. And thus you are condemned to live on deep layers of explosive which are lit from time to time by the very sparks of your loves and your fiery and violent emotion. Perhaps your greatest misfortune is precisely that you do not suspect just how much hatred there is in your loves and passions, traditions and pieties. And just as, under the influence of atmospheric moisture and warmth, the earth on which we live passes into our bodies and gives them colour and form, determining the character and direction of our way of life and our actions — so does the strong, underground and invisible hatred on which Bosnian man lives imperceptibly and indirectly enter into all his actions, even the best of them. Vice gives birth to hatred everywhere in the world, because it consumes and does not create, destroys, and does not build; but in countries like Bosnia, virtue itself often speaks and acts through hatred. With you, ascetics derive no love from their asceticism, but hatred for the voluptuary instead; abstainers hate those who drink, and drunkards feel a murderous hatred for the whole world. Those who do believe and love feel a mortal hatred for those who don't, or those who believe and love differently. And, unhappily, the chief part of their belief and love is often consumed in this hatred. (The most evil and sinister-looking faces can be met in greatest numbers at places of worship — monasteries, and dervish tekkes.) Those who oppress and exploit the economically weaker do it with hatred into the bargain, which makes that exploitation a hundred times harder and uglier; while those who bear these injustices dream of justice and reprisal, but as some explosion of vengeance which, if it were realised according to their ideas, would perforce be so complete that it would blow to pieces the oppressed along with the hated oppressors. You Bosnians have, for the most part, got used to keeping all the strength of your hatred for that which is closest to you. Your holy of holies is, as a rule, three hundred rivers and mountains away, but the objects of your repulsion and hatred are right beside you, in the same town, often on the other side of your courtyard wall. So your love remains inert, but your hatred is easily spurred into action. And you love your homeland, you passionately love it, but in three or four different ways which are mutually exclusive, often come to blows, and hate each other to death.

In some Maupassant story there is a Dionysiac description of spring which ends with the remark that on such days, there should be a warning posted on every corner: "*Citoyens*! This is spring — beware of love!" Perhaps in Bosnia men should be warned at every step in their every thought and their every feeling, even the most elevated, to beware of hatred — of innate, unconscious, endemic hatred. Because this poor, backward country, in which four different faiths live cheek by jowl, needs four times as much love, mutual understanding and tolerance as other countries. But in Bosnia, on the contrary, lack of understanding, periodically spilling over into open hatred, is the general characteristic of its people. The rifts between the different faiths are so deep that hatred alone can sometimes succeed in crossing them. I know that you could argue, and with sufficient reason, that a certain amount of progress can be seen in this direction; that the ideas of the nineteenth century have done their work here too, and after liberation and unification all this will go much better and faster. I'm afraid that this is not quite so. (In these past few months I think I have had a good view of the real relationships between people of different faiths and nationalities in Sarajevo!) On every occasion you will be told, and wherever you go you will read, "Love your brother, though his religion is other", "It's not the cross that marks the Slav", "Respect others' ways and take pride in your own", "Total national solidarity recognises no religious or ethnic differences."

But from time immemorial in Bosnian urban life there has been plenty of counterfeit courtesy, the wise deception of oneself and others by resounding words and empty ceremonies. That conceals the hatred up to a point, but doesn't get rid of it or thwart its growth. I'm afraid that in these circles, under the cover of all these contemporary maxims, old instincts and Cain-like plans may only be slumbering, and will live on until the foundations of material and spiritual life in Bosnia are altogether changed. And when will that time come, and who will have the strength to carry it out? It will come one day, that I do believe; but what I've seen in Bosnia does not indicate that things are advancing along that path at present. On the contrary.

I have thought this over and over, especially in the last few months, when I was still struggling against my decision to leave Bosnia for ever. Of course a man obsessed with such thoughts cannot sleep well, and I would lie in front of an open window in the room where I was born, while the sound of the Miljacka alternated with the rustling of the leaves in the early autumn wind.

Whoever lies awake at night in Sarajevo hears the voices of the Sarajevo night. The clock on the Catholic cathedral strikes the hour with weighty confidence: 2 am. More than a minute passes (to be exact, seventy-five seconds — I counted) and only then with a rather weaker, but piercing sound does the Orthodox church announce the hour, and chime its own 2 am. A moment after it the tower clock on the Bey's mosque strikes the hour in a hoarse, faraway voice, and that strikes 11, the ghostly Turkish hour, by the strange calculation of distant and alien parts of the world. The Jews have no clock to sound their hour, so God alone knows what time it is for them by the Sephardic reckoning or the Ashkenazy. Thus at night, while everyone is sleeping, division keeps vigil in the counting of the late, small hours, and separates these sleeping people who, awake, rejoice and mourn, feast and fast by four different and antagonistic calendars, and send all their prayers and wishes to one heaven in four different ecclesiastical languages. And this difference, sometimes visible and open, sometimes invisible and hidden, is always similar to hatred, and often completely identical with it.

This uniquely Bosnian hatred should be studied and eradicated like some pernicious, deeply-rooted disease. Foreign scholars should come to Bosnia to study hatred, I do believe, just as scientists study leprosy, if hatred were only recognised as a separate, classified subject of study, as leprosy is.

I considered whether I should devote myself to the study of this hatred and, by analysing it and bringing it to the light of day, make my contribution to its destruction. Perhaps I was in duty bound to try, since, although a foreigner by birth, it was in Bosnia I first "saw the light of day", as they say. But after my first attempts and much reflection, I realised I had neither the strength nor the ability to do it. I would be required to take sides, to hate and be hated; and that, I neither wanted nor was able to do. Perhaps, if it had to be, I could have consented to fall a victim to hatred; but to live in hatred and with hatred, to be a part of it — that I cannot do. And in a country like present-day Bosnia, the man who does not know how to hate, or, what is still better and harder, consciously does not want to hate, is always something of a foreigner and freak, often a martyr. That holds true for all you who are born in Bosnia, and even more so for a newcomer. And so on one of those autumn nights, listening to the strange chimes of the various and many-voiced Sarajevo towers, I concluded that I could not stay in Bosnia, my second homeland, and did not have to. I'm not so naive as to look for any town in the world that has no hatred. No, I only need a place where I'll be able to live and work. Here, I would not be able to.

You may now repeat your remark about my running away from Bosnia with mockery, perhaps even with contempt. This letter of mine won't have the power to explain and justify my action to you, but it appears that there are occasions in life when the ancient Latin maxim *non est salus nisi in fuga* holds true. I beg you to believe one thing only: I am not running away from my duty as a man, but only attempting to perform it more completely, without hindrance.

I wish you and our Bosnia the best of luck in its independent life in the new state.

Yours, M.L.'

Ten years passed. I rarely thought of my childhood friend and would have forgotten him completely, had not the basic idea of his letter reminded me of him from time to time. Some time around 1930 I found out quite by accident that Dr Max Levenfeld had stopped in Paris, that he had an extensive practice in the suburb of Neuilly, and that in our colony of Yugoslavs he was known as 'our doctor', because he examined workers and students free of charge and, when necessary, bought medicines for them himself.

Seven or eight years passed. One day, again by chance, I learned the further fate of my friend. When the civil war broke out in Spain, he abandoned everything and joined the Republican army as a volunteer. He organised a first aid station and hospital and became well-known for his keenness and expertise. At the beginning of 1938 he was in a small town in Aragon whose name none of us could pronounce properly. An air raid was carried out on his hospital in broad daylight, and he perished along with almost all the wounded.

Thus ended the life of the man who ran away from hatred.

THE HOUSE ON ITS OWN

Introduction

It is a two-storey house on the steep slope of Alifakovac, right near the top, a little distance from any others. On the ground floor, where it was warm in winter and cool in summer, there is a spacious hall, a large kitchen and two small, dark rooms at the back. Upstairs there are three quite large rooms, one of which, the one in the front that looks over the open Sarajevo valley, has a broad balcony. Its size and construction are reminsicent of the Bosnian 'divanhana', but it is not built as they are of natural wood, but painted dark green, and its balustrade is not made of round railings, but of flat boards cut as on the balconies of Alpine houses. It was built in the nineties — 1887 to be precise — when local people began to build houses 'according to plan', designed and laid out in Austrian style, and were half-sucessful in this. Had it been built just half a dozen years earlier, this house would have been built entirely in the old Turkish way, like most of the houses on Alifakovac, and not in the 'German' style of the buildings along the banks of the Miljacka. Then the broad entrance hall on the ground floor would have been called an 'ahar' and the balcony a 'divanhana' and the whole thing would not have had this hybrid appearance of a building in which intention and will had gone in one direction, towards something new and unknown, and hands, eyes and the whole inner being dragged in another, towards the old and customary. The nature and arrangement of the furniture, the colour of the walls, the Viennese chandeliers, of crystal and brass, the earthenware Bosnian stoves, with their ceramic tiles, and locally made rugs in the rooms symbolize that duality. Inside as well as out, one may clearly read the collision of two epochs and the arbitrary mixture of styles, and yet it all blends into the atmosphere of a warm human habitation. It is evident that the people who live in this house do not care much for the external appearance of things, or for their names, but that they know how to take all that those things have to offer for a modest, tranquil and comfortable life to people who care more for life itself than for what may be thought, spoken or written about it. Here things and buildings in their primeval namelessness and perfect modesty simply serve naturally modest and happily nameless people for their few, simple needs. Over it all reigns the kind of peace that we always wish for but rarely achieve in our lives, and that we even often run away from without real need and to our own detriment.

It is good to live and work in these Sarajevo houses. A few years ago I spent a whole summer in the one described here. These are my memories of that house and that time. More exactly, they are just some of those memories; ones about which I am able to say something.

A bright summer morning. The sun has been up for a long time and I have washed and had breakfast, but I am still full, from my toes to the crown of my head, of formless, nameless dreams, like a kind of mist. They fill me like this, once they have first devoured my whole inner being and drained all the blood from me.

Now people everywhere in this town are settling down to work. An ordinary working day is beginning for everyone, including myself. Only, while others sit down to a regular activity, with a more or less clear aim in front of them, I gaze absent-mindedly at the pictures and objects around me as though they were strange and new, and feigning awkwardness, I wait for my idea to begin to form in me. With naive cunning (whom am I deceiving, and why?) I seek the thread of my story, broken off the previous day, endeavouring to look like a man who is not seeking anything, I listen to hear whether the voice of the story can be heard within me, ready to turn myself completely into the story or part of the story, into a scene or one of its characters. And less than that: into an instant in a scene, into one single thought or movement of that character. In this endeavour, I circle round my target, indifferent and apparently innocent, like a hunter who turns his head away from the bird he is hunting but without in fact letting it out of his sight for an instant.

I have to proceed like this; it has become second nature to me. For the moment that a fragment of my everyday consciousness intrudes and I acknowledge my intention and all my aim by its true name, I know what will happen. Thinner than the least substantial mist, all this atmopshere of nameless dream will disperse and I shall find myself in this familiar room, just as I am in my identity card or in the list of occupants of the flats where I live, a man with recognised features, without any connection whatever with the characters and scenes in the story I was thinking about until a moment before . . . and then . . . my day which has barely begun will suddenly turn grey and, instead of my story and my work, there will be opened up before me the intolerable triviality of an existence which bears my name but is not mine, and the deadly desert of time which suddenly extinguishes all the joy of life and steadily kills each one of us.

But it can also happen that my day starts differently, that I do not lie in wait or anticipate my stories, but they seek me out, many of them at the same time. In a half-sleep, before I have opened my eyes, like the yellow and pink stripes on the closed blind of my window, there begin to tremble in me of their own accord the broken threads of unfinished stories. They offer themselves, waken me and disturb me. And later, when I am dressed and sit down to work, characters from these stories and fragments of their conversations, reflections and actions do not cease to beset me, with a mass of clearly delineated detail. Now I have to defend myself from them and hide, grasping as many details as I can and throwing whatever I can down on to the waiting paper.

Alipasha

Under my windows, in the freshness of early morning, there rides with his escort from time to time the former Vizier of Mostar — Alipasha Rizvanbegović of Stolac.

I can tell from the number of hooves and their clattering whether he is riding as the master and Vizier of Herzegovina, or as a defeated captive. When he comes as Vizier and despot he barely announces himself and never stops, while when he rides as a prisoner under sentence he pauses by my window and quietly exchanges a few insignificant words with me. But in either case, he is clearly admonishing me by these frequent visits to open the door of my story to him and to make him the room that he deserves.

He was born in 1783, the son of Zulfikar Rizvanbegović, captain of Stolac, who had six sons. Having somehow offended his severe and choleric father he left as a young man for Turkey, where he spent several years, and he returned to Stolac only after this father's death, bringing with him a handsome fortune in ready money. Where had he been? How had he come by it? There were many who asked, but no one ever discovered. Aliaga, as they termed him then, was one of those about whom you discover only what they want you to know.

Soon after his return he began the long and bitter struggle with his brothers and other nobles in the area for the position of top man in Herzegovina. The struggle was particularly long and difficult with his brother Mehmed, called Hadjun, 'the slaughterer of Hutovo'. Eventually he killed him near the fortress at Stolac, after a small real war in which the rayah helped Aliaga against the detested Hadjun. Then he stood alone on the field.

In the great revolt of the Bosnian nobles against the Sultan — around 1830 — Rizvanbegović was always firmly on the side of the Sultan. When the resistance of the Bosnian nobles was crushed, Herzegovina was divided administratively from

Bosnia, and captain Rizvanbegović of Stolac was appointed to Mostar as its first Vizier. This was his reward for fidelity to the Sultan, and the fruit of years of effort for Alipasha. From then on he would rule Herzegovina in the way he had said when he came to power: 'From today, no one need ago any longer to the emperor in Istanbul. Here in Mostar is your Istanbul, and here in Mostar is your emperor!'

He was one of those petty sultans who succeeded, for a longer or shorter time, in ruling various Turkish provinces in the first half of the nineteenth century when the central power was losing its remaining strength. He ruled 'his' country like a truly severe and wily tyrant, but also like a good husbandman. He irrigated the land, and made people plant and build. He constructed palaces — the majority, of course, for himself and his family — and erected mosques and tekkes; he introduced the cultivation of rice, olives and mulberry trees into Herzegovina and the raising of silkworms, and he even tried planting coffee. He felt the growing penetration of the Austrian capital: he was the first to establish connections with it, and began to sell Austrian firms concessions for exporting wood. All this time he was fighting and making peace with neighbouring Montenegro, and what was most important, reciprocally cheating and lying with the Viziers in Istanbul and pashas in Travnik. He bribed whoever needed bribing, giving them as much as they required. He was always for the Sultan, and even spoke in favour of the reforms: but in practice, in his pashalik, he was against them. He grew rich, arrogant and fat, producing a numerous progeny from four wives. So he ruled for almost twenty years, 'firmly and justly' (in his opinion) but wilfully and cruelly in the opinion of the majority of his subjects. Like many of these petty autocrats in the Turkish Empire, he genuinely wanted as many people in his pashalik to be as happy as possible — but the number of them, and the nature of their happiness, to be decided by himself. It looked as though he would rule like that till he died, leaving the country and power to his descendants; but at the end of his life the old magician was ensnared in his own tricks and contrivances. In 1850, when Omerpasha was sent to Bosnia to crush the resistance of the nobles for good, and to introduce *nizam*, direct rule, he attempted to frustrate himwith the cunning he had tried and tested so often. But this time nothing availed; not cunning, bribery or procrastination. The seventy-year old Vizier of Mostar, with his will-power already eroded and his strength diminished, was outwitted by the younger, wilier and more ruthless emissary of the Sultan, Omerpasha Latas. He overturned him unexpectedly and completely, stripped him of his Vizier's rank, confiscated all his estates and ordered him to be imprisoned, put on a donkey and led all round Bosnia and Herzegovina like the worst kind of criminal, so the people could see 'in whom they had trusted'; and then to be expelled to Asia. His orders were carried out. But in the course of his bitter journey, when Alipasha was in the village of Dobrinje near Banja Luka, he was unexpectedly killed while sleeping. It was said that one of the soldiers escorting him fired accidentally. He was buried in a handsome white turbeh beside the Ferhadpasha Mosque in Banja Luka. His family was sent to Istanbul, where some of his sons became prominent Ottoman civil servants and leaders.

Such was the fate of Galib Alipasha Rizvanbegović of Stolac, which is sufficiently familiar from history to be told only briefly here, and in part. But the reason why Alipasha wants to enter my story now, and for which he even stops sometimes to chat with me, is quite unconnected with the stormy years of his rise and even with the fortunate decades of his rule. It is not even his terrible death, for he realises now that sooner or later, every man is destroyed by his greatest passion; all he cares about, he says, are those two weeks when, as a prisoner surrounded by the soldiers of Omerpasha, he was led through scores of towns and villages in Herzegovina and Bosnia. During those days on the journey, it was revealed to him what it is that remains of a man who suddenly loses everything and, stripped of all he has, stands alone and naked on his own two feet, defying all the powers of this world that surround him — helpless but unconquerable.

Alipasha was informed in good time that Omer would be sent to Bosnia as military commandant with special powers. He knew who and what sort of man this was, and undertook all that was necessary to protect himself from this disaster, according to his own lights and his experience up till then. In the twenty-odd years he had spent as the ruler of Herzegovina he had, till now, always been successful; and doubtless there was no reason why it should be different this time.

The aged, self-confident tyrant and master of Herzegovina

trusted too far to his experience, tested across the years, and to his far-sightedness; he did not imagine circumstances could arise in which his innumerable wiles, already proverbial, might appear outdated and even be dangerous to him; or that a kind of man could come who saw through him completely, and to whom his adroitness would be unequal.

Now when the commandant's invitation arrived to come to Sarajevo and attend the official reading of the Sultan's firman, Alipasha was not surprised; he was only angered by the unusually dry and sharp tone of the invitation, but he quickly recovered himself, and realised that it was not worth getting angry and offended. He slept on the invitation, and the following morning, calm and resolute, he came to the decision not to go to Sarajevo in person, but to send his son Hafiz, who already bore the title of pasha, and with him the Orthodox bishop of Mostar, Josif.

That would be sufficient, in the old man's estimation. His oldest and best-loved son would be living proof and a weighty pledge of his good faith and sincere intention of serving the Sultan in all eventualities, as heretofore; and the bishop, by his presence, would show how rightly Alipasha understood the Sultan's plans for reform. Their task was to assure the commandant of Alipasha's devotion as strongly as possible, and convey his regret that on account of his old age and infirmity he could not come in person. He gave brief and clear instructions to both — one sort to one, and another sort to the other, separately to each. He was satisfied with his decision.

His emissaries set off immediately, not only equipped with instructions but with the necessary presents, and empowered to hint at new and greater offerings. But they came back faster than they went.

Omerpasha received them in an unusual way. They were met in the guardhouse of the commandant's temporary konak with well-feigned surprise, like unknown and unexpected visitors. There they were told, in none too pleasant a way, that their names could not be found on the list of leaders invited. After waiting a long time they were told to come early the following morning. They would probably be granted an audience by the commandant in the course of the day.

They came at exactly seven o'clock, prepared to wait, but the officer on duty reprimanded them for being late and immediately led them into the konak. But the real surprise was still awaiting them. In the large hall they almost collided with a group of smartly-dressed, high-ranking officers going towards the exit, among whom they immediately recognised Omerpasha.

The respected visitors from this country, he said, were invariably valued and welcome to him; but each man must stand before an emissary of the Sultan just as he is — not as he is not, or cannot, be. This, it seemed, was a case of misunderstanding, and he neither liked nor tolerated misunderstandings. Such important matters were at stake, and such sizeable state interests, that there could be no question now of health or illness, but only of life and death. Alipasha, as an old and faithful servant of the Sultan, knew that well. He wished him a quick recovery (the quicker the better!) and hoped to see him here soon, so he could complete what was necessary with him and the other leaders who had been invited. He wished them a good journey.

The audience was over.

The commandant bowed to the bishop as easily as a young man and went out, followed by his officers discreetly clinking their sabres and spurs.

The astounded emissaries could hardly find the exit. They stared at one another in silence, wondering dumbly whether it was all really over. Eventually they recovered sufficiently to see that the best thing was to turn back immediately. On the journey they had the opportunity, in the leaden silence, of thinking over the way in which they had been outplayed and repulsed, as well as about the commandant, his looks and carriage; and with every hour he seemed stranger and more unpleasant. But as they were nearing Mostar, one thought pushed all else aside: how they were to go before Alipasha, and what they would say to him.

However, the old Vizier received the news of their ill success as the most natural thing in the world, or pretended to do so. Two days later he left for Sarajevo, taking Hafizpasha with him again. There he went before the commandant as naturally and suavely as if this had always been his greatest single wish. Omer showed him particular respect among the leaders, but he retained him longer in Sarajevo than the others, and only let him return to Mostar when he set off for Krajina with his army. Alipasha promised he would help to introduce *nizam* in Herzegovina, and the commandant said that as soon as the matter was settled in Bosnia, he would come to Mostar himself. They embraced at parting.

While still in Sarajevo, Alipasha ordered his *kavazbasha* secretly to gather some good fighters and to man the entry into Herzegovina from Bosnia, but to seem to be doing it on his own account. As soon as he was dismissed from Sarajevo, he went to his estate at the source of the Buna to await the development of events there.

After initial setbacks, Omerpasha swiftly defeated the noisy, disorderly Krajishniks, and immediately sent Major Skenderbeg to Herzegovina with a strong combined army unit. Thanks to his superior weapons and the greater discipline of his army, Skenderbeg beat the *kavazbasha's* unit and came to Mostar. Alipasha had already repudiated his *kavazbasha* and proclaimed him a renegade and enemy of the state; now he sent his people to meet Skenderbeg and to congratulate him on his success. Skenderbeg thanked him and invited him to return to his konak in Mostar. Having no alternative, Alipasha did so. The commandant's emissary received him with great respect and had already arranged an official dinner for the following day in his honour.

In his usual fashion, Skenderbeg was already drunk at the start of the evening. But as the dinner approached its end he suddenly got up like the soberest of men, and clapped his hands twice. At this sign, a double door burst open and a wild-looking armed soldier rushed through. In the wink of an eye, both Alipasha and his sons were tied. The old Vizier wanted to ask Skenderbeg what was being done with him, but he turned his back on him and went outside without a word.

When they led the Vizier out he could see that all the members of his escort were tied up too.

Everything was well prepared and easily carried out. The forces surrounding Alipasha's konak immediately began to sack it and carry everything away. The same night Alipasha's family were also imprisoned at the source of the Buna. No one lifted a finger to help the old pasha, and he was incarcerated with his sons in the town's tower beside the bridge as easily, and with as little opposition, as if he had not been the Vizier and absolute ruler of Herzegovina for so many years.

This took place in the night between Sunday and Monday. The prisoners stayed in their prison only a day — as long as it took for the news of their imprisonment to spread among the people and take its effect. The very next day they were all led out of prison early in the morning. It was obvious that everything was being carried out in accordance with a previously-laid plan.

It was the end of February, when one begins to sense a certain restlessness in the air over Mostar; for spring starts to make itself felt here very early, and makes its appearance suddenly and unexpectedly, like a powerful but gentle explosion. This spring there was too much restlessness, for it did not only come out of the earth and sky, but from the heavy and confused movements and clashes of men and armies.

Even the man who had nothing to win or lose by all these disturbances and changes woke up early, wondering what anxious news or actual blows the coming day might bring; nor did he feel like going out on the street. And the slightly more prominent and richer people did not even sleep in their own homes but with trusted friends where, even so, they slept uneasily.

That Tuesday in Mostar was a sunny and ruthlessly clear day, cool, and transparent as if made entirely of the finest crystal, as if any word pronounced in it or any movement must ring through the blue and gold expanse with a cold, crystalline sound. It was not an ordinary Tuesday, to bloom and fade from dawn to dusk like all the others; no, it was Judgement Day, when light and shadow would not wax and wane, but everything would remain as fixed and unchanging as a backcloth so long as what had to be done had not yet been done.

On this day, early in the morning, Alipasha and his son were led out on to the terrace by the old stone bridge as if on to a kind of stage; and with them eight other prisoners, his personal friends or declared enemies of *tanzimat* and Omerpasha's mission in Bosnia and Herzegovina.

After them came a troop of thirty soldiers, mounted and on foot, and in the side streets there crowded and bumped an entire little field-train of loaded and unloaded mules and horses.

The attention of the army and the prisoners was entirely centered on Alipasha. Fat, ponderous and lame, unaccustomed to walking, he could scarcely get along: he leant his left hand on a stick, and his right on the shoulder of his son Hafizpasha.

This Hafiz was not the eldest son of the Vizier; that was

Nazif, who also had the rank of pasha. But he was prematurely fat, a spoilt little noble, already a heavy drinker and a great idler who took after his uncle Hadjun. Because of this, as soon as Hafiz grew up he took his father's place in all his affairs. This handsome man, unusually mature for his years, was his father's joy and hope. He showed an unusually well-developed sense of responsibility and family pride of the sort that does not seek its confirmation by denigrating others, but in self-restraint, nor its own preservation by power and plunder, but by work, skill and foresight. Now he suffered as only such people can suffer, and hid his suffering. He had left a wife of great beauty in enemy hands, the only one he had, who had recently borne him a second son; he had left her as if everything valuable he had remained with her. He suffered even more on his father's account, for whom he had always felt great filial affection and boundless admiration. He was ashamed — that was the right word — of this father who had become flabby and ponderous, in whom, for some time, he had already noticed the ugly and alarming signs of age: forgetfulness, irritability, a certain unbecoming frivolity, exaggerated self-confidence, slowness of understanding, and sluggishness in decisions. He was afraid that these weaknesses, which up till now only he had noticed and he had hidden as much as possible, would be visible to the whole world. He felt pity for the magnificent old man as well, and suffered for him, but he saw that he could help neither him nor himself. However, he did what he could and, setting his teeth, supported him as he walked with great care and tenderness.

Close together and separated from the others, the father and son made a striking ensemble. They moved slowly, but solemnly, with painful dignity, occupying much of the space around them.

When they stopped on the terrace, soldiers led before them a small pot-bellied donkey with the traces of a wooden saddle on its moulting coat. It raised its great, shaggy head from time to time and, anxious for the air and the view, waggled its ears restlessly at the spring sky.

A sergeant issued the hurried orders. Without addressing the old Vizier straight and directly, he ordered him sharply to mount the donkey, and Hafizpasha to lead it. A confused silence fell, and then, suddenly, there was a strange altercation. Hafizpasha tried to prove to the conscientious sergeant that it was impossible, physically impossible; for Alipasha, as he could see for himself, was one of the tallest men in Herzegovina — two fingers under three arshins — and he weighed more than ninety okas on the town scales.

Hafizpasha spoke softly but bitterly, his colour coming and going; it was obviously difficult and shameful for him to speak about the physical characteristics of the old man who was standing there, leaning on him in silence, in front of other people and to this little official The sergeant dully and persistently refused to talk, and impatiently demanded that the order be carried out immediately — that the old Vizier should sit on the donkey and be led like that on his journey.

A captain, the commandant of this strange caravan, came up and intervened; he listened to the son and took a better look at the father as well as the donkey, which was standing aside, blinking in the morning sun. It did not require much cleverness to see that, while the old man might straddle the young donkey, he could not ride it, with the length of his legs and his weight; nor could it carry him. It was evident that what was happening here was something that can always happen, and often does, with such armies in such times: someone somewhere far away, in an office, in accordance with some old regulation or custom, or inspired by hatred and zeal, had issued an order, without knowing either the man it applied to or his circumstances. And now they all stood as if at an impassable rock-face, in front of this strict order from above and the complete impossibility of carrying it out.

The captain went off to look for his superiors, and it took him a long time to find anyone and get authorisation for mounting his prisoner on a mule instead of a donkey.

The mule was bigger and stronger than the donkey, but sore, lean and shabby from bad feeding and the difficult months of the winter, during which it had carried gun parts from Konjic to the positions the *kavazbasha* had established against Skenderbeg. There was a dilapidated saddle on it.

Now the swarthy little sergeant appeared, and irascibly demanded that the second part of the order be carried out — that the Vizier mount backwards, and the son lead the mule. Again the captain had to intervene, and explain that his part of the order applied only to passing through towns, but as he was leaving Mostar immediately and going into the mountains, the old man could ride like everyone else; at least, till they reached the first town. This time, too, the sergeant had to give up his demand; but instead he took a malicious pleasure in ordering that, besides the horse and mule, the donkey should go along too.

They lifted the Vizier with great difficulty and placed him on the mule. Before that, someone threw a short blanket across the saddle, and everyone pretended not to notice. Eventually the procession set off and quickly disappeared in the bends of the grey karst. The sun was climbing and getting stronger, and people were beginning to appear cautiously at their yard gates, hitherto kept closed.

The first shops were starting to open up.

On the empty road or mountain track they rode and walked just as they wished or were able, but as soon as they found themselves entering a town or a large village, the sergeant established the prescribed order. The Vizier had to mount the mule backwards, while Hafizpasha led it. Children and idlers collected round the unusual procession whose pace was speeded up by Hafiz and slowed down by the sergeant. Then, the old Vizier would throw angry glances at the gathered crowd from the saddle, as if looking for witnesses to this unheard-of crime. Without fear or inhibition, growling like a captured wolf, he cursed Omerpasha aloud, calling him by his original Christian name 'Michael', and reviling him as an eater of pork; he threatened the swift arrival of the Sultan's justice, which was temporarily asleep and permitted this convert to play fast and loose and destroy true Muslims, who had preserved and protected this country always.

But only a few days later the Vizier suddenly altered. He fell silent. He grew visibly thin, hunched, he somehow dwindled. His large grey-green eyes whose glance all Herzegovina had once feared, turned white as if covered by cataracts; they still looked, but without seeing or wanting to. His untrimmed beard grew so much that his profile lost its former sharpness. His front teeth, formerly shaky, now suddenly began to fall out, and all his once firm and warlike face shrank, became stiff and bloodless, like the face of a cut-off head; and whenever a rare gleam of life illumined his face, it revealed the mild vagueness and devotion of a dervish beggar. The clothes he wore, carelessly thrown on and crumpled, began to fade in the rain, sun and dust: however, the entire man on the mule gained the look, which every day heightened, of calm, true greatness, such as he had never ever had even in the period of his greatest strength and power.

The passers-by mainly turned away their heads, from fear and compassion, for it was truly unbearable to contemplate such a sudden fall and such anguish, which no one could or dared help. Only one little shopkeeper in Donji Vakuf overcame his fear, and found in himself the strength to approach him in the middle of the market-place, to greet him politely, and ask him whether he needed anything. The soldiers pushed the man away, whipped the mule, and the procession quickly continued its journey. Alipasha, who had not properly seen his unknown well-wisher, answered him slowly and much later, when he was already far away. In husky, unintelligible speech from toothless lips overgrown by a beard and moustaches, he said that he needed nothing: for Allah had always supported him formerly, but now, when he was unjustly fallen into slavery and misfortune, He was helping him and giving him all he needed more than ever. This he uttered in the direction of the heavens, beyond the world surrounding him. All in all, Alipasha went through the last part of his journey as if in a kind of trance. Looking at the worried faces and bent heads of the peasants and townspeople around him he felt the need to comfort and cheer them, as if they were prisoners and he were healthy, powerful and free.

He looked down from the elevation of his suffering, he said, as from the highest mountain, and saw and grasped truths about men and human relations better and clearer than ever before in his life. But all that was extinguished by the bullet of the soldier in the tent at Dobrinje, spilt along with his brains and sight, and so lost for ever; and that, it seemed to him, was not right. There were things that could only be realised then, and in that way, from a wooden saddle and a shabby mule — things that needed to be known, for then his life and many of his actions would appear in another, truer light; and people would know better how to rule, and to behave, and that would be useful to them — he firmly believed that. This, and only this, was the reason he wanted his true and complete story to come to light. If it were possible — well and good, but he was not begging or insisting; in any case, it was all written down in heaven. But if it were possible, then, well, he would like it, especially for the sake of the others.

I listen to him at length and attentively, though from time to time I feel like interrupting his speech and telling him what I think about it. Yes, I feel like doing so, but I shall say nothing

— for I interrupt no one's story, and I don't correct anybody, least of all a sufferer describing his suffering. And where would I get to if I did? There would not be any stories then. And in its own way and proper time, every story is sincere and true, and should be listened to and accepted as such. Therefore, in the clattering of the procession as it disappears, I am listening to the weighty and unclear message of the former 'little emperor of Herzegovina', and I think about those sort of men for long afterwards. They are never finally reconciled to anything; and even after death something still remains of their passion — their longing to live in any guise and to influence the lives of the living.

A Story

Until a moment ago, one of my calm and pleasant visitors was sitting here, Ibrahim-Effendi Škaro. He is an exception among my guests altogether: he comes by rarely, and when he does stop, he does not stay long. From the first minute he sits and chats as if he could get up at any time at all, politely take his leave, and depart. But when it does happen that he sits back and gets carried away talking, it is a real holiday. He never talks about himself, he does not defend, or justify, or inflate, or impose himself; while the others are always wanting to come into my story and sometimes ask it inappropriately and aggressively, he, on the other hand, would prefer me not to mention him anywhere, and even if I borrowed one of his jokes, not to say whose it was.

I showed Ibrahim-Effendi out, came back, and sat down in my seat again, where I had been listening to him till then. It seemed to me he had not left my room; that something of him, invisible, but alive and real, was left behind and continuing to talk to me, not in words but directly, with the same vivid meaning Ibrahim-Effendi's storytelling had. I listened to the silence of my room telling me more of the story, and acknowledged what I heard from time to time with a nod of the head. Anyone observing me from outside would have thought me not in my right mind, but I was listening to the pure source, not otherwise audible, of all Ibrahim-Effendi's stories.

Hamidaga Škaro, his father, was one of the prominent people of this town in his day. His word, as the word of a just and fearless man, had influence with both the authorities and the people, and was often decisive. He married late, a famous beauty from the Suleimanpašić household, but he spent only half a year married to her.

It was something over a hundred years ago when Jelaludin Pasha arrived in Bosnia, invited the leaders of the whole country to come to him in Travnik, and slaughtered them all in his trap, like helpless lambs.

Hamidaga, who had also been invited to Travnik, but did not

want to go and had dissuaded others from the journey, spoke his mind openly and roundly condemned the vizier's wickedness. Frightened, but burning for justice and revenge, people listened to him as he spoke what everyone thought but no-one dared say. But that lasted only a few days. One Friday before dusk when the townspeople were going back to their homes, four men met him on Atmeidan near his house. To give him free passage they divided, two on each side. At that, the one who was closest to him on the left unexpectedly struck him in the breast with a dagger, and felled him on the spot. The murderers ran off in all directions with cries, to confuse the people who were still on Atmeidan, and the braver passers-by began to approach the victim and call for the guard.

Then something unheard-of happened. The heavy gate of the Škaros' courtyard banged and Hamidaga's lovely young wife ran out of it in her stockings, without a veil or yashmak, just as she had been in the upstairs porch of the house looking out for the aga's return. She ran halfway across the square, all uncovered as she was, and cleared a path for herself through the collected people with powerful thrusts of the arm; she fell on the prostrate body with a hoarse cry while the last weak trickles of warm blood flowed from his chest.

Embarrassed, people turned their heads away from the unveiled woman. Two Škaro servants soon rushed from the courtyard: one of them carried a broad white shawl and covered the woman's face and body in it, after they had first parted her from the corpse. The traces of her bloodstained hands immediately flared through the shawl. They led her into the courtyard and then, with the help of passers-by, brought in the dead man too.

That was how death came from Travnik — no-one doubted it — for Hamidaga.

It was a clear sign of the times. The Sultan's deputies in Bosnia had turned into common murderers who came, not to apply the law and protect the citizens, but to kill the leaders, whether in the vizier's own konak in Travnik or indirectly, through hired assassins, in every part of the country. The story was told throughout Bosnia in a bitter whisper; and the great love of the young wife was mentioned in addition, as a wonder and a terrible example: she had overturned all conventions and proprieties by rushing out into the public street uncovered. Some condemned her for it, others defended and justified her. None of this reached Hamidaga's wife, who was wholly sunk in wordless grief for her lost husband. Three months after the terrible event a male child was born.

It was only one year more that she cared for her son and nursed him with her milk poisoned with hatred and incurable grief; she pined and faded, and then left the world without having found words for what it was she died from. Her sisters took in the orphan child and brought it up.

From a child he became a youth, from a youth a man. A certain old man can still be found who remembers just how he was all his life: walking round Sarajevo and telling stories.

He was a strange fellow. He was from a good, wealthy home, and he studied at school, but he never concerned himself with any kind of business — the kind called 'serious business' — or took up any interest. His relatives ran his share of the estate for him. When you saw him you were amazed. What you had heard about him as a witty raconteur was in complete contrast to his appearance. Rather short, prematurely grey, with a good-humoured faun-like face, he was sparing of movement and this was slow and weighty, as if he was wholly bound up in invisible sticky threads from which he was endlessly and vainly extricating himself. Slow in himself, he even somehow looked slowly: he constantly blinked, and was always twitching a little, now in one eye, now in the other, now round his mouth. He prolonged every movement as much as possible. It was the same too with words. He filtered them and held them back as if he was choosing the kind of words which express nothing and do not commit the speaker in the least. It was only if he accepted an offered brandy after the coffee that he might begin to tell stories. I say 'might', because it did not happen often. Then, with the second glass, he would shake himself, as if throwing off all those invisible strings and threads, free himself from blinking and that nervous twitching of the face, drink not a drop of brandy more, and smoke little. His profile would grow sharp, his words connected and his voice steady; the whole man would come to life, as if growing wings; and then no one could surpass or touch him for speed, wit or invention. What was uncommon and exceptional in these stories was his power of always astonishing the listeners with something familiar. Regrettably, like many oral narratives, his stories are unrepeatable. Only a dry skeleton remains from any attempt at transmitting them, so you yourself are surprised and wonder how and when in the course of retelling the vital juices and enormous charm of an Ibrahim-Effendi story were lost. Even Ibrahim-Effendi himself did not like repeating them. In most instances he forgot his stories, which burnt away like the tobacco of a cigarette and had neither titles, nor beginnings, nor one firm, final shape.

So, sometimes, he would all at once begin to speak, sitting among his friends who, after a long and fruitless wait, were not hoping for a story any more; as if he were continuing some narrative begun long ago, warmly and confidentially, intended just for you.

From the very start, his auditors would be shaking with suppressed laughter, but they controlled themselves from the desire not to lose a single word. All the same, it rarely happened that Ibrahim-Effendi succeeded in telling a whole story to the end, because as soon as the auditors guessed the climax, which was always irresistibly funny, their self-control broke down and they would explode in hearty laughter in which nothing more could be heard. Later, when the laughter died away, Ibrahim-Effendi would already have finished his story and be sitting peacefully with a straight face.

Afterwards, he could sit for hours listening to the others and smiling innocently to himself, but he could equally suddenly begin to tell another story, again without a proper beginning, whose ending would similarly be lost in the general laughter of his listeners.

Listening to his narratives, it seemed to you that life itself, in all its richness and variety, was telling its own story, and Ibrahim-Effendi was only interrupting from time to time with a word or two at crucial places, as if he were himself a listener: 'Well, now!' 'Listen to that!' 'There, imagine!'

In these stories of his there were marvels by the hundred and sorrows of all kinds, but even more laughter; there were guilt and culprits, bullies, fools and swindlers; there were good folk, victims of human stupidity and the human need to deceive others and ourselves; but all of them were illumined by his special mode of telling which, although it might sadden a man, could not offend or discourage him. In any case, it made him laugh. Everything that happened in life or existed— people, events, animals or dead things — all had their value and their special place in it; and they all ended in a laugh free of pain or bitterness. Sometimes people who saw things round them in a black, bad-tempered way, according to their nature, would reproach Ibrahim-Effendi that in his peculiar form of story-telling everything was softened, embellished and elevated; but he would calmly answer them, 'I wouldn't say that. I don't embellish anything. Could it be your ugly way of looking, perhaps?'

But that rarely happened. He did not usually care about the fate of his stories, nor about how people received and interpreted them. He did not defend them and he did not explain them; he smiled silently, or he told new stories. Only from time to time he would be amazed himself: 'There, imagine!' But people loved his stories and accepted them just as they were; to many, who were accustomed from boyhood to hearing them, it seemed that a good part of life, with all its satisfactory and unsatisfactory happenings, only found its true form and full meaning in these stories. What did not get into them might be forgotten or changed, while Ibrahim-Effendi's stories lived on and passed from mouth to mouth round the whole of Bosnia.

Occasionally some leading citizens, civil servants and 'men of business' did not take kindly to either Ibrahim-Effendi or his stories, in which they saw cause for annoyance and criticism though they could not have said quite why. They often laughed at them themselves, but they appeared to be offended by the number of other people who laughed, and it seemed to them that laughter itself had something destructive about it, which lessened citizens' regard for order and obedience. They did not say so clearly or openly, but they often showed their disparagement of Ibrahim-Effendi as a crank and idler who turned everything into a story and made a joke of it, and they scoffed contemptuously at him, his stories, and the people who laughed at them.

None of that could influence Ibrahim-Effendi either to stop telling stories or to tell them differently.

So his life went by in stories, just like a story itself; and so he died too, after turning sixty, as quietly as a quail in the corn. He had not had any of his father's enterprise or fighting spirit. He had not married or left a family; he had not lived. Instead of what is called 'real life', whose blow he had felt while still in his mother's womb, he had constructed another reality for himself made from stories; and with these stories about what might have been, but never was, which is often truer and lovelier than all that has been, he sheltered, as it were, from the everyday 'reality' around him. Thus he avoided living, and tricked his fate. Now he has been lying in the graveyard on Alifakovac nearly fifty years; but he still lives on from time to time, here and there, as a story.

THE DAMNED YARD

It was winter, snow had enveloped everything up to the door of the building, depriving all things of their real shape and giving them all one colour and one form. Even the little graveyard had disappeared under this whiteness, with just the tips of the tallest crosses showing. It was only there that the trace of a narrow path through the virgin snow could be made out. It had been trodden down the day before by those attending Fra Petar's funeral. At the end of this path the thin track widened into an uneven circle, and the snow around it had the pink colour of softened clay. It looked like a fresh wound in the whiteness stretching as far as the eye could see, fading into the grey desert of the sky still heavy with snow.

This could all be seen from the window of Fra Petar's cell. The whiteness of the outside world merged here with the drowsy shadows filling the cell, and the silence blended with the quiet ticking of those of his numerous clocks which were still going. Some, unwound, had already stopped. The silence was broken only by the muffled bickering of two friars in the next cell making an inventory of the things left behind after Fra Petar's death.

The old friar Mijo Josić was mumbling something unintelligible. This was an echo of his former disputes with the late Fra Petar, a 'famous watchmaker, gunsmith and mechanic' who had a passion for collecting all kinds of tools: he would spend monastery funds on them, and guard them jealously from everyone else. Then Fra Mijo rebuked the young Fra Rastislav for suggesting that they light the stove so as not to make the list in a cold room.

'Oh, you youngsters today! You're all the same, poor old ladies. A warm room indeed! As though we hadn't wasted enough wood this winter!'

The old man stopped, sensing that this might sound like a reproach to the dead monk, before the earth had settled on his grave. But then he went on scolding the young man.

'I've always said your name should be "Brother Squanderer"! * Even your name bodes ill, my lad. It was all right when friars were called by plain names like Fra Marko, Fra Mijo, Fra Ivo — but now you all take names from novels, or heaven knows where: 'Fra Rastislav', 'Fra Vojislav', 'Fra Branimir'. I ask you!'

With a wave of his hand, the young monk dismissed these witticisms and reproaches. He had heard them dozens of times already and goodness knows how long he would have to go on hearing them. The work continued.

There is something special about the appearance of people making a list of belongings left by someone who was here, alive, two days ago. They represent victorious life which goes its own way, following its own needs. They are not exultant victors. Their only merit is that they have outlived the dead person. And when you look at them from a distance, they seem a bit like robbers, but robbers who are sure they will go unpunished, knowing that the owner cannot return and surprise them at their work. That is not quite what they are, but something about them suggests it.

'Carry on,' comes the curt voice of the older monk, 'write: "Pair of pliers, large, Kreševo make. One."'

And so they go on, tool by tool. At the end of each sentence the listed object thuds dully, thrown onto the heap of roughly jumbled tools on the little oak work-bench that had belonged to the late Fra Petar.

When we see something like this, all our thoughts turn unwittingly away from life towards death, away from the people counting and appropriating objects to the one who has lost them and no longer needs anything, for he himself is no more.

On this wide sofa from which the mattress and covers had already been removed, leaving only the bare boards, Fra Petar had lain or sat until three days ago — talking. And now, as the young man looked at the grave in the snow, he was in fact thinking of those stories. And, for the third or fourth time, he would have liked to say how good Fra Petar had been at telling stories. But that was something that could not be said.

For several weeks he had talked a great deal about the time he

---

* A play on the word 'Raspislav', suggesting a spendthrift.

once spent in Stamboul. A long time ago. The friars had sent Fra Tadija Ostojić to Stamboul on some difficult, complex business. He was their ex-definitor, and ex-guardian ('He was all "ex-es"!'), a slow and dignified man enamoured of this slowness and dignity. He could speak Turkish (slowly and with dignity), but could not read or write it. So they had sent Fra Petar as an escort since he was skilled in written Turkish.

They stayed in Stamboul just under a year, spent all the money they had, and even ran into debt, without achieving anything. All because of a misfortune that befell Fra Petar through no fault of his own. It was one of those things that happens in troubled times when the authorities cease to distinguish the righteous from the guilty.

Soon after their arrival the police happened to intercept a letter addressed to the Austrian Internuncio in Stamboul. It was a wide-ranging account of the state of the Catholic church in Albania, and the persecution of priests and believers. The bearer of the letter managed to escape. As there were no other friars from that region in Stamboul at the time, the Turkish police arrested Fra Petar, according to some logic of their own. He spent two months in prison 'under investigation' without anyone really interrogating him.

Fra Petar talked about these two months spent in the Stamboul remand prison more often and more vividly than about anything else. He spoke disjointedly, in fragments, the way a very sick man does when trying to conceal his physical pain or his frequent thoughts of death. These fragments did not always follow one from another in proper order. As he took up his tale, he would often repeat things or pass over whole periods of time. He talked like a man for whom time no longer had any meaning and who did not therefore attribute any importance to it or to its role in other people's lives either. His tale could stop, go on, repeat itself, anticipate, go back, and, once it was ended, be added to, explained and expanded, regardless of place, time and the real, forever established course of events.

Of course such a method of story-telling left many things unexplained, but the young man felt awkward about interrupting the story, going back and asking questions. It was best to leave a man free to tell his tale as he wished.

I

There is a whole small town of prisoners and guards known to Levantines and sailors of various nationalities as the *Deposito*. But it is better known as the Damned Yard, as it is called by the local people, particularly those who have any contact with it. This is where all those arrested every day in this sprawling, crowded city are brought, either because they are guilty of a crime or suspected of being guilty: there is plenty of guilt of all kinds here, and suspicion stretches far and wide. For the Stamboul police hold to the sacred principle that it is easier to release an innocent man from the Courtyard than to search for a culprit through the city's narrow lanes. Here a lengthy and elaborate process of selection of the detainees takes place. Some are interrogated before their trial, others serve out short sentences or, if it becomes quite clear that they are innocent, they are released, others are sent into exile in distant regions. It is also a large reservoir from which the police extract false witnesses, 'decoys', and agents-provocateurs according to their needs. So the Courtyard constantly sifts the motley crowd of its inhabitants, endlessly filling and emptying, yet always full.

There are both petty and hardened criminals here, from a boy who stole a bunch of grapes or a fig from a market stall to international swindlers and dangerous burglars. Some are innocent, some slandered, some feeble-minded and confused, or they may have been brought in by mistake from Stamboul or anywhere in the Empire. The great majority come from the city itself. The lowest of the low that skulk through the docks and markets or crawl into lairs in the suburbs. Burglars, pickpockets, professional gamblers; large-scale swindlers and blackmailers; destitute people who steal and cheat to survive; cheerful drunks who forget to pay for what they drink or tavern brawlers and trouble-makers; pale, shifty wretches who seek in addictive drugs what they have not been able to get from life, indulging in hashish, smoking or eating opium, and stopping at nothing to reach the poison they cannnot live without; depraved old men or youths ruined irredeemably by vice; people with all kinds of perverse drives and habits which they do not hide or embellish, but expose for all the world to see, and even if they try to conceal them they fail, because they are apparent in everything they do.

There are multiple murderers and people who have escaped from prison several times and are therefore chained even here, before being sentenced. They rattle their chains provocatively, furiously cursing both the iron and whoever invented fetters.

This is where everyone comes who has been sent from the western regions as a punishment, into exile. Here their fate is decided: either they are freed, with the help of Stamboul connections and return home or else they are despatched to Asia Minor or Africa. These are the so-called 'transients', usually older people, prominent in their own province, caught up in discord and conflicts there and accused by the authorities or slandered by their opponents as political criminals or rebels. They bring chests and saddle-bags of belongings, and have trouble in defending themselves from the Stamboul petty-thieves with whom they have to share a cell. Anxious and withdrawn, they try to keep well out of the way.

About fifteen buildings, some with two floors, built and extended over many years and linked by a high wall, enclose a huge, elongated, steep courtyard of irregular shape. There are some cobbles in front of the building for the guards and administrative offices; all the rest is grey, hard, trodden earth where not even a blade of grass succeeds even in sprouting, so many people walk over it from dawn to dusk. Two or three feeble, stunted trees, set randomly in the centre of the courtyard, always damaged, their bark stripped, live a martyred life unconnected with the seasons. During the day this uneven, spacious courtyard resembles a fairground of all kinds of races and peoples. But at night the whole crowd is driven inside, crammed fifteen, twenty or thirty to a cell. And their clamorous life goes on there. Peaceful nights are rare.

The hardened riff-raff of Stamboul, who ignore the guards and bow to no one, sing lewd songs and shout shameful propositions to their boyfriends in the neighbouring cells. Voices can be heard quarrelling over sleeping space; people who have been robbed call for help. Some grind their teeth and sigh in their sleep, some snore and wheeze as though their throats had been cut. The large cells live only through sound, like a jungle at night. One moment there will be a strange shriek, then a sigh, then, like a recitative, two or three long drawn-out words from a song, the sad and barren substitute for all kinds of sensual desires, then incomprehensible voices, guttural and heavy.

And knocking is heard at the main entrance. For it is by night that the ancient double gate creaks and rumbles to receive or thrust out its inmates, either individually or in groups. By night the sentenced are taken off to serve their punishment or into exile. And often after some great fight in the docks people are brought in foaming, dishevelled and bloody, still hot with fury, alcohol and blows given and received. They growl at each other, threatening, and trying to deliver one last blow, as they stumble between the hurrying guards. And after they have been separated and locked up, they take a long time to settle down, shouting terrible threats to each other from cell to cell.

With the dawn right-minded people feel a little better. Only a little. Then all the prisoners surge out of their stuffy cells into the spacious courtyard and there, in the sun, they pick the lice from their heads, bandage their wounds, continue their crude jokes and endless, strident arguments, or settle their sinister scores. Groups form which are either subdued or noisy. Each of these circles has its centre. This may be a group of gamblers or jokers, or perhaps a single man singing softly or reciting bawdy comic songs. It may be a naive chatterbox or a madman lost in his own world of whom the circle round him makes cheap, brazen fun.

Fra Petar would approach some of them, listening and watching from a slight distance. ('What a good thing I'm not wearing my habit and no one knows who I am!')

Here, outside his building a small circle formed every morning, in the shade, around a certain Zaim. He was a short, bent man with a frightened expression, who spoke quietly but confidently and enthusiastically, always about himself. He always talked about the same aspect of his life, but exaggerating so much that a man would have needed at least a hundred and fifty years to experience it all.

The sun had just begun to come up, and the conversation was already under way.

'My, you've certainly seen the world, Zaim-Aga.'

'Yes, I have, but what good is that to me. My life's ruined because people are so vile they won't let a decent man live. I've certainly seen a lot of places and I've done well everywhere.

People have respected me and invited me to their homes. I've always behaved properly and known how to get on with everyone.'

He gazed straight ahead of him in silence, as though reading a cue board, then started again with no preamble:

'In Adabazaar I got rich and married. I had a good, clever wife. People respected me and my painter's shop was the best in town.'

'So why didn't you stay there?'

'Ah, why! The devil got into me and I took another wife. And from that day everything started to go wrong. She did satisfy me the first few days. I have to say that. But she had such a temper! It wasn't enough for her to quarrel with my first wife and make my home a hell. She went out and about, as the saying goes: in one hand straw, in the other a light. Wherever she went she brought discord and hatred. She would have set two eyes in a head against each other, as they say. My first wife's brothers started persecuting me. People began to hate me. So, seeing that I was losing my reputation and my customers, and that I would lose my life as well if things went on like that, I sold off all my goods and tools, discreetly, for a song, and set off into the blue.'

'What a shame!' said someone sympathetically.

Zaim shook his head sadly as though only he knew what a shame it was.

'Eh, you old runaway, why didn't you send that bitch packing, why run away yourself, when you had so much!' said an athletically built man from the circle in a husky voice.

'"Send her packing, send her packing"! It isn't as easy as that. You don't know what kind of a woman she was. You can't tear yourself from her although you're wasting away.'

'So what! I'd have sent her packing even if she had the sun between her legs and the moon on her belly.'

That was the athlete again. Then he angrily left the circle, with a wave of his hand.

'Eh, women, so what! They're all the same when you blow out the candle.'

But the little man went on talking about how he had gone as far as Trebizond and there married a rich widow.

'She looked after me as though the sun shone out of my eyes, what a life I had for four years! But, just my luck, she got ill and died, I was too upset to stay, so I sold up and set off again. I did all kinds of jobs and everywhere I was valued and loved because of my golden hands. I went as far as Salonika. And there I got married . . . '

'Again!'

'I know four trades and I've been married eleven times.'

'And then what happened?' people asked.

'What happened? Her relatives, Jews, cheated me. If I charged them even half what they owe me I'd be rich. I'd easily throw off the slander and get out of here.'

The 'slander' was that he had accused of passing forged coins. This was not the first time he had been charged with this crime. It was a kind of sickness. As soon as he cleared himself of one charge or served one sentence, he started again, and, as he was inept, he was caught at once. But he never stopped dreaming (and lying) about being happily married and pursuing his 'four fine trades'. Now he was terrified of a severe punishment, if the charges were proved, and he kept fooling himself with lies, half-lies and half-truths which he would tell all day to people ready to mock. As soon as one circle dispersed, he would wander around the courtyard like a lost soul, and then approach another group. He listened with a funeral, sorrowful expression on his face to jokes which made everyone else roar with laughter. He listened patiently to all that was said, waiting meekly for his opportunity. And when the moment seemed favourable, he joined in. Someone would mention a country, Egypt for example. And Zaim broke in with a ready tale.

'I had an Egyptian wife. She was older than me, and she really cared for me, my own mother couldn't have done better. We lived well for two years. I had a good reputation among the townsfolk. But, what can you do? One day . . . '

And there would follow another story about some imaginary place and marital misfortune, which some listened to with mocking interruptions, while others moved away at the very start, with a wave of the hand, not sparing poor Zaim.

'That'll be his eighteenth.'

'Bye! Tell us when he gets to the end.'

But the story told by the crazy, incurable conterfeiter Zaim, who dreamed of a quiet life and perfect marriage, was soon lost in the deafening shouts of the group beside them where a quarrel had broken out, with oaths which no one outside the Courtyard has ever heard.

The very position of the Damned Yard was strange, as though calculated for the greater torment of the prisoners. (This was a theme Fra Petar used to return to.) From the Courtyard nothing could be seen of the town or docks or the abandoned arsenal on the shore below. Only the sky, vast and merciless in its beauty, in the distance a little of the green Asian shore beyond the invisible sea, and just the occasional tip of an unknown minaret or gigantic cypress behind the wall. It was all vague, nameless, and foreign. A stranger felt all the time that he was on some devil's island, outside everything that had been his life until then, and with no hope of soon seeing it again. The prisoners from Stamboul, on top of all their other troubles, had the additional punishment of not being able to see or hear anything of their town. They were in it, but they might have been hundreds of leagues away; and that apparent distance tormented them as much as if it were real. For all these reasons the Courtyard would break a man's will, quickly and imperceptibly, subordinating him to itself, so that he began to lose himself. He forgot what had happened before and thought less and less of what was going to be, so that past and future merged in one single present, the strange, terrible life of the Damned Yard.

And when it happened that the sky clouded over and a damp, unhealthy southerly wind began to blow, bringing the smell of decay from the sea, the filth of the city and the stench from the docks somewhere below, life in the cells and in the courtyard became really intolerable. The sickening stench did not come only from the docks, but rose from all buildings and objects; it seemed that all the soil weighed down by the Damned Yard was slowly decaying, giving off a poisonous odour that made food bitter and life hateful. The wind howled, seeming to spread disease everywhere. Even the most even-tempered people flared up and began roaming angrily around, looking for trouble, in a state of inexplicable aggravation. A burden to themselves, the prisoners provoked each other or the guards who were equally irritable during these days. Nerves were painfully stretched and they suddenly snapped in dangerous explosions and senseless acts. Virulent, pointless conflicts broke out, there were scandals unusual even for the Damned Yard. And while some raved like this, quarrelling with everyone, others, older, more withdrawn people, squatted for hours alone, arguing with invisible opponents in an inaudible whisper or with just a grimace or feeble movement of the hand and head. They looked like ghosts.

At these moments of general aggravation, madness, like an epidemic or swift flame, spread from cell to cell, from man to man, and was carried over from people to animals and inanimate objects. Dogs and cats became uneasy. Large rats began to scuttle swiftly from wall to wall. People slammed doors and banged spoons on their tin plates. Things dropped out of hands of their own accord. At times everything would fall silent in general, morbid exhaustion. But immediately afterwards, with the first darkness, such a racket would break out in some of the locked cells, that the whole courtyard resounded and shook. Then other cells would join in. It seemed that everything in the Damned Yard that had a voice was howling and yelling with all its might, in the sick hope that somewhere at the peak of this din it could all burst and die down, once and for all.

At such times this whole Courtyard moaned and clattered like an enormous rattle in a giant's hand while the people in it danced, jerked, knocked into one another and beat against the walls like grains in the rattle.

The governor and his men knew the effects of this rotten south wind, they avoided conflict as far as possible, for they were themselves on edge. They guarded the gate, increased the number of sentries and — waited for the wind to die down. They knew well, from experience, that any attempt to 'restore order' would be both dangerous and impossible, for no one could have carried out the order and it would have been ignored in any case. And when the wholesome north winds began to prevail, the sky to clear a little, the sun to break through and the air to freshen, the prisoners began to spread through the courtyard cheerfully in groups, sunbathing, joking and laughing, as though they had been ill and were now cured or saved from a shipwreck, and everything that had happened during those two or three days of madness slipped into oblivion. No one could remember anything, even if he had wanted.

The governor of this strange and terrible institution was Latif-Aga, known as Karagöz. This nickname had long since become his real name, the only name he was known by, not just here but far beyond the walls of the Damned Yard. It exactly suited his appearance and everything about him.

His father had been a teacher in a military school; a quiet, pensive man who loved books, who married quite late in life and had only one child, a boy. The child was lively and bright. He liked reading, but particularly music and all kinds of games. Up until his fourteenth year the boy did well at school and seemed set to follow in his father's footsteps, but then his liveliness began to change into rage and his quick wits to take him in the wrong direction. The boy began to change, even physically. He became suddenly thickset and unnaturally heavy. His clever brown eyes began shifting rapidly around. He left school and started to associate with café musicians and conjurors, although he did not have any particular gift for such skills, and with gamblers, drunks and opium smokers, without himself having a real passion for gambling and drink. But he was attracted to those people and everything connected with them, just as he was repelled by everything that belonged to the world of quiet, ordinary pursuits, steady habits and normal responsibilities.

Unruly and still inexperienced, the young man soon became involved in the dubious activities and foolhardy exploits of his companions and came into conflict with the law. And more than once. His father got him out of prison several times, relying on his reputation and his acquaintance with important people, particularly the Chief of Police, an old school friend. 'Is it possible that a son of mine should break into houses, rob merchants and abduct girls?' the desperate father wondered. And the old, seasoned Police chief answered calmly but truthfully: it was not that he himself broke in, or robbed merchants, nor did he abduct girls, but wherever these things were happening, you could be sure you would find him somewhere nearby. And if nothing were done about it, he would himself soon drift into crime. A solution had to be found in time. And the Chief of Police had found a 'solution', which he believed was the only one possible, therefore the best: to take the young man who had begun to go wrong into his service. And so, as often happens, the young man who had already taken up with gamblers and rich layabouts became a good, zealous Stamboul policeman.

This did not happen overnight. For the first few years he was uncertain, trying to find his place, but then he found it where it could least have been expected, working against his former companions. He turned implacably on tramps, drunks, pick-pockets, smugglers and all kinds of wretches and idlers from the dark quarters of Stamboul. He worked with passion, with inexplicable hatred, but also with skill, with a knowledge of that environment that only he could have had. His old contacts enabled him to extend the range of his activity, because petty criminals betray the big ones. Information about people accumulated, his network of informers spread and was strengthened. Ten years later his exceptional zeal and success brought him to the position of assistant governor of this large remand centre. And when the old governor died of a heart attack, he was the only person who could take over. That was when his rule over the Damned Yard began. And it had been going on now for twenty years.

The former governor, a hard man with years of experience, had an inflexible, conventional method of control. For him the most important thing had been that the world of vice and lawlessness should be identified as such as clearly as possible and separated as far as possible from the world of order and law. He was not particularly interested in the individual or his crime. In the course of many years he had looked on the Damned Yard as a quarantine and saw all its inhabitants as dangerous patients whom it was hard to cure, but who must be kept away, in physical and moral isolation, from so-called healthy, honest people by various measures, punishments and fear. Apart from that, they could be left entirely to their own devices. They must not be allowed to break out of their circle, but they should not be interfered with unduly, because nothing good or sensible could ever come of such contact.

The new governor immediately adopted quite different methods: in his whole attitude and all his actions.

The very first year, when his father died, Latif sold the fine, spacious family house in the New Mahala and bought a large neglected estate just above the Courtyard itself. Overgrown with cypress trees, it looked like an abandoned island or an ancient cemetery. It was separated from the Courtyard by a shady gorge full of fine trees and a whole system of various fences and high walls. Here, beside abundant running water, among the old trees, he built a beautiful house, which faced the opposite side of the slope and so was protected from the south wind and the unhealthy stench from the arsenal and docks. The house had the great advantage of being both very remote from the Damned Yard and very close to it. Its whole appearance, its calm and cleanliness, made it seem another world, thousands of miles away, and yet it was right next to the Courtyard, invisibly connected with it. Using shortcuts accessible only to him, Karagöz was able at any time of day to enter the Courtyard, straight from his house, unobserved. (As a result no one could ever know for certain whether he was there, or where he might suddenly appear.) The governor made frequent use of this situation. He watched over both the prisoners and their guards personally. And, as he knew most of the inmates, their past and their present crimes, he could say with some justification that he knew 'how the Courtyard breathed'. And if he did not know an individual personally, he knew his vagrant's or criminal's soul and at any moment he could stop in front of him and *continue* the discussion of his or someone else's crime. And in the same way, and even more closely, he knew every guard and his good and bad, public and secret traits and inclinations.

At least that is what he himself boasted. And so he remained his whole life in close touch with the underworld of crime which he had abandoned forever in his youth. But at the same time he was above it and remote from it, separated by his position, his overgrown gardens and by iron fences and gates inaccessible to others.

From the very beginning Karagöz 'worked from inside'. This unusual method made him both far more difficult and dangerous, and in a certain sense, sometimes more humane than the earlier governors. Out of the impenetrable intertwining of these opposites was forged his individual attitude to the Courtyard and to all those human beings who passed through it like a murky, sluggish river. Not even the oldest and wiliest guests of the Damned Yard could ever quite grasp the rhyme or reason of this game Karagöz played, a game that was entirely personal, full of unexpected, daring twists and inventions, very often the opposite of all rules of police work and procedure and social customs in general. It was in his very first year that he acquired his nickname — 'Karagöz' * And really this Courtyard, and everything that lived in it and happened there was a great theatre in which Karagöz acted out his life.

Dark-skinned, with abundant hair, he had put on wieght and aged early, at least apparently. But his appearance could be deceptive. For all his bulk he could be as swift and agile as a fox when he wanted, and then his heavy, flabby body would develop a bull's strength. His sleepy, lifeless face and closed eyes concealed constant alertness and a fiendishly restless and inventive mind. No one had ever seen a smile on this dark olive-coloured face, not even when the whole of Karagöz's body shook with inner laughter. This face could stretch and contract, altering from an expression of absolute revulsion and terrible threat to deep understanding and genuine sympathy. The movement of his eyes was one of Karagöz's great skills. The left eye was usually almost completely closed, but between the closed lashes one was aware of a watchful gaze, sharp as a razor. And his right eye was wide open, huge. It lived a life of its own, sweeping around like a searchlight; it could leave its socket to an unbelievable extent and just as quickly retreat back into it. It attacked, provoked, and confused its victim, pinning him down, penetrating into the most hidden corners of his thoughts, hopes and plans. This gave the

---

* Character in Turkish shadow puppet theatre

whole hideously cross-eyed face the appearance of a grotesque
mask — at one moment alarming, the next comic.

When they talked about Karagöz, discussing every detail about
him, the prisoners always spoke most about these eyes. Some
maintained that he saw nothing with his left eye, others that it was
in fact with the right, wide-open one that could not see. And in
twenty years they could not agree, but they all shuddered at the
gaze of those eyes, avoiding it as far as possible.

There was nothing of the heavy dignity of an Ottoman high
official in Karagöz, in his speech or movements. In each
individual case, with each suspect, he would play a different
game. He showed no shame or consideration, no respect for the
other man or for himself. Whatever he did was unexpected,
inspired. He would burst in at various times of day or night,
approaching an individual or a whole group of prisoners.

'Pshee, pshee, pshee, psheeee!'

He pronounced these sounds in a varying pitch and intonation,
always differently and always sounding as though he was amazed
and disgusted by this person, by himself and by the whole 'affair'
between them.

'What is it? You're still here? Pshee! So, come on, what
happened?'

That is how the conversation would begin, but it was never
clear what was coming next. It could have been a long
interrogation, in which every detail was known, with grave threats
which were often only threats, but each one of which could at any
minute be transformed into a terrible reality. It might take the form
of tenacious, ominous and irresistible coercion, but also of
heartless clowning with no obvious sense or purpose.

If, in his anxiety to be free at least for a moment from Karagöz's
pressure, the cornered, tormented man began to beg and assure
him of his innocence, with either genuine or feigned tears,
Karagöz could all at once change his behaviour, smacking his
palm against his brow.

'What are you saying, you're completely innocent? Ah, why are
you telling me now, for god's sake, man. Pshee . . . If you'd told
me you were guilty, I could have let you go, because there are a
lot of guilty people here. They're all guilty. But it's precisely an
innocent man that we need. So I can't let you go. If you hadn't
said so yourself, something could have been done. But as it is,
now you'll have to stay here until I find another innocent man
somewhere, someone like you, to take your place. Now, sit still
and keep quiet!'

And moving on through the Courtyard, accompanied by a few guards, Karagöz continued his game, for his own sake now, shouting so that everything around echoed, unable to stop.

'Just don't let anyone tell me someone's innocent. Not that. Because there's no one innocent here. No one's here by chance. If he's crossed the threshold of the Courtyard, he's not innocent. He's done some wrong, even if it was in his sleep. If nothing else, then his mother had evil thoughts when she was carrying him. Of course, everyone says he's not guilty, but in all the years I've been here, I still haven't found anyone who's been brought here without any reason or without some fault. Whoever comes here is guilty, or has at least brushed up against a guilty person. Pshee! I've let enough of them go, both on instruction and on my own authority, certainly. But each one of them was guilty. There's no one innocent here. But there are thousands of guilty people who're not here yet and who never will come, because if all the people who're in any way guilty were to come here, this Courtyard would have to stretch from one ocean to the next. I know people, they're all guilty, only it's not written that all of them should eat their bread here.'

Bit-by-bit this whole monologue, spoken as he walked, grew increasingly animated, until it became a mad shout, cursing everyone the Courtyard enclosed and all who lived outside it. In his voice, under all its surliness and revulsion towards everything, there trembled, barely perceptibly, something like a tearful twinge and sorrow that this was the way things had to be.

And that 'innocent' man now knew that he would have to sit here for weeks more without Karagöz so much as glancing at him again.

It happened that a week or so after this event, a group of prominent people from the city arrived to plead with Karagöz. They were the relatives of a wealthy young man arrested together with the bad company he kept. They asked Karagöz to release him because he was innocent. All of a sudden the governor changed completely, as though he had remembered something. He became thoughtful and serious, closed both his eyes for a moment, so that his face grew longer and his expression changed, and bent politely down towards the petitioners, to say in a thin voice:

'Did you tell the people who arrested him he was innocent?'

'Yes, of course we did, but. . . .

'Ah, now that was a mistake. Pshee, pshee, psheee! That's bad. Because right now they're catching innocent people and letting the guilty ones go. That's the new procedure. But as you have yourselves declared to the authorities that he hasn't committed any crime, he'll have to stay here.'

The people looked at his calm mask, puzzled, expecting Karagöz to laugh and turn the whole thing into a joke. They even began half smiling themselves. But he remained implacably serious, cold and polite. And sent them away. It took them a long time to get over it. They told their friends the whole story, they went to complain to influential acquaintances who shrugged their shoulders dismissively, like people who firmly believed that the devil himself, or perhaps more than one, lived in Karagöz and spoke through him.

But perhaps as soon as the next day, on his way across the Courtyard, Karagöz would come across that first 'innocent' man and suddenly take up the conversation of three weeks before. He would stride right up to him, pressing up against him as though he were going to devour him.

'Pshee! What's got into you, how much longer are you going to stink the place out? As though there wasn't enough stench without you adding to it. Get out of here this minute, d'you hear? Collect your bits and pieces and get out of my sight. If I see you again I'll have you whipped like a dog.'

At first rigid with amazement, the man would then suddenly gather his strength and just slip out of the Courtyard, leaving his few belongings for the guards and prisoners to fight over.

In this 'game' Karagöz could spend hours with a man accused of robbery or embezzlement, of rape, grievous injury or murder, he could act the fool, yell or whisper, play an idiot or bloodthirsty executioner, or a man of feeling and understanding, all in turn and all with the same sincerity and conviction. He would sometimes wrestle with such a man and sometimes embrace him, hit him or caress him, and keep thrusting his face into the other man's: 'Confess, damn your eyes! Confess and save your skin, otherwise you can see you'll end up on the gallows. Confess!'

And when he had achieved his aim, dragged a confession out of the prisoner and information about accomplices or the place where the stolen money was hidden, he would simply rub his hands together, like a man who had finally completed an unpleasant dirty task. Then he would throw off all those masks and let the affair take a normal course. But even then he did not completely abandon the man who had confessed, but spoke up for him, making things easier.

This endless, strange game of his was unfathomable. It seemed, in fact, that he did not ever believe anyone. Not merely the accused or witnesses but not even himself. And that was why he needed a confession as the only at least partially fixed point from which it was possible in this world, where everyone was guilty, to maintain at least the semblance of some kind of justice and order. And he sought a confession, hunted it, squeezed it out of a man with a desperate effort, as though he were fighting for his own life, squaring his inextricable accounts with vice and crime, cunning and disorder.

In most cases the game looked unnecessary, impenetrable and undignified, it was so twisted and distorted, but in fact it was carefully calculated and regularly achieved its aim. There was no repetition or routine in it, it was always new, growing of its own accord, so that it confused even the most hardened and frequent guests of the Damned Yard. At times it perplexed even those who had been working with Karagöz for years. Stories were told about it all over Stamboul, his behaviour seemed at times so inhuman and mad, and then at others unaccountably considerate.

This all led to frequent complaints against Karagöz, of the most varied kinds; at one point there was even a possibility of his being dismissed; the viziers discussed him at the Divan, more than once. But in the end, nothing changed. They all knew that Karagöz was an arbitrary, idiosyncratic governor, but they also knew that it was not easy to find a man who would spend his life, day and night, with a whole underworld of criminals, vagrants and degenerates of all kinds and keep them in his Yard in some kind of discipline and order. So Karagöz remained in his position, governing the Damned Yard in his own way.

Everyone felt that this was the most natural solution. Everyone, including the inmates of the Yard. Here Karagöz was a constant topic of conversation, gossip, mockery, curses, hatred, sometimes even of physical attack. (Oaths involving the name of Karagöz's daughter on every possible occasion were an established custom in the Courtyard.) All the inmates followed and interpreted Karagöz's every action and glance, his every word, as though bewitched. They were afraid of him, and avoided him as far as they could. But these same people spoke of him and recounted his exploits with unacknowledged admiration. They were all accustomed to Karagöz, somehow adapted to him. They cursed him, but in the way one curses the life one loves and one's wretched fate. He was part of their damnation. In their constant fear and hatred, they had become one with him and it was hard to imagine life without him. And since there had to be a Damned Yard with a governor, then this one, the way he was, was the best they could hope for. His way of working was monstrous and sometimes, for the individual concerned, terrible, but there was always the possibility of surprise, in a bad but also in a positive sense, it was like a kind of endless lottery and constant suspense for the inmates. This made everything, including Karagöz himself more bearable, or at least that was how it seemed, for the prisoners all liked gambling: certainty always weighed heavily on them. This whole metropolitan underworld of vice and disorder regarded Karagöz as their own; he was their 'swine', their 'bloodsucker' and 'scum', their 'bastard and son of a bitch', but their own.

That, then, was Latifaga, known as Karagöz. Perhaps it would be better to say that is how he had been, because he had aged considerably, grown still heavier and lost much of his former zeal. He had wearied, it seemed, of astounding the Courtyard with his imagination and inventiveness, his witty and capricious actions and his judgements of Solomon. Now he spent more time on the beautiful, wholesome side of the hill, in his fine house where he had seen his sons and daughters married.

From time to time the old Karagöz would reappear and perform one of his great exploits of ten or fifteen years before in front of the amazed and superstitiously fearful Courtyard.

With a strange mixture of wonder and bitterness which could be felt in his tone even after so many years, Fra Petar spoke at length about how he had watched with his own eyes as the 'old villain' extracted a confession from some Armenians, arrested for embezzlement from the state mint.

Precious metal had been steadily disappearing from the mint. Eventually, the matter came to the attention of the Sultan himself, who threatened the senior officials with the most terrible punishment unless the thefts stopped, the criminals were found and the state compensated for the loss. The government immediately arrested several culprits from the mint who were directly involved, and then a whole wealthy, extensive Armenian merchant family, for the threads of the investigation led to their shops. Eight adult male members of the family were brought into the Damned Yard. Here these overweight, olive-skinned men arranged their life as rich people are able to do in all circumstances. Whole piles of rugs and furniture were dragged in, lavish meals were brought each day. No one bothered them or interrogated them. And when it seemed that was how the whole affair would end, the aging Karagöz performed one of the feats he was renowned for in his younger days.

One morning, while the head of the family, the elderly, asthmatic, overweight Kirkor, was sitting in the courtyard on a little bench in a recess in the prison wall, the governor suddenly appeared and sat down beside him on the bench on which there was scarely room for one. Without a word, he began to lean his considerable bulk against Kirkor, who in any case had difficulty breathing, pressing him against the wall. When he had driven him completely into the stone corner, he said, without any introduction, in a low but terrible voice:

'Listen, this case is important (a matter of state!) and it has to be solved at once, or innocent people, high officials, are going to lose their heads because of you. You're Armenian, in other words sly and astute, but I'm worth at least three Armenians. So why don't *the four of us* look for a way out of this dangerous mess. These few thieves they've caught are nonentities. They can't make up the loss. They'll pay with their lives. But you're accomplices. You've bought the stolen stuff for nothing. You can still save your skins and buy yourselves off. I know you yourself aren't guilty, but one of your lot is. And until the stolen stuff is found and returned to the Imperial treasury, that one is you. So let's do it, because otherwise, by my faith and my honour, you'll be tortured till this flesh falls off you. There'll be less of you left than a ten year-old boy!'

Crushed against the wall, the old Armenian could neither breathe nor speak. Karagöz continued talking to him in a whisper. First he mentioned the huge sum the family would have to pay the state. The figure made the merchant's eyes grow dim and a gasp form in his throat. But Karagöz went on squeezing him into the corner.

'Never mind, never mind. The loss is certainly great, it may even be more than that, but that is roughly a quarter of all your liquid assets. But since you always give false information about your possessions, declaring at least four times less than you have, that means in fact it's only a sixteenth. Do as I say and give it back. Then the whole business can be forgotten. But if you don't . . .'

Then Karagöz presented his whole devilish plan to the merchant, who was listening to him panting, his eyes closed.

There had recently been two cases of illness in the family's households. There was a suspicion that it could be the plague. That had only to be stated and all of them, from the youngest to the oldest, would be shut up in the Armenian hospital for plague victims. There at least half of them would really become infected and die. During that time people would be found, either from outside or among their servants, who would raid the abandoned houses and shops and steal whatever came to hand. And after that, the usual procedure with regard to plague victims, their houses and possessions, would be carried out.

As he said this, he squeezed the almost unconscious Armenian against the wall, who wheezed and rolled his eyes, trying to say something, to ask for a little time and a little space to think, to discuss it with his family. But Karagöz would not give him either, repeating in a terrible whisper that everything had to be decided this moment, on this bench.

The other prisoners who had, as always, withdrawn into their cells when Karagöz appeared, or into the most distant corners of the Courtyard, could not have seen or heard any of this. They were aware only that a duel to the death was taking place between old Kirkor and Karagöz here in this recess. Eventually they saw the governor going into the supervisor's office above the gate, and Kirkor stumbling as though in a coma, staggering in fits and starts towards the cell where his family was. For a while there were the sounds of loud argument — the bitter but vain resistance of the younger members of the family, and then all at once it all fell silent. Old Kirkor emerged, supported between two of his eldest sons, and went to the supervisor to discuss how the money should be paid.

In the course of the following few days, they were all released, two or three at a time.

For weeks the Courtyard talked about the way Karagöz had forced the heavy fine out of Kirkor, repeating the whole story with details that only the two of them could have known, but which the prisoners had discovered in a miraculous way, or had added by way of decoration themselves.

Fra Petar often talked about Karagöz, always with a mixture of bitterness, revulsion and a kind of reluctant admiration, with bemused amazement, endeavouring to give a picture of this monster as best he could in words, so that it would become clear to the person listening and so that he too should be amazed. And he kept returning to him at least with some ironical word, as though he felt that he had not yet done with him.

But he spoke equally vividly about the life of the Courtyard as a whole and about the interesting, comic, pathetic, deranged individuals in it. They were closer to him and more familiar than the brigands, murderers and sinister criminals whom he avoided as best he could.

Nevertheless, that did not seem to be the most important thing or to take up the most space in Fra Petar's memories of the Damned Yard about which, in the last days of his life, he had talked so much to the young man beside him.

II

As with every affliction, it was the first days in the Damned Yard that were the hardest and the most painful. The nights were particularly unbearable. In order to protect himself, at least up to a point, from the fights, quarrels and distasteful night scenes, Fra Petar had chosen the remote corner of a spacious cell, behind a large ruined chimney, and he secluded himself here with the few possessions he had with him. There were already two Bulgarians there, also 'transients', destined for exile. They received Fra Petar well, without many words. They were certainly glad that the place had been taken by this quiet man from Bosnia in urban dress, about whom they knew or asked nothing more, but they guessed that he was a 'transient' like themselves and that it was as hard for him as it was for them in this ugly, threatening crowd.

Evidently prosperous people, as far as could be ascertained they were the victims of a rebellion that had broken out in their region because of excessive taxes and tributes and the inhuman way they were collected. They were more a kind of hostage. But they did not talk about the charges against them. They were anxious and frightened, but you could not tell even this from their faces. Nothing. Everything about them was restrained and cautious. Always fully dressed, with their belts and shoes on, so that their summons to leave should not find them unprepared. (While the Stamboul prisoners, whatever their crime, regarded the Damned Yard as part of their lives, and behaved accordingly, these two were not really living here, just enduring: their lives were out there, in Bulgaria. Now they were waiting for a decision. If they succeeded in returning they would live, but as long as they were far away from what was theirs, there was no life for them. And they needed none. That was how all the 'transients' were.) Only one of the two of them would ever leave the cell at a time, and then only rarely and for a moment, while the other stayed on the mat, beside their belongings. They mostly sat or lay, silent and motionless. They did not look up without need. They ate little, and only when no one was looking, and they drank only water, turning aside even then. They spoke to no one and secretly disapproved of the fact that Fra Petar listened to the prisoners' jokes and stories in the courtyard, and even talked to some of them himself. And they asked him not to smoke in the dark because that attracted unwanted visitors.

But still, after a few days they did acquire a guest who immediately became their neighbour. Here was someone else who had been drawn to this corner of orderly, quiet and withdrawn 'transients'.

Thinking about him later, often, Fra Petar could not remember exactly either the time when he had arrived, or how he had come, looking for a little space, nor what he had said. With people we grow close to we usually forget these details of our first contact with them; it seems as though we have always known them and they have been with us forever. All that remains are a few unconnected images that sometimes come into our memory.

One early dusk the silhouette of a tall, stooping, evidently young man bent over him. He had a blanket over one arm and a leather bag in his other hand. The two Bulgarians exchanged swift, sidelong glances first between themselves and then both of them with Fra Petar. A fleeting but unambiguous expression of displeasure, caution and antagonistic solidarity: a Turk! The new arrival settled himself without fuss, almost without movement; you could not hear him breathe. And whenever he woke up that night (there is no one here who does not wake frequently), something about him made Fra Petar aware that the 'new one' next to him was not asleep.

Waking at daybreak, in the pale light of dawn, which must already have been abundant outside, Fra Petar turned his eyes to his right, where the Turk had spent the night. The first thing he saw was a small, yellow leather-bound book. An intense, warm feeling of joy ran through his whole body; something of the lost, human, true world which had been left far beyond these walls, as beautiful but as nebulous as a vision. He blinked, but the book was still there and it really was — a book. Only then did he look further and see that the book was lying in the lap of a man who was half lying and half sitting, leaning against his little trunk. It was the man from the night before. Beside him was a travelling bag of bright, tanned leather, under him a dark blanket, splendid and even to the eye warm and soft as fine, expensive fur. Given his origins and upbringing, within the narrow limits of his quite modest needs, Fra Petar never thought much about the value and form of objects around him, nor did he attribute great importance to them, but he could not fail to notice this. He had never seen objects of ordinary, everyday use made so skilfully and of such refined material; had he remained in Bosnia and not by misfortune happened into this Courtyard, he would not have known nor been able to believe that they really did exist.

He looked further. The man's face was a new surprise. A young man's face, soft, slightly puffy, white with the pallor that comes from being indoors — unlike anything that could be expected here — overgrown with a red, whispy beard of some ten days growth and a lighter, drooping moustache. What stood out most were the large sockets, sunken and dark as bruises, of his blue eyes, moist and shining. To Fra Petar, who had seen many sick people of all kinds in the course of his life, this was all suddenly familiar. He had seen eyes just like these before. There are people like this who are afraid or ashamed of something, who have something to hide. They always try to attract and hold another person's gaze, endeavouring to fix it firmly with their eyes and so stop it going further and examining the lines of their face or the parts of their body or the clothes they are wearing. Without blinking, the young man looked enquiringly, but calmly, at the friar's open, broad face with its thick, black moustache and wide-apart large brown eyes of tranquil gaze.

The conversation began of its own accord. These are the best conversations. First something like a greeting, a few vague words which seek each other and examine each other when they meet. That was enough for Fra Petar to see that the Turk was not arrogant or distant as he might have been. He was restrained, certainly, but in a different way.

In the course of the morning they met and parted several times. And each time they exchanged a few insignificant words. This is what prison conversations are like: they begin hesitantly, and then, when they do not find new sustenance, they are easily extinguished in a mistrustful silence in which each of the speakers examines what he has said or heard.

Around the time of the midday meal they lost one another from sight. It was not until the afternoon that they resumed their conversation. They discovered that they both knew Italian and they exchanged a few words in it. More as a joke than anything else. But nevertheless, this somehow separated them from the people around them and brought them closer together. They talked about various cities and parts of the world, then about books, but since they had not read the same books, the conversation came to an end. They told each other their names. The young man was called Kamil. Fra Petar gave his, without mentioning his vocation. Otherwise they did not say a word about themselves or what had brought them here. Their talk ran in closed circles and on the surface of life. The young Turk was particularly reticent. In his deep, dark voice, and a slight nod of his head, he simply confirmed whatever Fra Petar said. And he confirmed evrything, without reflection. He did not himself fully express a single thought, not even the most ordinary. He often stopped in the middle of a sentence and his gaze kept straying into the distance.

Fra Petar spoke more animatedly. He was glad to have found a companion, but he had at once thought: this is a sick man! It was not necessary to know people as well as he did, to reach this conclusion.

'Yes, yes,' said the young Turk with somewhat Western politeness, but this seemed to confirm Fra Petar's idea of him rather than the words he had spoken.

Even such as they were, however, it seemed that these conversations were agreeable to both prisoners. They welcomed them as the unexpected gift of what they most lacked here; and so kept resuming them after every interruption.

The two merchants watched them with concealed surprise and still better concealed suspicion.

And when it began to get dark, the young Turk and Fra Petar had their evening meal together. Or rather, Fra Petar did, for the young man ate nothing, chewing lengthily and absently on the same mouthful. In his direct and open way, Fra Petar remarked:

'Kamil Effendi, forgive me, but it isn't good for you not to eat.'

And he tried to convince him that one should eat more in adversity and be stronger and more serene than when things were good.

'Yes, yes,' replied the young man, but he ate no more after that than before.

The next day their conversations began to be longer, more lively and more natural. The time passed more pleasantly and evening came more quickly. But with the dusk their talk slowed down again. Only Fra Petar spoke. Even that absent 'yes, yes' became rarer. The young man withdrew increasingly into himself, confirming everything by a mere lowering and raising of his heavy eyelids, without really participating in anything.

The reddish light in the sky and on the rare tips of the cypress trees behind the high wall showed that the sun was going down rapidly somewhere out there on the other side of the invisible city. For a time the whole courtyard was filled with a pink glow, but it quickly emptied like a square bowl tipped on its side, and began to collect the first shadows of dusk.

The guards started driving the prisoners inside, while they slipped away, like a disobedient and scattered herd, to the seclusion of the far ends of the courtyard. No one felt like abandoning the day or going into the stifling cells. Shouts and blows were exchanged.

At that moment a guard came running up to where the friar and the young man were still sitting. He shouted the young man's name. A second guard came up a few steps behind him, shouting the same name, only with more vigour. In all places like this junior servants are faster if they have the sharp command of their superiors behind them, faster to do both good and ill, depending on the nature of the order. In this instance it had to be good. With an attentiveness which is rare here, the two of them invited the young man to move immediately into a different room that had been arranged for him. They helped him collect his things. It was clear that he was going somewhere better.

The young man accepted this unexpected attention as a command, without much surprise and without question. Before he left, he turned to his companion as though for the first time he were going to tell him something solemn and clear, but he only smiled and nodded as though he were greeting him from a distance.

And they parted without a word, like good, old acquaintances.

For a long time that night Fra Petar thought about the unusual Turk. He seemed both like a Turk and not, but it was certain that he was an unhappy man. At times, when Petar fell into a half-sleep, it seemed that he was here beside him, awake but silent, with his book and his unusual, fine possessions. At the same time he was aware that he had gone. And he regretted this. When he did succeed in falling into a proper sleep, which was always deep and sound as long as it lasted, without dreams, without consciousness of himself or the world around him, his sleep engulfed his neighbour on the right and his thoughts about him too. But as soon as he woke in the course of the night, he was aware of a vague, distant, but strong sense of deep regret for the years of his youth, when he had had to part with good friends and be left to live and work with indifferent strangers. And when day broke, that nocturnal fluctuation of dreams and visions came to an end, and in the light of day there was only the simple truth: his neighbour really had gone. He was conscious of the empty space on his right as a discomfort and a special pain in this life which was full of pain and discomfort, both major and minor. To his left were the two merchants, silent and always ready to depart.

As soon as it was light, the empty space was filled. It was taken by a lean, gaunt man, unshaven and unkempt, with black, curly hair. He excused himself, speaking rapidly and at length. He did not want to get in anyone's way, but he could no longer bear the improper behaviour of the people he had been sleeping among up to now and he had been obliged to find a quieter place, among better people. He put down his wickerwork basket and some threadbare clothes, and went on talking.

Lengthy, ceremonious introductions were not the custom here, but this man talked, immediately, about everything as though he were among old, trusted acquaintances. And it was clear that he was talking more on his own account, because he could not do otherwise, than because of the people he was speaking to or what he was saying.

The two merchants withdrew still further into themselves, pressing up against each other. But Fra Petar both listened and observed the strange man. His whole bearing seemed to encourage this loquacity. (And he thought to himself: I'm a little like my uncle, the late Fra Rafo, who could listen tolerantly to everyone, and who always joked: 'I could manage somehow without bread, but without conversation, that I really couldn't do.') The man talked.

He was a Jew from Smyrna. His dark face looked sad. A large nose, big eyes with yellow, bloodshot whites. He looked altogether sad, or anxious and afraid, but his need to talk was stronger than his misfortune and fear. As though he were continuing some conversation of the night before, he talked to Fra Petar, as they went out of the cell into the courtyard, in a lively half-whisper about himself and his sufferings.

'First they rob you, then they charge you and lock you up! And, I ask you, how come we belong with this riff-raff? I wonder . . .'

And he listed all the things he wondered about; and he wondered about all kinds of things. As he did so he looked around him timidly, but without ceasing to talk. It's his talkativeness that has brought him here, thought Fra Petar to himself, listening now with only one ear to this strange man's feverish chatter, when he suddenly mentioned the name of Kamil Effendi.

'I saw yesterday that he had found refuge with you, beside decent people. But now they've given him a room in the so-called white porch, there by the gate, where the guards sleep and where the more prominent prisoners have separate cells and special food. And, really, it is terrible. Is a man like that for this ... this ... '

Fra Petar was startled.

'You know this ... Kamil Effendi?'

'I? Of course I do! I don't know you, I'm sorry, we've just met . .. I don't know you, but I can see that you are a man of propriety and honour, and for me that is ... You no, but him, him, yes. From sight, very well. The whole of Smyrna knows him. Everyone knows everything in Smyrna.'

In the course of that very first day Fra Petar discovered a great deal about the young Turk and his family, and about what had brought him into this unusual place. Of course he learned all this in the way it could be learned from Haim, as the man from Smyrna was called. Everything was jumbled up and fragmented, some things left out, and some things on the other hand repeated three times, colourful, lively, not always clear, but with a mass of all kinds of detail. For this man, who had to talk, could never talk about just one thing. He would stop for a few seconds, think for a moment, frowning sadly, as though it were a torment to him himself and as though he could see that it was not good manners or appropriate to talk about everyone, everything and everywhere, but his need to talk about other people's lives, particularly about the lives of those whose social position was higher, or whose destiny was exceptional, was stronger than everything else.

Haim was one of those people who spend their whole lives waging a hopeless dispute they have lost in advance with the people and society around them. In his passion to say and explain everything, to reveal all the mistakes and all the crimes of humanity, to unmask the wrongdoers and give the good their due, he went far further than what an ordinary, healthy man could ever find out. He could relate scenes which had taken place between two people, without witnesses, in unbelievably fine detail. And he did not only describe the people he was talking about, but entered into their thoughts and desires, frequently those of which they themselves were not aware and which he disclosed to them. He spoke through them. And he had a strange gift of imitating the speech of the person he was speaking of, by the slightest adjustment in his voice, so that he was one moment a dignitary, the next a beggar, and the next a Greek beauty; and with quite slight movements of his body or the muscles of his face he could recreate completely the gait and bearing of a person or the movement of an animal or even the appearance of lifeless objects.

In this way Haim talked rapidly and at length about the large, prosperous Jewish, Greek and even Turkish families from Smyrna, pausing always at major events and difficulties. And every account of this kind would end with curious sounds, almost a cry: 'Eh? Ah!', which was meant to convey roughly: 'There you see what kind of people there are! And what is my poor life and my case compared to them and their complex destinies!'

And where one story stopped, the next began. There was no end.

(We are always more or less inclined to judge those who talk a lot, particularly about things that do not affect them directly, we even speak with contempt of such people as tedious chatterboxes. But as we do so, we do not think that this human, so human and so common a failing has its good sides. For, what would we know about other people's souls and thoughts, about other people and consequently about ourselves, about other places and regions we have never seen nor will have the opportunity of seeing, if there were not people like this who have the need to describe in speech or writing what they have seen and heard, and what they have experienced or thought in that connection? Little, very little. And if their accounts are imperfect, coloured with personal passions and needs, or even inaccurate, we have reason and experience and can judge them and compare them one with another, accept or reject them, partially or completely. In this way, something of human truth is always left for those who listen or read patiently.)

That was what Fra Petar thought to himself, as he listened to Haim's wide-ranging, roundabout account of 'Kamil-Effendi and his fate' which took still longer to tell because of Haim's strange caution. For, despite all his liveliness and his fervent need to talk, he would at times lower his voice to the point of inaudibility, glancing enquiringly around him, like a man who is pursued by many and suspects everyone.

Kamil was a man 'of mixed race', Haim explained, his father was Turkish and his mother Greek. His mother had been a famous Greek beauty. Smyrna, a city of beautiful Greek women, had never seen such a form, such bearing and such blue eyes. At sixteen she was married to a Greek, a very wealthy man. (Haim mentioned a long Greek surname, pronouncing it as one speaks the name of a generally known dynasty.) They had only one child, a daughter. When the little girl was eight years old, the wealthy Greek suddenly died. His relatives rushed to cheat the young widow and to withold as much as they could of his estate. The woman defended herself. She travelled all the way to Athens, to save at least her inheritance there. As she was returning to Smyrna by boat, her daughter was taken ill and died. The sea was rough, the boat was sailing slowly, it was still a long way to Smyrna. According to regulations the little girl's body should be thrown into the sea. And the sailors absolutely insisted as well, because according to some ancient belief of theirs a dead body on a ship brought bad luck: the dead person's soul dragged the boat to the bottom like lead. Beside herself with pain, the mother refused. She insisted that the body be left alone and buried when they reached Smyrna, so that she would at least know her child's grave. The captain of the ship had a hard time with her. Caught in an awkward position between the mother's pain, which he did not have the heart to withstand, and the strict regulations, which he did not dare ignore, the captain and the first officer of the ship planned to deceive her. They had two identical coffins made. The child's body was placed in one, which the sailors secretly lowered into the sea, while the captain gave the other, filled with an appropriate weight, firmly nailed down and sealed, to the mother, as though he had given in to her entreaties. When they reached

Smyrna, she took the coffin and buried it in the graveyard.

She mourned her child long and painfully, going every day to the grave. And when, with time, young and beautiful as she was, she began at least up to a point to forget her loss, something terrible occurred. The wife of the first officer from the ship on which the child had died, discovered from her husband the secret of the well-intentioned deception they had carried out with the child's dead body. One day she divulged this secret to her best friend. After some women's quarrel, in her stupidity and desire for revenge, this friend passed it on to others. In an inexplicably cruel way the mother came to hear. It was only then that the unfortunate woman was maddened with grief. She ran to the graveyard, digging the earth from the grave with her nails. They had to drag her away by force and shut her up, because she wanted to jump into the sea after her daughter. This was real madness. It was several years before the woman recovered from her new grief. And she never recovered fully.

Many Greeks asked for the hand of the beautiful, unhappy widow, but she refused them all, angry with her relatives and all her fellow countrymen. It was only several years later that she did marry, choosing, to everyone's surprise, a Turk. Much older than she was, a rich, respected and educated man, who in his younger years had held high office in the state service, this Tahir Pasha lived quietly, in summer on his property near Smyrna, and in the winter in his large house in town. He did not ask his wife to change her faith, only that she did not show herself in the street with her face uncovered. Nevertheless this marriage created a great stir among the Greeks. But, despite all the cursing of the Greek women and the priests, the marriage of the young Greek woman to the sixty year-old Pasha was not only happy but fruitful. In the first two years they had two children, first a daughter, then a son. The son was strong and grew well, but the daughter was sickly, and when she was four years-old she died of an unknown disease, after an illness lasting just two days. The mother, who had never really recovered from the first grief, now fell into a deep, incurable melancholy. She looked for and found the hand of supernatural forces in the death of her second daughter. Feeling cursed and unworthy, she began completely to neglect her husband and son. She withered and faded abruptly. And the following year her death came as a release.

The boy, who was called Kamil, was handsome (his mother's good looks, only in masculine form), clever and strong, the best swimmer among his friends and the winner of all their wrestling matches. But he began very early on to neglect the games and amusements of his contemporaries. He devoted himself increasingly to books and learning, and his father supported him in this, acquiring books and teachers for him, and enabling him to travel. He even learned Spanish from an old Sephardic Jew, a Rabbi in Smyrna.

And when, one winter, old Tahir Pasha died as well, the boy was left alone, with a considerable fortune, with no close relatives or experience of the world. The great respect Tahir Pasha had enjoyed was a protection. He was offered the chance of preparing for state service, but he declined. Unlike his contemporaries, he had never fought over women or sought female company. But that summer it happened that in passing, through the fence of a small, lush garden, his eye fell on a Greek girl. Instant love changed him entirely. The girl was the daughter of a Greek small-scale tradesman. The young man was determined to marry her just as Tahir Pasha had once married his mother. He offered everything, with no conditions of any kind.

The girl, who had seen him two or three times, definitely wanted to marry him; she even found a way of letting him know. But her parents were adamantly opposed to letting their daughter marry a Turk, especially one with a Greek mother. The whole Greek community supported them. It seemed to them all that this was Tahir Pasha, even though he was dead, taking yet another Greek girl from them. The girl's father, otherwise a philistine, small in stature and mind, behaved like someone deranged, suddenly beset by delusions of grandeur, heroism and a desire for martyrdom. Spreading his arms as though he were being crucified, he shouted in front of his fellow countrymen: 'I'm an insignificant man in position and possessions, but I'm not wanting in my faith and the fear of God. And I would rather lose my life and send my daughter, my only child, into the sea, than hand her to an infidel.' And he went on and on. As though he and his faith were the main thing, and his daughter incidental.

This heroism did not cost the little merchant from the steep street much, in fact. He was not given the opportunity of becoming a martyr. They married off the girl by force to a Greek from outside Smyrna, secretly, without a wedding, hiding the place and day of her departure. They were afraid that Kamil would abduct her, but he had already withdrawn after the first blow he received. It was only then that he could see clearly what he could never have guessed before, in his youthful elation: just how much could separate a man from the woman he loved, and in general people from one another.

After that Kamil spent two years studying in Stamboul. He returned to Smyrna changed and far older in appearance. And he found himself isolated. He was divided from the Greeks by everything and he had little in common with the Turks. The contemporaries with whom, even a few years before, he had spent many carefree hours, were now alien and distant as though they belonged to a different generation. He became a man who lived with books. At twenty-four he was a wealthy eccentric who did not know what he owned or where it was, nor how to manage it all. He travelled along the coast of Asia Minor, went to Egypt and the island of Rhodes. He avoided those he belonged to by name and social position, who had begun to regard him as a recluse, and he spent time only with people of learning, regardless of their faith or origin.

The previous year a strange rumour had begun to circulate round Smyrna, a vague whisper that books had turned Tahir Pasha's son's head and that all was not well with him. People said that in studying the history of the Turkish Empire he had 'overdone it' and, imagining that the spirit of an unfortunate prince lived on in him, he had begun to believe that he himself was some would-be sultan.

'Eh? Ah!' Haim interrupted his story for a moment to explain what Smyrna was like: it had not only slandered him, Haim, and driven him into this gaol, but even such respectable and blameless people as this Kamil Effendi. But he went on straight away.

'When I say that rumours began to circulate through Smyrna', went on Haim, 'you should not, of course, imagine that this refers to the whole town. What is Smyrna? When you look at it from down below, from that plain below Kadifa Kala, it seems as though it has no end. And it is big. A lot of houses and a lot of people. But if you really look at it, there are a hundred or so families, fifty Turkish and as many Greek; and those few higher authorities around the Vali and the harbour master, a thousand or two souls altogether. And that's all, because they are the ones who make all the decisions and count for anything, everyone else just muddles along, struggling to maintain themselves and their family. And those hundred or so families don't always socialise and mix with one another, but they know all there is to know about each other, observing each other from generation to generation. Kamil belonged to that minority through both his father and his mother. The unusual destiny of his family and his unusual way of life had always attracted attention and curiosity.

And in Smyrna people talk, repeat stories, gossip, and exaggerate everything, like everywhere in the world, and a bit more so.'

In his absence and just because of it, they talked a lot about Kamil, who in the past few years had taken no part in the life of his peers, the wealthy, land-owning youth. They talked about his historical studies; some with amazement, others with ridicule.

On a terrace where a dozen well-bred young men were drinking and smoking with a simlar number of girls from the port, someone happened to mention Kamil, his unhappy love and his curious way of life. One of the others said that Kamil was making a detailed study of the time of Beyazit II, and especially the life of Cem-Sultan, and that was why he had travelled to Egypt and Rhodes, and was now preparing to go even to Italy and France. The girls asked who this Cem-Sultan was, and the young man explained that he was Beyazit's brother and rival, who had been defeated in a struggle for the throne, escaped to Rhodes and given himself up to the Christian knights. After that the Christian rulers of the time had held him prisoner for years, using him constantly against the Ottoman Empire and the lawful ruler Beyazit. Somewhere there he died, and the Sultan Beyazit took the body of his unfortunate usurper brother and buried it in Bursa, where his tomb could still be seen today.

At that point a frivolous young man joined in the conversation, one of those whose vivid imagination and thoughtless talk can do harm both to themselves and, more often, to others.

'After his unhappy love for the Greek girl, Kamil fell just as unhappily in love with the history he was studying. Secretly he has become Cem. That's how he behaves and interprets everything around him. And when they talk of him now, his former friends, mocking and pitying him, never call him anything other than Cem-Sultan.'

Whenever the name of a Sultan is pronounced, and particularly if disputes or conflict in the Emperor's household are discussed, even in the distant past, it never stops there, in the company where it was mentioned. There is always a bird that flies off and informs the Emperor or the Emperor's people that his name has been mentioned, and who spoke it and in what circumstances. So it happened that, through the mouth of a fool and the ear of an informer, Kamil's innocent passion reached the Vali of Izmir, where it met with a quite different reception and acquired a new meaning.

The Vali of the Izmir vilayet at that time was a hard, zealous official, a stupid and morbidly suspicious man, who trembled even in his sleep lest he had failed to notice some political irregularity, plot or the like.

(But all this zeal in 'political and state affairs' did not prevent him from accepting plentiful bribes from merchants and shipowners. That was why the Izmir Cadi said of him that he was a man short on ideas and long in the fingers.)

The first thing the Vali thought as he listened to the report on Kamil, was something that had never remotely crossed the young man's mind: the fact that the present Sultan had a brother, whom he had declared simple-minded and whom he kept locked up. Everybody knew this, although no one ever spoke about it. The similarity disturbed him. And when just at that time, in connection with some disturbances in the European part of Turkey, a stern circular from Stamboul was issued to all the Valis reminding the authorities in all parts of the country to be on their guard against all the numerous trouble-makers and agitators who discussed state affairs without being asked and even had the effrontery to sully the name of the Sultan, the Vali, like every bad official, felt personally affected. It seemed clear to him that this reprimand could refer only to his vilayet, and since there was no other 'case' in the vilayet, it could only be Kamil's 'case'.

One night the police surrounded Kamil's house and carried out a raid. They took away all his books and manuscripts, and imprisoned him in his own house.

When the Vali saw the heap of books in various foreign languages, and the numerous manuscripts and notes, he was so astounded and furious that he decided to arrest their owner on his own authority and send him, with all his books and papers, to Stamboul. He could not make out why books, especially foreign books and in such numbers, provoked such hatred and such anger in him. But his hatred and anger did not seek any explanation, they fed on and increased each other. The Vali was convinced that he was not mistaken and had hit just the right spot.

Many prominent people, especially the Ulema, were angered by the news of Tahir Pasha's son's arrest. The Cadi himself, a learned, older man and a friend of Tahir Pasha, went in person to the Vali. He laid Kamil's whole situation before him. He was entirely without vice, his way of life could serve as the model of a good man and a true Muslim, an unhappy love had driven him into a kind of melancholy trance and he had given himself over completely to learning and books. And if the young man had perhaps overdone that, it should be seen as an illness rather than some ill-intentioned deed. He deserved consideration and pity and not persecution or punishment. The whole business was obviously a great misunderstanding. What he was concerned with was history and scholarship, and scholarship could never be harmful. But all of this crumbled to nothing in the face of the stupidity and mistrust of the official.

'I'm not going to bother my head with all of this, Effendi. I don't know history, or whatever it's called. And it seems to me that it would be better for him not to know either and not to spend time investigating what some Sultan once did, but to listen to what the present Sultan decrees.'

'But that's learning, those are books!' the Cadi interrupted bitterly, knowing from experience how harmful it could be, and how dangerous for an individual, when, because of their limitations, people had unlimited faith in their own intelligence and perceptiveness and in the accuracy of all their judgments.

'Well, in that case, his books are no good! Cem-Sultan! A pretender! A struggle for the throne!' The word had been spoken, and once a word is set in motion, it can no longer be stopped, but goes further, growing and changing on its way. 'I didn't invent these words, he did; now let him answer for them.'

'But they can often quite misrepresent a person!' the Cadi tried again to defend the young man.

'If he's been slandered, let him wash and it'll be washed away. I don't read books nor do I want to think for anyone else. Let everyone think for himself. Why should I worry about him? In my vilayet everyone has to watch what he does. I know only one thing: order and law.'

The Cadi raised his head and looked at him sharply and reproachfully: 'Why, I believe that is what we are all of us defending!'

But the heedless man could not be deflected or stopped: 'Yes, order and the law. And whoever pokes his head above that, I'll have it off, on my imperial honour, even if it were my own son's. I won't tolerate the slightest infringement here, and I won't put up with the shady learning of this young Effendi.'

'The whole thing could be looked into and cleared up here.'

'No, Effendi. Regulations are regulations, and that is not what the regulations lay down. He has talked about Sultans and the affairs of Sultans, let him answer for it on the Sultan's doorstep. There's Stamboul for him, let him explain there what he has read and written and what he has said about it all to the outside world. Let them bother their heads with that. If he's innocent, he's got nothing to fear.'

And that was all. The old Cadi looked at the Vali in front of him. A beardless, puny man, weak and impotent, and he could do so much evil. Always sour and suspicious, of two possibilities he was always inclined to the worse and when, as now, something frightened him, he became terrible. The Cadi realised that there was no point in going on talking to this Vali, who would do what he had resolved. He would have to look for other ways of helping the young man.

And Kamil was sent to Stamboul, under secure, but discreet, guard. (This was the only concession the Vali made to the Cadi.) And his books and manuscripts went with him, all under seal. As soon as they discovered this, the Cadi and other friends sent their man after him, to explain the affair and help the young man in Stamboul. When the man arrived in the capital, Kamil had already been despatched to Latif Effendi to be held in remand until his interrogation.

That was Kamil Effendi's story, the way Haim was able to know and envisage it. It has been related here briefly, without Haim's repetitions and comments and his numerous cries of 'Eh? Ah!'.

IV

Karagöz had always disliked political detainees. He would rather wrestle with a hundred ordinary criminals from the underworld than have anything to do with one political suspect. His hackles rose at the very thought of them. He tolerated them in his establishment, because that is how it had to be, as 'transients', but he never wanted to have to deal with them. He gave them a wide berth, as though they had the plague and he endeavoured to get rid of everything 'political', or that came to him under that name, as fast as he could. Everything about this prisoner they had brought from Smyrna was strange: he came from a respected Turkish family, he was accompanied by trunks full of books and papers, and no one quite knew whether he was clever or mad. (Madmen, and everything connected with them, filled Karagöz with a superstitious fear and instinctive revulsion.) But he could not refuse to take him. So Kamil was put into one of the communal cells, where, as we have seen, he found a place for the first two days.

On the second day the man sent by the Cadi of Smyrna arranged with higher authorities for Kamil to be given a room of his own and decent conditions in the Courtyard until his interrogation and until the whole thing was cleared up. And that was done.

During the next few days Fra Petar walked slowly round the large courtyard, as though he were looking for something or expecting someone, and he kept glancing up at the windows and balconies of the buildings round it. From time to time Haim would come up to him. He had already given up his place beside Fra Petar and the two merchants and found another, even more secluded. He said it was because of the draught. But just two or three days later he admitted to Fra Petar in confidence that he suspected the two merchants of being spies. Fra Petar smiled, dismissing such an idea. Then he looked more closely at Haim's thin face and for the first time noticed on it the strangely concentrated expression of people who are struggling with their own false assumptions and imaginary fears.

Two days later Haim appeared again, his head bowed, and touching Petar's ear with his long, pointed nose, he whispered something about some other spy, warning Fra Petar to be careful.

'Come on now, Haim, you mustn't say that kind of thing to anyone.'

'It's only you I'm telling.'

'Well, don't tell anyone, not even me. You shouldn't talk about such things at all.' Fra Petar fended him off, finding Haim's sudden great confidence in him uncomfortable.

This happened several times. Fra Petar began to get used to it. He would pat him on the shoulder and soothe him, trying always to give the conversation a humourous, innocuous tone. Which one? That tall, fair man? Why, my dear fellow, he's half dead with fright, can't you see? He's not up to anything! He's as innocent as a lamb. You fear and suspect people for no reason.'

Haim was calm for an hour or two, but he would not hold out long before coming up to Fra Petar again and assuring him that he was the only person he trusted and continuing the conversation of a short time before.

'All right, it's not the one I mistakenly — let's say "mistakenly" — thought it was, all right, but it's someone else you couldn't imagine it being. And who's that? The man who stands beside the gate, looking straight ahead, pretending nothing interests him? The man who brazenly examines everyone from top to toe? That harmless one who looks so stupid? Or perhaps it isn't any of these, but someone quite else? And since you can't be sure of any one of these whether it's him, but you're also not certain that it isn't, it could be any of them. Any one.'

'Come on, Haim, for goodness' sake, forget this nonsense,' said Fra Petar becoming a little impatient.

'No, no! You're a good man, my respected friend, and you think everyone's good.'

'Well, if you expect good, you will find good, my dear Haim'

'Ah, good! Good?' whispered Haim doubtfully and went slowly off with bowed head, his unwavering gaze fixed on the ground.

And the next day he came again, early in the morning, as though to confession. But even when he had rid himself of some of his fear, he still could not relax. Always irritated for some reason, he would talk in his vivid way about the injustice and injury he had suffered, about people in his town and their ways. And Fra Petar would always take advantage of the opportunity to ask him some question about Kamil Effendi. Haim was never stuck for an answer. He could still talk at length about things he had already talked about, with a lot of new, plausible details. Fra Petar listened carefully to all of this, observing Haim's thin face and high brow. The skin on this brow was so taut that you could trace the slightest indentation and the whole arrangement of the bones of his skull. The hair that framed it in strange wisps was unhealthily stiff and dry as though it were being burned up by an invisible flame somewhere at its roots.

And when, after his stories, Haim skulked off, stooped and anxious, Fra Petar would follow him for a long time, with a pitying gaze.

Two days went by and there was no sign of Kamil. Haim, who, for all his own problems, somehow succeeded in discovering or at least guessing everything, explained this by saying that the young man was probably under interrogation. Detainees were never let out during that time so as not to come into contact with anyone. When the interrogation was over and the whole affair had been submitted to the court, they would start letting him out into the courtyard again.

This Haim from Smyrna knew everything and predicted everything (even if not always accurately). In this case he was right.

That morning, Fra Petar was sitting on a rock, deep in thought, half-listening to the racket reaching him from all sides of the yard, fragmenting and merging in his hearing.

To his left a small circle of gamblers had formed. They were settling an old gamblers' argument, but this was like a kind of court. They were grim-faced, and their speech dry, hard and factual.

'Just give him the money. Now,' said a tall man who was evidently the gamblers' leader, in a thin but terrible voice.

'This is what I'll give him!' shouted a short, thickset man with burning eyes, making a sign with two fingers.

'Just look at him! And he injured the man, he almost killed him,' joined in voices from the side.

'And why not kill him!'

'They'll lock you up!'

'So what! I'll kill him as soon as I get out, and . . .'

The angry voices grew louder. Beneath them you could just

make out that of the tall man, unwavering and threatening.

'You give the money back! D'you hear?'

The din coming from the circle on the right was still greater and at times it quite drowned that from the left. Here were Zaim, that talkative man of athletic build with the thundering hoarse bass, and a new, slightly built prisoner, whom they called the Student. As always, the conversation was about women. Zaim was not saying anything; he was presumably preparing a new story. It was the athlete and the Student who were having the argument.

The slightly built man was shouting, and you could tell from his voice that he was capering about, as small people do, to give what they are saying more importance.

'Armenians, Armenians, now, those are women!'

'What do you mean Armenians? What Armenians? You're telling me about Armenian women. You? Why you're under-age.'

'I'm thirty-one.'

'Oh I don't mean that. It's not a matter of years, it's just the way you are. You're under-age, and you'll be under age when you're fifty. Do you follow? You're under-age, and under-sized, and under-weight, and under-developed, altogether everything about you is — small.'

'And everything about you is "big",' said the little man drily and unwittily, while everyone laughed uproariously.

'There, you see, you haven't even got that right. Everything about me is — excessive, if you really want to know, and that's why I'm no use. No, I'm no use either. But you, yoouu!'

The hoarse bass voice said something, one single, brief word, which was lost in general laughter.

Then the bass voice came again. On and on about women and women's love. He did not know how to talk about anything else: 'Armenian women are like forest fires: it's hard to set them alight, but once they flare up, no one can put them out. They aren't women, they're hard labour. A blight that attaches itself to a man, and you are enslaved to her and her whole family. And I don't mean just the living either, but the dead and unborn. They devour you, and all honest and lawful, and only as long as it's honest and according to God's law. (They all have God as their accomplice). Armenian women go unwashed for six days of the week and only wash on holidays. And they are covered in hair up to their eyes and stink of garlic. Now, what about Caucasians?'

'Ah, they're women!' said someone from the crowd, supporting him.

'Caucasians?' the bass disagreed, and his words became an

irritable sigh. 'They're not women, brother, they're a summer's day. A summer's day, and you don't know which is more beautiful, the earth or the sky above it. You need all your strength. But then again nothing helps, even the greatest master falls short. It's not like a bird: when you catch it, you have it. You can't hold onto them; they overflow like water; and when you've had them, it's as though you had never had anything. They have no memory and no heart and they know nothing of reason or mercy. And you can't begin to grasp their ways.'

And again came the short, unintelligible word that provoked loud laughter. Fra Petar roused himself from his thoughts and decided to go and sit down a little further off. He rose, but then stopped in surprise. In front of him, with a quiet, embarrassed word of greeting, stood Kamil.

That is how it usually is. Those we wish to see do not come at the times when we are thinking of them and when we most expect them, but appear at a moment when our thoughts are far from them. And our joy at seeing them takes a little time to surface from the depths, where it has been supressed.

They moved some distance away from the shouting and laughter.

'Well, well,' said Fra Petar first, and he repeated the exclamation several times, as though confused, when they were sitting beside one another. (His joy found satisfaction in seeming less than it was.)

Suddenly everything looked far away and long ago, although only a few days had passed since they had last met. The young man was visibly thinner, as though wrung out. The dark rings under his eyes were darker, and his face smaller, with a faint, hovering smile which seemed to illuminate him from somewhere outside, giving him an expression of slight confusion. His clothes were a little crumpled, his beard longer and neglected, and his whole appearance still more restrained and fearful, but in a different way now.

The unusual friendship between this young gentleman, a Turk from Smyrna, and the foreigner, a Christian from Bosnia, seemed to have grown steadily during the few days they had not seen each other, strengthening in this curious prison, rapidly and unexpectedly as can happen only in such exceptional circumstances. Their conversations now took the form only of the leisurely relating of what they had once seen or read. (They never spoke about themselves.) But these conversations were different from everything they could hear and see around them. And that was the main thing. They spent the whole day talking, from morning to evening, when the prisoners had to go each to his own cell, and with interruptions, when Kamil would go off to his noon or afternoon prayers. As before, Fra Petar spoke more, but the young man's participation in the conversation increased, gradually, imperceptibly, but constantly, although his voice still sounded like the echo of someone else's firmer, more definite voice, and after the first few words kept dropping to a whisper.

In such a voice, at a certain time, on a certain day (again Fra Petar could never remember when or how), Kamil, who had spoken so little until then, began to tell the story of Cem-Sultan. And from that moment to the end he never talked about anything else.

The starting point was fortuitous, or at least it seemed so. Quietly, as though he were talking about something quite ordinary, Kamil asked: 'Have you ever come across the name of Cem-Sultan, the brother of Beyazit II in history books?'

'No,' replied Fra Petar calmly, thinking with excitement of Haim's story and hiding every trace of his excitement.

'No? You haven't. . . .?'

The young man was evidently hesitant. And then, after a few introductory words which he pronounced with forced indifference, he began.

V

This was the age-old tale of two brothers in a new and solemn form.

Ever since the world began there have been two rival brothers, constantly born anew. One is older, wiser, stronger, closer to the world, to real life and everything that links and motivates the majority of people, a man who succeeds in everything, who always knows what should and what should not be done, what can be asked both of others and of himself. The second is his exact opposite. A man of brief span, ill fortune and a misguided first step, a man whose ambitions constantly bypass what is needed and surpass what is possible. In his conflict with his elder brother — and conflict is inevitable — he has lost the battle before it begins.

The two brothers found themselves face to face, when in 1481, on a spring day, in the course of a military operation, Sultan Mehmet II the Conqueror suddenly died. The older brother, Beyazit, was thirty-four and the younger, Cem, just twenty-three. Beyazit was the Governor of Amasya, with his seat on the Black Sea, while Cem was Governor of Karamania in Konya. Beyazit was dark-skinned, tall, slightly stooped, composed and reticent, while Cem was burly, fair and strong, quick-tempered and restive. Although he was still so young, Cem had gathered in his court in Konya a circle of scholars, poets and musicians, and he himself wrote good verse. In addition he was a fine swimmer, athlete and huntsman. 'A wild head' with no sense of measure in his ideas or diversions, so that his days were short and he snatched what he could from the night and sleep, so as to prolong his day. He knew Greek and read Italian.

Beyazit was one of those people about whom little is said. Impassive and courageous, an excellent marksman in war, he was not only older and more experienced, but his interests made him far more familiar with his father's extensive empire, its laws and regulations, its sources of income and relations with the rest of the world. He was one of those people who at any given moment are occupied with only one thought and one task, always the most essential.

In the race for the empty throne, Beyazit was swifter and more astute. Cem had more supporters at court and in the army. (It was known that Sultan Mehmet had favoured his younger son and wished him to succeed him.) But Beyazit's people had better lines of communication, both with him and among themselves, and they worked faster. Beyazit was the first to reach Stamboul where he took power. He immediately began to prepare the army to attack his brother, who was on his way to Stamboul with his army from Karamania.

Cem's army, under Gedik Pasha, reached Bursa, the ancient centre of Ottoman power, a beautiful green city on the slopes of a high mountain and captured it, after a battle. But Beyazit's army under Ayas Pasha was waiting in the plain. Negotiations began. Each of the two brothers had adequate proof of his right of precedence. Beyazit was older and more stable, he had already been acknowledged ruler in Stamboul. Cem based his claim on other evidence. Beyazit was born during the reign of their grandfather Murat II, while their father was still only heir to the throne. His mother had been a slave. Cem was born when Mehmet II was Sultan. And his mother was of Serbian royal blood. Without saying anything openly, Sultan Mehmet himself had shown that his younger son was closer to him, and in his heart he had intended the throne for him. Both of them were supported by powerful pashas, driven by genuine loyalty or their own selfish aims.

And as always happens, each of the two brothers found in everything around him sufficient confirmation and belief in both his right and his strength to pursue what he had long since resolved.

In such circumstances negotiations could not bear fruit. Cem sought part of the Empire, in Asia, for himself, while Beyazit calmly replied that the Empire was indivisible and that there could only be one Sultan. He invited his brother to retire with his harem to Jerusalem and to live in tranquillity there with a large sum of money which would be paid to him every year. Cem did not want even to consider this. There was a battle. Beyazit had succeeded in infiltrating one of his men, Jakub-Beg, among Cem's advisers.

Cem was defeated and barely escaped with his life. He fled to Egypt, where he was well received by the Egyptian Sultan who welcomed this strife between the brothers. He tried his fortune once more, supported by the Sultan of Egypt, but he was again defeated. He found himself on the coast of Asia Minor, without an army, with just a few of his most devoted men. (His mother and his wife, with three small children, had remained in Egypt.) Pressed from all sides, knowing what awaited him if he was captured, he decided to flee to the island of Rhodes and seek refuge among the Christian authorities there.

Rhodes, which Mehmet II had besieged in vain a few years earlier, was in the hands of the powerful Catholic order of St. John, the Jerusalem Knights Hospitallers, and it represented an important fortified point in the western Christian world. Cem knew the Knights from before, because he had carried out negotiations with them on the order of his father the Sultan. He turned to them with a request for refuge and they were only too glad to send a special galleon to transport him and his whole retinue of some thirty people to Rhodes.

The renegade and pretender was received with royal honours by the Grand Master of the Order, Pierre d'Aubusson, all the Knights Hospitallers and the whole population of the island. The Grand Master repeatedly assured Cem that he guaranteed him freedom and the right of asylum. They came to an agreement that it would be best to choose France as the country in which to live, until fortune should favour his return to Turkey as Sultan.

Cem was despatched to France with his retinue. And d'Aubusson began to work on all sides to exploit the position of this unfortunate prince to the best advantage of his Order, the whole of the Christian world, and his own interests. He was well aware of what an important pawn he held in his hands. On his arrival in France, Cem was not granted his liberty. On the contrary, despite the assurances he had been given, he was held captive in fortified towns belonging to the Order of the Knights of Jerusalem.

A whirlpool of intrigue and calculation was stirred up around the 'Sultan's brother' in which all the European states of the time took part, including the Pope and, of course, the Sultan Beyazit himself. Matthew Corvinus, the King of Hungary, and Pope Innocent VIII wanted Cem handed over to them, so as to use him as a tool in their struggle against Turkey and Beyazit II. But the shrewd Pierre d'Aubusson held the precious captive in his power and used him with great ingenuity to blackmail everyone —

Beyazit, the Sultan of Egypt, and the Pope. Beyazit paid d'Aubusson a large sum for Cem's maintenance, or rather to ensure that he did not release Cem or hand him over to anyone else. The Pope promised d'Aubusson the rank of Cardinal if he delivered Cem to him. The Sultan of Egypt gave him considerable sums of money. Even Cem's poor mother, who lived in Egypt and never ceased working for her son's release, sent him money for Cem, but the money went no further than the Grand Master.

This dispute over the 'Sultan's brother' and d'Aubusson's shrewd game went on for eight years. During this time, Cem was moved from one French fortified town to another, always under the strong guard of the Jerusalem Knights. Little by little, he was deprived of his retinue, so that in the end he had only four or five loyal attendants left. All his attempts to escape from the grip of the faithless Jerusalem Knights were futile. For his part Sultan Beyazit did all he could to free himself from the pressure being exerted on him by the whole Christian world through his unfortunate brother who had become its pawn. He gathered information about his brother from the Venetians, from the Ragusans, from the King of Naples, he maintained constant contact with Pierre d'Aubusson, making him considerable concessions of all kinds. Despite everything, however, in a certain sense their interests coincided. D'Aubusson wanted to keep Cem as long as possible and use him to blackmail virtually the whole world, while for Beyazit the main thing was that his rival was in a secure prison, and not at the head of an army marching against Turkey.

In the eighth year of Cem's stay in France, in 1488, the diplomatic battle over him reached its climax. Delegates arrived in France from all directions and the main focus of all their attention was the person of Cem. Beyazit's envoy, a Christian Greek Antonio Reriko, assisted by the envoy of the King of Naples, offered the French King and his courtiers large sums, publicly and in private; he offered power over Jerusalem, once Beyazit had conquered the Sultan of Egypt and captured that city; he brought gifts for which the courtiers and the court ladies were voracious. At the same time the Hungarian King Matthew Corvinus sent a glittering delegation, seeking the Sultan's brother for himself, so as to attack Beyazit with a greater chance of success. But the most energetic delegation was that of Pope Innocent VIII who, despite his age and ill-health, would not give up his intention of urging the Christian rulers to a crusade against Turkey. And for this he needed the Sultan's usurper brother as a weapon.

But the Grand Master from the island of Rhodes was pursuing his own aim. He succeeded in enlisting the French King's support for his idea that Cem should be handed over to the Pope. In February 1489, the Knights put Cem with his small retinue aboard their galleon in Toulon, and after a long and difficult journey they arrived in Civitavecchia, where they were met by emissaries of the Pope. Cem entered Rome with a splendid escort and was received by the cardinals and the whole papal court, together with diplomatic representatives. Both he and his retinue wore picturesque oriental dress, and rode fine horses. The following day, the Pope graciously received the long awaited Turkish prince in a solemn audience. Cem refused to bow before the Pope as everyone else did, but embraced him as an equal and a fellow ruler.

Pierre d'Aubusson became a Cardinal, and his Order received not only recognition, but other real powers and benefits from the Pope.

A few days later the Pope received Cem at a private audience. Here they spoke more openly. Cem informed him that the Knights of Rhodes had deceived him by keeping him in captivity until now. He asked the Pope to let him go to Egypt, where his mother and family were living. Cem spoke so movingly that he brought tears to the Pope's eyes. He consoled Cem with kind words, but words were as far as it went.

The elaborate diplomatic game around Cem continued and became increasingly animated. The Pope developed his plans for the formation of a league of Christian rulers against Turkey. Cem was to play an important role in this crusade, and the Vatican was a gilded cage for him. Matthew Corvinus wanted Cem for his own campaign against Turkey. The Sultan of Egypt wanted him as well, and offered a ransom of six hundred thousand ducats, with a further sixty thousand from Cem's mother.

In 1490, Matthew Corvinus died. This was a severe blow for the idea of a general Christian campaign against Beyazit. Then, discovering that Cem was in the Pope's power, Beyazit sent a special envoy to Rome. The Pope received him at an audience and here all d'Aubusson's lies and intrigue were revealed and the sums of money he had received from Beyazit came to light. Beyazit asked the Pope to keep Cem with him under the same conditions that the Knights of Rhodes had held him. In other words, in addition to certain political concessions, the sum of 40.000 ducats a year. Before paying out the sum of 120.000 ducats for the following three years, the envoy had to see Cem in person to assure himself that he was alive and really there. Cem agreed to receive the envoy, but only as Sultan, with the full ceremonial. He sat cross-legged on a special throne, surrounded by his retinue. One of the cardinals was with him. Beyazit's envoy fell prostrate before Cem-Sultan and handed him the letter and gifts sent him by his brother. The contents of the letter were whispered to Cem, and he distributed the gifts, without looking at them, for his retinue to share among themselves.

Innocent VIII continued to work on the formation of a league against Turkey, and Beyazit went on with his plans against Hungary and Venice. Cem played a major role in all of this. The Sultan sent the Pope the 'stake with which Christ was pierced on the cross' and other precious relics, asking him only one thing: to keep Cem captive and not hand him over to anyone else. And the Pope asked Beyazit not to attack Christian countries, otherwise he would make use of Cem by placing him at the head of a great campaign against Turkey.

And then Pope Innocent VIII died. While the new Pope was being elected, Cem was shut in the fortress of St. Angelo for greater security. The former cardinal Rodrigo Borgia was elected as the new Pope, known now by the name of Alexander VI.

It seemed as though better times had come for the royal Turkish captive. He made friends with the Pope's sons, moved about with greater freedom, took part in festivities. In chronicles and letters and in the paintings of his contemporaries, Cem is described as a man of about thirty, but who looked more than forty. Overweight, sombre, with his left eyelid completely closed, so that he looked 'like a man taking aim', he was dejected and irritable, merciless to his servants, and devoted to pleasures, especially drink, seeking in it sleep and oblivion.

New intrigues began among the Western Christian rulers. The young French King, Charles VIII, moved against Italy with his army to capture the kingdom of Naples which he claimed, with the declared intention of leading the armies of the Christian league into a crusade against Turkey. The Pope did all he could to prevent his advance on Italy. At that time Alexander VI was negotiating with Beyazit, seeking his support against the French King. Beyazit sent him the agreed sum of 40,000 Venetian ducats for Cem's annual maintenance, and in a special personal letter he offered 300,000 ducats for Cem's body. This correspondence was seized by opponents of the Pope's in Italy and made public.

Charles VIII penetrated into Italy. He rapidly captured city after city and on the last day of 1494 he entered Rome. The Pope had no choice but to come to an agreement with the young conqueror, with as little damage and loss as possible. One of Charles' demands was that the Pope should hand over 'the Sultan's brother', whom he intended to use in his struggle with Beyazit. They came to an agreement that Charles should take Cem with him on his campaign against Naples and then on to Turkey. But the Pope asked the French King to guarantee that, once the war was over, he would return the precious prisoner. Likewise the Pope secured an agreement whereby the 40.000 ducats which the Sultan regularly sent should continue to come to him.

At a solemn audience, before numerous witnesses, the Pope delivered Cem and his by now quite meagre retinue over to the French King. When the Pope informed him of this decision, Cem announced that he was a slave and it was of no consequence to him whether he was enslaved by the Pope or by the King of France.

The Pope endeavoured to dissuade Cem from this view and to soothe him with fine words, and Charles VIII behaved with consideration towards him, treating him like a ruler.

When Charles VIII set off to attack the King of Naples, he took with him both Cem with his retinue and the Pope's son Cesare, the Cardinal of Valentia, as a hostage. But on the journey the wily Cesare escaped, and Cem was taken ill. He was ill for just a few days. He died in Capua, before they reached Naples.

He had asked his escort, who had shared all the years of his captivity with him, to ensure that his body was taken to Turkey, so that the infidel would not be able to exploit him even when he was dead. He also dictated a letter to his brother Beyazit requesting him to permit his family to return to Stamboul and to be merciful to those who had been his faithful retinue throughout his long captivity.

Charles VIII ordered that Cem's body be embalmed and placed in a lead coffin.

The word immediately went round that the Pope had poisoned Cem and that he had already been poisoned when the Pope handed him over to the King of France. The Venetian Senate hurried to inform the Sultan Beyazit of Cem's death, wanting to be the first to give the powerful Sultan this pleasant news.

The campaign waged by Charles VIII ended pathetically. Charles returned to France, where he soon died. Cem's body remained in the hands of the King of Naples. There was a long correspondence about this dead body. The King of Naples blackmailed Beyazit. Pope Alexander VI also sought his share.

But the King of Naples extracted all the benefit for himself. The dead body helped him to make an advantageous agreement with the Sultan, and it was not until September 1499 that it was finally handed over to Beyazit, who gave it a solemn burial in the tomb in Bursa, where the Turkish rulers lie buried.

VI

This was the bare skeleton of Kamil's story, briefly and drily told. What Fra Petar heard from his new friend was far longer, far more vivid, and spoken to a different effect. But it all amounted to one thing: there are two worlds, between which there can never be any real contact or possibility of understanding, two terrible worlds condemned to eternal war in a thousand forms. And between them was a man who, in his own way, was at war with both these warring worlds. An emperor's son and emperor's brother, himself an emperor according to his deepest conviction, and yet the unhappiest of men. First betrayed and defeated, then deceived and deprived of his liberty, isolated and separated from his family and friends, held in a tragic impasse for all the world to see, as in the stocks, but proudly resolved to survive and be true to what he was, not to lose sight of his purpose, and not to give in either to his gaolor brother or to the unbelievers who tricked, blackmailed, sold and resold him.

Fra Petar heard innumerable names — of foreign cities and powerful world figures, emperors, kings, popes, princes and cardinals — which he had never heard before, as he followed all the fluctuations of Cem-Sultan's unusual life. He could not possibly have remembered or repeated all these names. It often happened that as he listened he lost the thread of the young man's tale and no longer knew who was related to whom nor who was deceiving, buying or selling whom, and he even stopped following the story, thinking instead about his own misfortune. But he still pretended to be listening, for he felt sorry for this man for whom it was evidently very important to tell the whole tale to the end, in detail.

And there were many things he found quite incomprehensible, such as Cem's verses about destiny, about wine and drunkenness, about beautiful young boys and girls. Kamil recited them by heart as though they were his own. There were words and ideas that troubled and upset him, such as Cem's caustic judgments of the popes and other church leaders. But Fra Petar considered that this was not the place or the time to discuss these things. The more so since there was so much of it he could not himself follow. You have to let a man say everything. People had always, everywhere, been able to approach him freely, make contact with him quickly and confide in him easily, and that was how it must be here too. He accepted this as natural and endeavoured always to hear everything attentively to its end.

This business with the young man from Smyrna went a long way and lasted a long time. He would forget himself entirely for hours, relating the destiny of Cem-Sultan as though it were something that had to be told as soon as possible, this very minute, for tomorrow it would be too late. He used Turkish one moment and Italian the next, forgetting, in his haste, to translate the French and Spanish quotations which he knew by heart.

The conversation would begin early, in the warm shadow of the eaves, which soon began to shrink, and they continued it in other secluded parts of the large courtyard, avoiding the heat of the sun and the loud, intrusive games and quarrels of the prisoners.

Fra Petar noticed that Haim never came up to him during these conversations, but only when he found him on his own. But it did happen that one of the prisoners would approach, as though in passing, trying incidentally to catch something of the young man's whispering. Then Kamil stopped at once and, like a sleep-walker woken from his dangerous trance, fell into a dull silence, interrupted by a mechanical, insincere 'yes, yes!', then, abruptly and coldly, he would mutter some meaningless words of farewell and walk away.

The following day he would appear in that same mood, with the vague traces of regret and decisions made in the night, taciturn and completely withdrawn. With a faint smile which erased everything and conveyed nothing, he would utter ordinary words about quite ordinary things. But that did not last long. As they spoke his bad mood changed imperceptibly, unnoticed by either himself or Fra Petar. Not knowing how or why, he would abandon himself once again to his passion, and talk, softly and vividly, as though making his confession, of Cem and his destiny.

By the third day the whole story had been told, to its sad and solemn end, to the bright, dignified tomb in Bursa, whose white walls were inscribed with the most beautiful verses from the

Koran, stylised in the form of strange flowers and crystals. But then came the account of individual scenes in full detail. Cem's happy and unhappy days followed one another, his meetings and conflicts, loves, hates and friendships, his attempts to escape from Christian slavery, his hopes and despair, his reflections in long nights of sleeplessness and the jumbled dreams of his brief hours of sleep, his proud and bitter answers to high dignitaries in France and Italy, his furious monologues in his solitary imprisonment, spoken not in Kamil's but in a different voice.

Without introduction or visible connection, with no chronological order, the young man would begin to relate some scene from the middle or end of Cem's captivity. He spoke quietly, his eyes lowered, not taking much account of whether his companion was listening or could follow.

Fra Petar could not quite remember when this tale without order or end had actually begun. Nor could he recall the exact moment, the grave and crucial moment, when Kamil first moved from the indirect narration of another's destiny to a tone of personal confession and began to speak in the first person.

(I! — potent word, which in the eyes of those before whom it is spoken determines our place, fatefully and immutably, often far beyond or behind what we know about ourselves, beyond our will and above our strength. A terrible word which, once spoken, links us and identifies us with all that we have imagined and said, with which we never dreamed of identifying ourselves, but with which we have in fact, in ourselves, long been one.)

In ever increasing uncertainty, with trepidation, pity, and an unease it was hard to conceal, Fra Petar continued to listen to the tale. When he left Kamil in the evening and thought about him and his case (and it was impossible not to think of it), he would reprimand himself for not having stopped him clearly and decisively on a path which obviously could not lead to any good, for not having shaken him, jolted him out of his delusion. But nevertheless, when they met again the next day, and when the young man again gave full reign to his morbid imaginings, he would listen again, with a slight shudder of alarm but profound compassion, wondering all the time whether he should interrupt him and bring him back to his senses. And when, remembering his decision of the night before, and seeing it as his duty, he did try to turn the conversation to some other subject or, as though by chance, by some passing remark to separate the Kamil who was speaking from the dead Cem-Sultan, he did it feebly and indecisively. He felt too sorry for him. His innate directness and forthrightness, which otherwise always enabled him to say anything to anyone, seemed to be paralysed by the young man's persistent narration. And it would always end with the friar giving in and listening in silence, without approval but without spoken dissent, to the young man's passionate whisper. What was not, what could not and should not be, was stronger than what was — obvious, real and the only possibility. And afterwards Fra Petar would reprimand himself once more for having succumbed again to this irresistible wave of madness and for not having made a greater effort to turn the young man back to the path of reason. At these moments he felt like an accomplice in the madness and resolved that the very next day he would do what he had so far omitted to do, at the first suitable opportunity.

This went on for five or six days. It began every morning at roughly the same time, like some established ceremonial, and lasted, with two or three short interruptions, until the evening. The story of Cem-Sultan, his sufferings and exploits seemed inexhaustible. But one morning Kamil did not appear. Fra Petar searched for him and waited, anxiously walking through all the different parts of the Courtyard. Twice that day Haim came up to him with always the same fretful complaints and fears about injustice in Smyrna, spies and all kinds of traps here in the Damned Yard. Fra Petar listened to him inattentively. And thought all the time of the absent Kamil.

He imagined he could see him and heard him saying as he had the night before, when they parted, speaking rapidly as though he were reading:

'Standing upright, in his splendid ceremonial dress, on the deck of the ship coming into Civitavecchia, and looking at the motley array of the papal army and church dignitaries aligned by protocol, Cem thought quickly and clearly, as we think only at moments when we have moved from one place where we have been living and have not yet stepped into the next. He thought coldly about his misfortune, seeing it distinctly and pitilessly, in a way that you can only do when, unnoticed, you hear it from someone else's lips.

Wherever he went he was met by foreign people who formed the living wall of his prison. And what could he expect from these people? Perhaps pity? This was the one thing he did not need and had never needed. The compassion he had sometimes been shown by a few good and noble people was for him simply a measure of his ill fortune and unparalleled humiliation. Pity is insulting even for the dead, but how was he to bear it, still alive and aware of everything, when he looked into the eyes of living people, and read in them only one thing: pity?

Of everything the world contains, I wanted to make a tool with which I would rule and conquer the world, and now this world has made a tool of me.

Yes, what is Cem Cemshid? A slave, that is not saying much. A slave, a simple slave led on a chain from market-place to market-place, may still hope for the mercy of a good master, for a ransom, or escape. But Cem could not expect mercy nor could he have accepted it even had someone wanted to offer it. A ransom? People did not collect a ransom for him, on the contrary, whole fortunes were paid out by both sides not to ransom him, but to keep him a slave and a tool. The exception was his mother, a steadfast, wonderful woman, a being above all beings, but her ineffectual efforts simply increased the burden of his humiliation.) Escape? It was hard for a nameless slave to escape from his chains, but if he did escape he always had some hope of eluding his pursuers and reaching some world of his own where he could live as a free and nameless man among other free and nameless men. But for Cem there was no posibility of escape. There was no refuge for him anywhere in the whole inhabited, known world, divided as it was into two camps, Turkish and Christian. For, there or here, he could be only one thing: a Sultan. Victorious or defeated, dead or alive. That was why he was a slave for whom there was no longer any escape, not even in his thoughts or dreams. That was the path and the hope of lesser and more fortunate people than himself. He was destined to be a Sultan, enslaved here, alive in Stamboul, or dead under the earth. Always and only a Sultan, and it was only in there that his salvation could lie. A Sultan, and nothing less, for that would mean the same as not being, and nothing more, because there was nothing beyond that. This was slavery from which there was no escape even after death.

The ship's fenders knocked dully against the harbour wall. The silence was so great that it was audible and passed like a slight shudder along the shore where everyone, from the cardinals to the grooms, was unblinkingly watching the tall man with the white, gold-embroidered turban on his head, standing apart, three steps in front of his retinue, like a statue. And there was not one who did not see in him a Sultan and who did not realise that this man could not be anything else, even though it was destroying him.

As he spoke, Kamil himself stood up. (Not to allow the guards to drive him into his room like the others, he usually set off of his own accord, a little before the appointed time.) After his usual meek words of farewell, he disappeared in one of the bends of the Damned Yard, where the first shadows of twilight had already begun to gather in the remote corners.

VII

The young man did not appear the next day, nor the next. But around noon on the third day Haim came and, glancing cautiously all around him, said that 'something bad' had happened to Kamil. Even he did not know any more than this.

It was not until two days later that Haim, who had not rested all that time, came with the story of Kamil's disappearance fully composed.

To start with, scowling, his head bowed, he skirted the space around Fra Petar in wide and then increasingly narrow circles and elipses, looking round him out of the corner of his eye, evidently trying to give his conversation the appearance of a chance encounter and, of course, quite unable to see how transparent these 'precautionary measures' of his were. When he came quite close, he asked in a muffled tone:

'Have they interrogated you?'

'No,' replied Fra Petar out loud. Haim's 'measures' had begun to bore him.

But in the hope that Haim had learned something about Kamil, he at once added more gently:

'No, they haven't. What's happened?'

Then Haim began to talk. At first he still behaved like a man who had stopped in passing, by chance, and who was about to move on. And he went on glancing around him, but little by little he forgot himself and talked increasingly animatedly, without raising his voice.

There were a few unclear and inexplicable places in his account, but then some other things were related in such abundant detail that he might have seen them with his own eyes. Haim knew everything, and he saw what could not be seen.

When, with the first twilight, Kamil had withdrawn into his cell

and the guard had locked it after him, it was light in the spacious
room. In two bright, covered dishes, a dinner such as the other
prisoners never received was already getting cold. Everything was
the same as every evening. Pacing from corner to corner and
waiting for the sleep he knew would not come. Little by little the
last sounds died away down in the courtyard. Darkness engulfed
the white walls and objects and gripped the cell around the
wakeful man. A new, night world was coming into being and in it
tiny, unreal sounds began to be heard, echoes of the game of
hearing and looking in the dark and in his sleeplessness. At one
moment, he did not himself know when, he heard the sound of a
key seeking and finding the keyhole. But this was no longer a
trick of his hearing. The door really did open and a faint light
appeared in the doorway. Without a sound two dark figures
entered the room. Behind them came a boy carrying a small oil
lamp. He stood to one side, raised the lamp and stayed like that,
motionless.

The light spread over them all. One of the two was fat;
everything about him was round and soft: his outer appearance,
his voice and movements. And the other was thin, all bone and
muscle in a dark skin, large eyes hidden in shadow and huge,
terrible hands that stood out in the light. They looked like the two
faces of the Sultan's two-faced justice. Only the first of them said
good evening politely (a blood-chilling politeness). And it began.

In a dangerously quiet voice the fat official said that the first
interrogation had been more of a formal nature and so had his
answers. But, of course, things could not rest there.

'We need you to tell us once and for all, Kamil-Effendi, who
you have been collecting information about Cem-Sultan for. And
working out the details of plans for a revolt against the rightful
Sultan and Caliph. And ways to seize the throne with the help of
enemies from abroad.'

'Who for?' echoed the young man softly, already entirely on the
defensive.

'Yes, who for?'

'For myself, not for anyone else. I studied what is known in our
history books. I did extensive research . . . '

'And how is it, that of all the numerous subjects people write
about in books, you should have chosen precisely that one?'

Silence.

(By now Haim had forgotten all his caution and was talking
rapidly with facial expressions and gestures.)

'Listen,' the fat official went on calmly and with exaggerated solemnity, 'you're an intelligent, educated man from a respected household. You can see for yourself you've got mixed up in an unpleasant business — or someone else has got you into it. You know that there is now, as then, a Sultan and Caliph on the throne (God grant him long life and every success!) and that that's not a good topic even for thinking about, let alone for studying, writing and discussing. You know that a word doesn't stay in one place even if it's spoken in the deepest forest, let alone when it's written down or uttered to others, as you've been doing all over Smyrna. Just explain the whole business to us. Tell us everything. It'll be easier for us and better for you.'

'Nothing of what you say has anything to do with me or my way of thinking.'

The young man's voice sounded candid, with just a hint of resentment. Then the official abandoned his solemnly polite attitude and adopted a tone that came far more naturally to him:

'Now, wait a minute! What d'you mean it has nothing to do with you? Everything's connected. You're a man of learning, but we're not entirely ignorant either. No one embarks on such a huge undertaking quite accidentally or without some aim.'

It was only the fat one who spoke. And Kamil began to mull over what he was hearing, replying increasingly indistinctly, like an echo.

'An aim. What sort of aim?'

'Why, that's exactly what we want to hear from you.'

The young man said nothing. Thinking that he was wavering, the fat man continued, confidently drawing out the syllables:

'Come on, then.'

This was spoken still more harshly and drily, in a new way, with a hint of impatience and threat.

The young man glanced into the dark corners around him as though looking for a witness beyond the circle of this dim light. He wondered what he could say to clear up this whole stupid misunderstanding, to explain everything and prove that there was nothing behind it and that he neither needed nor was able to account for it all, particularly not at this moment, here, like this. He thought that was what he was saying, but he said nothing. But the two officials spoke (now the thin one had joined in), rapidly, insistently, in turn.

'Talk!'

'Come on, it'll be better for you and — simpler.'

'Come on, now you've begun.'

'So, what was behind it and who was it for?'

They bombarded him with questions. The young man blinked in the light and kept looking uneasily into the dark corners. He was finding it hard to keep going, not managing even to make out the questions or distinguish one from another. All at once he noticed that the thin one had come closer, that he had raised his voice and that he was addressing him with the familiar form of 'you'.

'Speak up now, I'm waiting.'

All his attention fixed on this point. He felt shamed, diminished, weakened and still less capable of defending himself. His guilt and misfortune did not lie in any 'aim', but in the fact that they had put him (or he had put himself) in the position of being interrogated about it, and by people like this — that was what he wanted to say. He thought that was what he was saying, but he said nothing.

So it went on and it lasted a long time. Somewhere in the course of that night outside time measured by the rising and setting of the sun, and outside all human relationships, Kamil confessed openly and proudly that he was the same as Cem-Sultan, that is the same as that unhappiest of men who had been driven into a corner with no way out, and who would not, who could not, deny himself, could not stop being what he was.

'I am he!' he said again, in the quiet but firm voice in which fateful confessions are made, lowering himself into a chair.

The fat official took a sudden, unwitting step backwards, and fell silent. But the thin one did not seem to feel anything of that awesome horror at seeing a man who was obviously lost, and had placed himself forever outside the world and its laws. In his stolid, short-sighted zeal the thin policeman greedily exploited the empty space his cleverer companion had left him. He asked new questions, hoping to drag out of the young man a confession that there had nevertheless been some sort of plot in Smyrna.

Sitting on the low stool, Kamil looked completely drained and withdrawn into himself. The thin official danced around him, pressing right up against him. He felt that he now had before him a body without will or consciousness with which he could do what he wanted. This incited him to behave increasingly impatiently and boorishly. At one moment, it seems, he placed one of those two terrible hands on Kamil's shoulder. And the young man pushed him sharply away, presumably outraged and sickened by this insulting intimacy. In a flash it developed into a real fight. The other policeman became involved. Kamil defended himself and attacked with a strength and fury that no one could have expected. In the fray the boy was knocked over, together with the lamp he was holding. And when he was able to drag himself out of the mad tangle of arms, legs and blows, he rushed outside, and, while the struggle raged in the dark of the cell, he roused the whole building. (It was from this boy and the prisoners woken by the noise that people in the Courtyard learned of the night scene with the young man from Smyrna, and whatever was whispered in the Yard was immediately known to Haim.)

That same night they took Kamil out through one of the side gates of the Damned Yard.

Dead or alive? Where had they taken him? — Fra Petar could think of nothing else, in his shock. But Haim was already answering these questions too.

If he was alive, they had probably taken him to the Timarkhane, near the Süleymaniye, where mental patients were locked up. There, among lunatics, his stories about himself as heir to the throne would be the same as all the words of madmen, the innocuous ravings of the ill to which no one paid any attention. And such a deranged, sick person did not in any case live long but slipped quickly and easily out of the world, together with his morbid imaginings, without anyone having to account to anyone for it.

However, if the fight had been serious and if the young man had gone too far in defending himself and wounded one of them (and it seemed that this was the case, for traces of blood had later to be washed from the room), then it was possible that the emperor's men had gone even further, for blows are not measured here and they easily go beyond what is required. In that case Tahir-Pasha's unfortunate son was already in his grave. And such a grave, with a white stone and no inscription, says nothing, even about emperors, or their quarrels and battles with their rivals.

Only when he had told the whole story to the end, did Haim again recall the 'dangers' that surrounded him and without saying goodbye, glancing enquiringly around him, he walked away, endeavouring to look like a man strolling aimlessly through the spacious courtyard.

Fra Petar clenched his teeth with bitter anger at his destiny, at everything about him, even at the poor innocent Haim and his eternal need to know everything, and pass it on, elaborating it in the smallest detail. He stayed standing in one place, wiping the icy sweat from his brow. Looking with incomprehension at the grey trodden earth and the white walls in front of him as though he were seeing them for the first time, he felt a thin, cold wave of fear run through his whole body. Might they not start interrogating him because of his conversations with Kamil and so drag him, innocent as he was, into a senseless investigation for a second time? It was true that Haim was unbalanced and saw dangers where there were none, but everything was possible.

Soon afterwards this thought was replaced by another: what could have happened to Kamil? Now a painful rush of heat ran through him. A heavy pity that could not be endured like this, motionless and in complete uncertainty. He felt a keen need to move around, to see and hear different people who were far removed from these tortuous, sombre tales from Smyrna; to see people, no matter who, just as long as they were outside this insane net that was being woven, drawn tight and twisted by sick people who had lost their reason and imperial policemen without heart or sense, in which, through no fault of his own, he now found himself caught.

He set off down the courtyard towards the secluded corners and shadows, where he could hear the loud noise of quarrels, games or jokes from scattered groups of prisoners.

VIII

After two or three days it was clear that Fra Petar was not going to be interrogated because of his long conversations with Kamil. That meant that everything was over and — buried. His fear and anticipation left him, but things were no easier. On the contrary. There began a time without Kamil. He did not forget him, but he was aware that he did not expect to see him again.

It was still very hot summer weather. Everything in the Courtyard was just the same. Some were released, others came in their place, but that was not perceptible. They were all incidental and unimportant. The Yard lived for itself, with hundreds of changes, and always the same.

Each morning the same or similar groups of prisoners gathered in the shade. Fra Petar stopped by the first circle of his 'neighbours'. Here everything was just the same. Zaim was still marrying and divorcing new, affectionate, women, and there would always be people to goad him into his lies while others listened. He was pale, with a greenish tinge and black shadows in his face, as though suffering from jaundice. And, regardless of what he was talking about, his eyes wandered, pitiful and mad with fear and hidden thoughts of the punishment that awaited him, if the charge against him was proved.

Others talked about women as well, but in a different way. The athletically-built man with the hoarse bass voice was heard most. But even he was silenced for a moment to listen with the others to an elderly sailor talking about a young Greek girl who had served in his bar.

'I've never seen a bigger, firmer woman. A galleon. She bore her breasts before her like two pillows. And behind her went two massive spheres; grinding. Everyone reached out a hand to grab what they could and as much as they could. She tried to shove them away, and the innkeeper, a toothless Greek, tried to as well, but who can tie sailors' hands? A little while later they were pinching her again.. And in the end she had to leave her job. At least that's what the landlord said. But that wasn't it, he, the old fox, had hidden her in his house and was keeping her for himself. The sailors chided him, sighing: "Oh, what a shame, a woman like that, like a haystack!" ("Like a haystack, like a haystack!" muttered the Greek to himself, "but if it had gone on like that, everyone pinching where they could, what would have happened? Straw by straw, they would have taken the stack. Wretches!")

'Come now,' grumbled the hoarse bass.'Come, come, what sort of people are you! You only know how to talk about these coffee house whores! And only about that kind of filth! Come now!'

There was an argument, out of which the bass emerged the winner: they all urged the sailors to be quiet, asking the bass to go on with a story he had begun earlier. He went on relating something vague and tantalising about a woman of exceptional beauty, of Georgian origin, who had made a great stir here in Stamboul and died young.

'She was that kind of person. Her grandmother had been a renowned beauty. The whole of Tiflis was wild abut her. They hid her away with relatives in a little hamlet some distance from Tiflis. The hamlet is still called "Seven Stretchers" today because of her, it was called something different before, I don't know what. Because on account of her and her beauty in half an hour seven men fell dead around her house. Suitors and would-be abductors all killed each other. Three families were in mourning. And she died of grief. She did not slowly fade, but was struck down as though by frost. Overnight. But not even when she was dying did she want to say who it was that *she* loved, nor whether he was one of those who died. There, it was from this grandmother that she inherited her beauty, her figure, her eyes . . .'

'Yes,' said someone from the circle, 'everyone knows Georgian women are famous for their wonderful eyes.'

'Who knows? How do they know? What do you know about these things, you fool!'

'Why shouldn't he know? You're not the only person in the world!' some voices protested.

'Don't interrupt the man, let him talk!' demanded others.

'Just you carry on, brother, don't take any notice of anyone.'

The big man, with his big voice, refused, with an angry gesture and an expression of disgust on his face: 'I can't be bothered to talk. What's the use of talking to this blind puppy?'

But they all insisted and in the end, as always, they managed somehow to soothe him, so that he went on talking gruffly about the Georgian woman and her eyes.

'When someone says "she had wonderful eyes", I get really mad. What sort of eyes, damn yours! When you look at two eyes like those, you don't even think of the two lights each of us has in our heads, but of two Elysian fields bathed by the sun and the moon. What stars and clouds, what wonders there are in those two fields! My poor brother! You look, and you are struck dumb, you melt. You aren't there! Are those just "two eyes" then? They do see, of course, but that is the least of it, that is the last thing they do. Eyes! What are these mere eyes we carry in our heads, that stop us bumping into doors and missing our mouth with our spoon? And what are those two heavenly miracles? There's no comparison. That occurred once on this earth: once and never again. And so much the better. Less sorrow and strife. Such eyes ought not to die like others, or they should not be born in this world.'

The man suddenly fell silent. His voice had given out. There was no comment from the circle. That lasted a moment. And then an argument began as did the laughter and confused murmur of mingled voices and oaths.

As he followed the course of the conversation in the group from a little way off, Fra Petar became aware of someone behind him. When he turned to go away, Haim was standing there.

On his walks through the courtyard he regularly ran into Haim who, constantly on edge, kept moving restlessly from place to place. Wherever he came with his bundle of belongings, his suspicion of everything and everyone was already waiting for him there. He immediately undertook his 'precautionary measures'. And after a day or two he would abandon that spot and seek a different, more secure place to sleep. When he met Fra Petar he would sometimes pass by as though he did not know him, sometimes just greet him with a slight movement of his head, blinking meaningfully, and sometimes go up to him and talk freely, until he remembered something again and went on his way.

This time he had stopped of his own accord beside Fra Petar and began to talk about the man with the hoarse bass voice. And he knew everything about him.

He was a man of humble origin who had worked his way into higher society by means of his great strength and ability. For some years he had been a champion wrestler, known throughout

Turkey. He was an army supplier, the owner of inns, and a middle man in all kinds of business. Large sums of money had passed through his hands. Otherwise, a gambler and a drunk and above all a womaniser. That was how he had caught some disease. Always involved in some shady deal, he did not distinguish what was his from what was other people's, but somehow he had got by as long as he was in full strength of body and mind. Some two or three years before he had begun to fall lower and lower, to lose control. Women had unhinged him and he grew weak. In the end his former companions abandoned him. He became involved with the lowest criminals. And so he had ended up here, as a multiple bankrupt and fraud. This was only the second month he had been here, under investigation, but you could clearly see him deteriorating from day to day, and the little good sense he had melting away. He could no longer distinguish what was possible from what was not. And he only talked about women. That was a disease. He evidently could not imagine that there should be anywhere a woman's love, passion or the mere thought of it, without him participating. And he was melting, disappearing like a piece of sugar in water. There was virtually nothing left of his former violence and extravagance other than this empty arguing with idlers and his constant need for conversation and story-telling. Recently he had become increasingly sensitive, he had grown somehow thinner and more refined. His stories were livelier and fuller. His once famous big voice was now hoarse, constantly excited and emotional, with tearful, abrupt breaks which he tried in vain to hide and disguise by yelling at the people around him.

'He can't talk any more. The hoops have burst and you can see him leaking in all directions. He's had it!'

Haim went on talking in a raised, assured voice, almost gaily, about all kinds of things. But then he suddenly gave a start, looked around him as though he had just woken up, blinked both eyes, which was intended as a mysterious and unintelligible sign to his companion and without a word of farewell he went off with slow step, his head bowed, like a man looking for something he has not lost.

And Fra Petar continued his walk though the Courtyard, to another corner, wondering whether there was a sensible person anywhere he could talk to, and searching, as one searches for a cure, for a little diversion and forgetfulness.

It was said earlier, and it is true, that life in the Courtyard did not ever really change. But time changes and with time so does the picture of life before each of us. It begins to get dark earlier. One begins to fear the approach of autumn and winter, the long nights and the cold, rainy days. Life was always the same for Fra Petar, it stretched before him like a narrow and increasingly poorly lighted corridor which does not alter visibly, but of which one knows that with each day it is a finger or two narrower. This brought the prisoner brief but overwhelming moments of panic which would have made the strongest falter, at least for a moment or two.

Fra Petar spoke at length about those days. Raising himself up from time to time and settling himself on his pillow, staring into the snowy distance and following the footsteps of his memories, he spoke in a low, but clear voice:

'I thought to myself, this imprisonment of mine, an innocent man, has gone on a long time. As long as I was passing the time with poor Kamil and worrying about him, I somehow thought less about myself and my misfortune. But now I couldn't protect myself from those thoughts. I told myself to be patient, but my patience was beginning to let me down. Long nights, still longer days, and heavy thoughts. The worst was that I knew I was innocent, but neither did they interrogate me nor did anyone from outside let me know anything. When I thought about that, the blood rushed to my head and I was blinded and I felt like shouting at the top of my voice. But I repressed it, saying nothing, consuming myself inwardly, and only wondering what else was in store for me. All kinds of things came to mind, only I didn't see a way out. There was no one to talk to anywhere, and the idleness was killing me. That was the worst thing. I wasn't used to it. No books and no tools. I asked whether there was any work for me, a coffee mill to mend, a clock to adjust. Anything. Because that's my craft. But the guard just looked at me without a word. I asked him to ask the supervisor. The following day he told me: "Just you sit there and don't say another word about it!" And turned his back on me. I tried to explain, but he turned round and contemplated me with an ugly expression.

"It does sometimes happen that someone gets hold of a file or a chisel, so as to get out of here more easily, but if you think we're going to give them to a prisoner ourselves, you're out of your mind! The very idea!"'

So saying, he spat and walked away. I was dumbfounded. I wanted to shout after him that I was innocent. It hadn't even crossed my mind to escape. Tears of shame came to my eyes. I didn't myself know why. But when I thought a bit more about it, I could see that the man was right. And I was angrier with myself than with him. What had I been thinking of? When people are in the kind of situation I was in, no one can believe anything they say. I had forgotten where I was!

And so again, idle and anxious, I just sat and waited for the day to pass and the night to come. And the night would pass even more slowly.

One day they let those two merchants from Bulgaria go and instead of into exile they set off home. According to custom and as an act of charity they gave me the mat they had lain on. Take it, said one, and may the sun shine on you as well! In a whisper, his head turned away. They went like two shadows. They did not even dare be pleased. It was even harder without them. But despite all my cares I keep on thinking of Kamil, the story he had told, and his ill fortune. He began to appear to me.

I rose early, with the dawn, and could hardly wait for the door to open. I left the oppressive stench, washed at the tap, and sat down to savour this time, before all those people came tumbling out of their cells. Daybreak in Stamboul! It can't be described. I had never seen anything like it before nor will I ever again. (Did God really mean to give everything beautiful to the enemy!) The sky glows pink and then descends to the earth; there's enough for everyone, for rich and poor, for the Sultan and the slave and the prisoner. I used to sit, revelling in it and smoking, if I had something to smoke, and the tobacco turned my head. Smoke surrounded me, and in its billow Cem-Kamil seemed to appear beside me, unslept, pale, with tearful eyes. And I talked with him warmly and simply, as I could never do when he was here and we used to meet, just as I would have talked with some young monk from my monastery if he was overcome by *taedium vitae*. I took him by the shoulder and gave him a shake.

'So you're up early, with the birds! It's dawn, Kamil-Effendi. Eh!'

But he shook his head.

'Not for me,' he said, 'midnight and dawn, they're all the same. There's no daybreak.'

'But of course there is, my dear boy! What nonsense! Don't blaspheme. As long as there is darkness there will be dawn. Do you see this beauty of the Lord's?'

'No,' he said, his head bowed and in a broken voice.

And I felt sorry for him and I didn't know what to do to help him. Around us the whole Damned Yard was bathed in brilliance.

'Come, my poor lad, don't say what you shouldn't and sin

against your soul. God willing, you'll recover from your illness and look your fill in health and freedom on every good and every beauty.'

He simply bowed his head.

'I can't recover, you good man,' he said, 'for I am not ill, I am what I am, and one cannot recover from oneself.'

And he went on talking nonsense, involved and obscure, but sad; it was enough to make the hardest man weep. I consoled him to no avail. I reproached him like a father for not seeing what was around him, and for seeing what was not there. And to tell the truth, somehow the bright morning grew dark for me as well. I tried to make a joke again. I took out my tobacco.

'Let's smoke together and drive our troubles away, devil take it all! Shall we?'

'Yes,' he said, more for my sake, 'let's.'

And he started to smoke, but who know where his thoughts were. And he smoked as though with dead lips and through his tears the unhappy Cem was looking at me. His cigarette went out.

Somewhere someone shouted (two people were having a fight) and roused me. I started, and there was no one beside me. My cigarette had gone out, but my hand was still outstretched. Why, I'd been talking to myself! I was afraid of madness as of an infectious disease and of the thought that in this place with time even the sanest man starts seeing things. And I began to resist. I defended myself, forced myself to remember who and what I was, where I had come from and how I came here. I reminded myself that apart from this Courtyard there was another, different world, that this was not all there was and it was not forever. And I endeavoured not to forget this, to hold on to this idea. But the Courtyard was like a whirlpool dragging a man into its dark depths.'

It is not easy for the toughest man to spend the day and wait for dusk with such thoughts; but the days brought neither change nor hope. Only Haim when he happened to come. He came every day, but there could be no real conversation with him. He, poor man, was sinking ever more deeply into his gloomy tales and imagined fears. In vain did Fra Petar ask him every time whether he had heard anything of Kamil. He knew nothing and he was no longer interested. It seemed that he had forgotten the young man from Smyrna. Everything in him was seething with new, different horrors and accusations which he expressed as briskly and with as much detail as though he had experienced it all himself, forgetting it all just as quickly. It seemed that the universe did not contain enough misery, injustice and suffering for him. He re-worked it all rapidly in himself, related it and forgot.

Haim came up, after the whole ritual of his 'measures', sat down beside 'the only man you could trust here', and Fra Petar forced himself to be cheerful, patting him on the shoulder.

'What is it, Haim, my old solace, what's new?'

But Haim looked at him with the fixed dark stare of his unevenly placed pupils, and as though he had not heard his words, said in a gruff voice:

'Listen, I don't know whether you've thought about it, but I keep thinking the same thing: there's not a single man in his right mind here. Believe me! They're all crazy, the guards and the prisoners and the spies (and almost all of them are spies!), not to mention the greatest madman, Karagöz. In every other country in the world he'd have been locked up in a madhouse long ago. In other words, everything is crazy, apart from you and me.'

His voice quivered. This obliged Fra Petar to raise his eyes and look at him better. Haim was even thinner, just as unshaven, with red, moist eyes, as though he had been sitting for a long time beside a smoky fire. His head trembled slightly, and his muffled voice rasped.

'Nothing but madmen, honest to God!'

Fra Petar felt uncomfortable, and a slight shudder ran down the back of his neck. For an instant it seemed there really was no way out of the Damned Yard.

But it happened that that same day he received his first joyful news from outside.

He was walking, as every morning, through the courtyard. Two young prisoners, virtually boys, were chasing one another, circling round Fra Petar and hiding behind him. He felt awkward, and the circles were growing tighter and tighter. But before he had succeeded in moving away from the wild youths, one of them, as he ran, pushed right up against him, as against a living shelter, and Fra Petar felt him press a piece of folded paper into his hand. Then the youths continued their chase further away from him, while he, confused and alarmed, retreated to the end of the yard. On the paper was written in Turkish, in an unknown hand: 'Pete will be released in a day or two.'

He spent that day and the following night uneasily. Everything pointed to the fact that no one but Fra Tadija could have sent that message.

The following day the guard really did come and tell him to

collect his things and prepare for a journey. Towards evening he was led out and sent away — to exile in Acre. Even if he had not been sure before that the note came from Fra Tadija, he would have been convinced now, because Tadija was a man who never predicted anything accurately.

That night from the Asian shore, where the exiles had to gather before they set off, he saw Stamboul for the first and last time, in all its power and glory. The air was tepid and sweetish. He felt confused and lost in the crowd of some two dozen fellow travellers. A night without stars or moon. And in front of him along the whole unfamiliar dark horizon rose the evening Stamboul, resembling a firework that had stopped in its flight. It was Ramadan and oil lamps burned on the minarets of all the mosques, flickering like regular constellations above the innumerable lights of the city. Most of the exiles were sitting with bowed heads. Some had already lain down for the night. For a time Fra Petar looked at what was Stamboul by day but which now rose up provocatively like a powerful, sparkling wave towards the invisible sky, into the endless night. How long did it take to light so many lights? Who would ever be able to put them out?) It looked as though there was no room anywhere for a Damned Yard, and yet it was there somewhere, in one of those small dark spaces, between the densely scattered lights. Exhausted, he turned at last to the other side, to the dark, silent East, but here too, as on the bright side, was the thought of the Damned Yard. It was going with him on his journey and it would accompany him, awake and asleep, throughout his stay in Acre, and afterwards.

'And in Acre I saw and experienced all manner of things. I've told you about some of them, and there would be more to tell. I met quite a few exiles there, of every faith and every race, criminals, but far more innocent people. Many of them had spent a few months in the Damned Yard and knew Karagöz. And one young man from Lebanon had caught his voice and walk exactly, and he would make us roar with laughter by walking up and down in front of us, shouting: 'What did you say, you're completely innocent? Well, good, good, that's exactly what we need!' He was a plump man, broader than he was tall, with a large shaved head and thick glasses, and somehow all composed entirely of jokes and laughter. He was a Christian. And when we got to know each other a little better, and I told him who I was and where I was from, I saw that he was far cleverer and more dangerous than he let one see. Some sort of politician, it seemed.

He joked and joked, then sat down beside me, saying through his laughter: "Ah, he's a good man, a good man is Karagöz." I was surprised: "What do you mean 'good', devil take that kind of goodness!" "No, no, he's the right man in the right place at this moment," he replied. And then he whispered in a quite different tone: "If you want to know what a state and its government are like, and what their future holds, just try to find out how many decent, innocent people there are in prison in that country, and how many criminals and villains go free.That's the best guide." He said all this as though in passing. Then he stood up and with his hands in his pockets walked off shouting like Karagöz and made us all laugh again. And as he joked and laughed I thought constantly of Kamil and I regretted having no one to talk to about him. Because I don't think I have felt more pity for any man.'

Fra Petar spent eight months in Acre. And it was only on the intervention of the friars and some prominent Turks that he was released and returned to Bosnia, at the same time of year in which he had set out twelve months before, with Fra Tadija Ostojić who had stayed the whole time in Stamboul, working strenuously for his release.

And this is the end. There is nothing more. Only a grave among the invisible graves of the friars, lost like a flake in the deep snow spreading like an ocean and turning all things into a cold desert without name or sign. There are no more stories or story-telling. As though there were no world any more for which it would be worth looking, walking and breathing. There are no Stamboul or Damned Yard. There is no young man from Smyrna who died once before his death, when he imagined that he was, that he could be, the Sultan's unfortunate brother Cem. Nor wretched Haim. Nor black Acre. Nor human evil, nor the hope or resistance that always accompanies it. There is nothing. Only snow and the simple fact that one dies and goes under the earth.

That is how it seemed to the young man by the window, who had been carried away for a moment by memories of the story and overshadowed by thoughts of death. But only for a moment. First feebly and then more loudly, as though he were slowly waking, the voices from the next room reached him increasingly clearly, the uneven sound of metal objects falling dully onto the heap and the firm voice of Fra Mija Josić, dictating the list of tools, left by the late Fra Petar.

'Next! Write: steel saw, small, German. One!'